VAPOR TRAILS

TERRAN SCOUT FLEET
-BOOK THREE-

JOSHUA DALZELLE

©2021

First Edition

1

"Your old man is looking for us. He wants his ship back."

"Where the hell did you hear that?" Jacob asked. "I haven't heard anything."

What was left of Scout Team Obsidian sat at the galley table in their current home, the ship Jacob had stolen from his father. The *Phoenix* was the property of Jason Burke and used by his merc crew, a group calling themselves Omega Force.

The gunship was an older vintage, but she'd been overhauled and rebuilt so many times that not much of the original ship was left. Her armament and flight systems were heavily—in some cases illegally—modified to make her one of the nastiest killing machines Jacob had ever flown on.

The *Phoenix* had been left on the planet his estranged father called home now. An out-of-the-way world near the edge of the Delphine Expanse called S'Tora. When Obsidian had found themselves on the run, out of options, and burned by their chain of command, taking the ship had seemed like an easy solution to their problems. But if Burke wanted his ship back, that could be a problem.

For all his insistence he had little use for his father, he also had a healthy respect for him and didn't want him or his crew on the wrong side of his rage. Jason Burke was a dangerous, unpredictable man.

"I still have some friends in the community," Murph said. Alonso "Murph" Murphy was actually Special Agent Murphy of the Naval Intelligence Section. He'd been embedded with Obsidian in a deep-cover operation, posing as an enlisted Marine, and found himself stuck in the assignment. It was a strange dynamic since, in real life, he was an assimilated O-4 and outranked Lieutenant Jacob Brown, but he was acting as a Marine NCO for his mission.

"They said Burke reached out to Captain Webb and asked where we were at."

"Damn," Jacob said.

"They're coming back," MG said over the intercom.

The weaponeer had been sitting in the *Phoenix*'s cargo hold, watching out the back ramp, waiting for the alien members of their team to come back. Since Obsidian hunted rogue humans, they tried not to muddy the waters by being seen waltzing around starports asking questions. Instead, Jacob had sent his two battlesynths to poke around.

The problem with battlesynths was twofold. They were not subtle beings and tended to stick out wherever they went thanks to how rare the species was. They also generated strong fear and panic reactions in some due to their deserved reputation. Jacob had weighed his options and decided the stir two battlesynths would cause would be preferable to someone remembering they'd seen another group of humans running around.

"Let's go down and meet Tin Man and his sidekick," Murph said.

"You're really playing with fire fucking with them like that," the team's pilot, Ryan "Sully" Sullivan, said from where he lounged in an overstuffed chair. "They don't like nicknames, and they're capable of killing you in the span of milliseconds."

"I think 707 is warming to the name," Murph said. "I'm going to get him to open up. You'll see."

"It was nice knowing you." Jacob shrugged. "I'll be sure to let NIS know you died as a moron."

"Appreciate it."

Jacob walked out of the hatch and onto the mezzanine in the cargo hold, the hot, dry air of the planet blasting him in the face. Sergeant Angel "MG" Marcos sat on a transit crate with a cold beer in his hand as the two battlesynths made it to the bottom of the ramp.

"Any luck?" Jacob called.

"Some. The Ull we are looking for was here," 707 said, "but we cannot determine if it has left or is still in the area."

"The usual bribes didn't work, Tin Man?" Murph asked. He couldn't speak any further because 707's hand shot out and clamped over his entire face. Jacob winced as he saw the hand squeeze.

"I have repeatedly told you not to call me that," 707 said. "I would suggest you respect my wishes."

"Let him go," Jacob ordered. "Murph, stop being a dumbass."

707 released Murph, who fell to the deck, rubbing at the side of his face where the alloy digits had dug in. The idiot still had a smile on his face.

"It's just our friendly way of welcoming you to the team," he said. "It's a human thing."

"I assure you, I have no desire to be human," 707 said.

The other battlesynth, who went by 784, just stood impassively as his commander abused Jacob's people. The two had agreed to come with him to watch his back when he disobeyed his orders and set off to try and hunt down a woman named Margaret Jansen. They actually had little interest in Jacob himself and were holding up their end of a blood pact they had with his father, Jason Burke.

He hadn't gotten the entire story but, apparently, Burke had rescued them from imprisonment on their home world of Khepri. When they found out he was in mortal danger, they'd come to his aide. When he said he was going to hunt down Jansen, they promised to help.

The Jansen problem had seemed simple at first—she was just some bureaucrat after all—and had quickly snowballed into a cluster fuck of impressive proportions, even by Obsidian standards. It didn't help that Omega Force was now hunting them, too.

His old man had made a few overtures over the years, all of which he'd rejected, but he wasn't sure Burke would just smile and ruffle his hair for stealing his beloved gunship. Again, seemed like a good idea at the time.

"If we can't find this Ull, we're dead in the water," Jacob said. "This mission is dragging on with little to show for it. At this point, I feel like we're just delaying our inevitable court-martials."

Obsidian had obtained detailed specs on Margret Jansen's communications network from one of her right-hand men, the now-dead Elton Hollick. The former NIS agent had kept tabs on her as a sort of insurance policy since nobody in their little One World faction seemed to trust each other, but once they'd dug into it, they saw Hollick had only breached the first few layers of security.

They saw the message routing and were able to decode a few drop locations but, for the most part, One World's com traffic remained encrypted and beyond their ability to break. The real problem was that their entire mission hinged on their ability to track Jansen through her communications network.

"This is how these things tend to go." Murph shrugged. "Intelligence and counterintelligence work are often long and boring. You've had a string of kinetic, fast-evolving ops that I think have skewed your perception as to what this job is about."

"Not sure what's more boring...watching an empty starport ramp or listening to you try and show off your vocabulary," MG said.

"The fact you think that's showing off my vocabulary is truly frightening," Murph said.

Jacob opened his mouth to head off the inevitable fight that comment would spark but stopped as something flew into the cargo hold. It bounced off some transit crates and rolled around on the floor in the middle of the deck. They all just stared at the small, blue sphere dumbly for a moment.

"What the fuck is that?" MG asked. Then the object exploded.

Jacob was flung back and felt something dig into his abdomen on the right side. As he slammed into the crates strapped to the deck behind him, he saw MG and Murph had also been launched away from the blast like ragdolls. He struggled to remain conscious as he lay in a heap on the deck. His teammates appeared to be down for the count...at least the humans were.

707 and 784 had both leaned into the blast and anchored themselves with the mag-locks built into their feet. As loose debris was blown around in the cargo hold from the force of the blast, both battlesynths switched to combat mode. The glowing crimson of their eyes stood out amidst the swirling dust and gave Jacob something to focus on as his brain insisted he just lie down and switch off for a bit.

Apparently, the munition had been some sort of anti-personnel stunner, but the battlesynths were impervious to such things. The rangy Ull that came bounding up the ramp learned that fact too late as both armored warriors turned on it before it could bring its weapon to bear, appearing to be going specifically for Jacob. The Ull raised its weapon and trained it on a still-incapacitated Jacob when it saw the two battlesynths bearing down on it.

The Ull got two shots off with its plasma carbine, one hitting 784 in the chest and splashing ineffectively against his armor, the second shot hitting the armory door, scorching the alloy. 707 reached the alien first, ripping the weapon from its hands and snapping it in two before tossing both halves back out the rear of the ship.

The Ull spun to flee, but 707 clamped onto its left arm and spun it about. As it tried to get its bearings, the battlesynth threw a savage punch that crushed into the pink, rock-hard thorax of the Ull, cracking the dermal layer and causing it to let out a warbling screech.

784 reached the fray just as the Ull dropped to its knees and hit it at close range with a stunner shot from his arm cannon. The alien collapsed on the deck, its keening cries mercifully stopping. Jacob climbed up onto shaky legs and walked over to where the battlesynths picked through the Ull's belongings.

"Interesting," he said before walking to the bulkhead panel and hitting the intercom. "Mettler, get your ass down here. MG and

Murph are hurt. Some sort of concussion grenade tossed them into some crates."

"On my way."

"Any idea who we're looking at?" Jacob asked as he rejoined the other two.

"Feature recognition scans indicate this is the Ull we have been searching for," 707 said.

"Convenient," Murph coughed as he struggled to sit up. "We could have saved a lot of time by having the LT sit outside the ship as bait."

"You good?" Jacob asked.

"Broken arm, I think," Murph said. "Mettler will patch me up. I think MG hit head first, so he'll be okay."

Jacob stepped back to allow the battlesynths to secure their Ull prisoner. Mettler came flying out of the upper hatch into the cargo hold, and Murph waved him over to MG. The team's medic went to work with a portable scanner, checking the weaponeer's vitals and making sure there wasn't anything that would pose a risk to him being moved.

Murph cradled his left arm, and the forearm had an odd bend to it, but the bone wasn't protruding from the skin. The *Phoenix*'s advanced med-bay would be able to patch it back up in short order. Thankfully, the computers already had detailed files on human treatments given how many times its owner, Jason Burke, had to be patched up.

"Murph, go ahead on up to the infirmary, and I'll meet you there," Mettler called. He'd put MG into a neck brace and rolled him onto his back. The Marine's chest rose and fell regularly, and his color looked good, so Jacob was hopeful it was just a precaution.

"What about him?" he asked.

"Med nanobots are reporting at least a moderate concussion they can treat," Mettler said. "I put the brace on just in case. He banged his head pretty good on that crate, and I want to do a full scan in the infirmary. I'll go get the board, and then have one of the battlesynths help me carry him up. You okay?"

"Bell rung," Jacob grunted. "I'm feeling alright now."

"Let me treat these two, and then I want you up there as well, LT," Mettler said. "Let's not take any chances."

"Will do, Corporal," Jacob said. "Go patch them up."

"Jacob, you will want to see this," 707 said.

Jacob walked over and saw the Ull had been carrying a small device with a screen not unlike their own com units, but with an oval shape and screen instead of rectangular. 707 had accessed the device and flipped through pictures and documents written in a language Jacob's neural implant couldn't identify. The pictures told the whole story, however. Most were of him, some were of his team, and two were of their old ship, the *Boneshaker*.

Boneshaker, a ship that lived up to its name like no other, sat in a rented hangar on S'Tora and would probably not get back into orbit without a major overhaul. The Eshquarian combat shuttle had been stolen by the team when they'd been in a pinch, and they had kept it far longer than they'd intended.

Once they'd gone rogue and were outside of Naval Special Operations Command's logistical system, they'd not been able to do anything about it. The mangled ship had been the reason Jacob had taken bold action and stolen the *Phoenix*. The powerful Jepsen gunship had already made their current mission easier by actually making it all the way to their destination without dropping out of slip-space with a mechanical emergency.

"The data is old. The shuttle is out of date, as is the fact they're still showing Taylor," Jacob said, his chest tightening. "He was killed months ago."

"The text on this device indicates this Ull has been instructed to capture you not kill," 707 said.

"This is a strange turn of events," Jacob said. "I thought we were hunting down a burned member of the Ull faction helping Jansen. Now, it looks like he was hunting us. Was this a counterintelligence op, and they know we have their com system cracked?" He rubbed his temples to relieve the pain of the massive headache that started to kick up right behind his eyes.

"Unclear at this time," 784 said. The second battlesynth had come back up the ramp after doing a quick check around the *Phoenix* for any other potential attackers. "It is also unclear how they knew you were on this ship."

"Probably saw one of those morons out there taking a leak by the fence or something," Jacob sighed. "Damnit! That means we've lost the advantage this ship had given us when it comes to sneaking in on Jansen."

"That was always a dubious advantage, my young Lieutenant," 707 said. "Your father was known to Jansen. He attacked her with this ship multiple times. I believe she would recognize it but possibly draw the wrong conclusions."

"What are we going to do with him?" 784 asked, nudging the Ull with his foot.

"Secure him and let's question him," Jacob said. "Do we need to treat that wound?"

"If it is not oozing blood, the dermal plates will fuse again without any help from us," 707 said. "Without the proper infirmary, you would be unable to treat him."

Ull were somewhat unique looking in a part of the galaxy that boasted almost a hundred different star-faring species. They were thin and tall with an almost pipe-like appearance. Their limbs and torsos were tubular, pink, and hard as nails. They had an almost rubbery texture to them, but it wasn't an exoskeleton, just a thick, strong skin adaptation.

They tended to be minimalist when it came to clothing, and this one was no different, wearing a utility belt and what looked like a cross between a kilt and cargo shorts...and that was it. Not even any shoes, which was insane on an active ramp full of starships that leaked all manner of caustic fluids.

784 propped the Ull up on the transit crate Jason dragged over while 707 strapped it down to the cargo loops on the deck. Ull were incredibly strong despite their willowy appearance, but the straps 707 had used should be more than enough to keep it in place if it went crazy. Jacob also figured the spidery cracks in its torso skin would

slow it down a bit. Once they were done, it took another twenty minutes and some hard slaps to get the alien's eyes to flutter open.

"I see I have severely underestimated my prey," the Ull said, wheezing a bit.

"Why did you use a concussion stunner against two battlesynths?" 707 asked. "Are you unfamiliar with my kind?"

"I didn't know you were with him," it said. "I know all about you, of course. I'd even seen you poking around the starport. My intel said nothing about the human having battlesynths on his crew."

"We saw your information was dated," Jacob said, waving the oval device at him. "Any chance you're going to tell us why you tried to kill me?"

"Capture not kill," it said. "I switched my weapon to plasma shots when I saw the battlesynths coming at me. It was why my shot went wide, for all the good it'd do against them. I'd originally been set to stun again and get you out of here before your team could react."

"Who sent you?" 707 asked.

"That answer is a little more complicated than you would think. To be brief, I'm a private contractor. I was sent out to grab you and hand you over. They don't give me much more information than that."

The Ull's demeanor was unlike any of the others Jacob had encountered. Its speech patterns were relaxed and familiar, and it didn't look at the two species in front of it with the open derision and contempt he'd seen in the others. He asked his prisoner about that.

"Oh, I am much more indicative of our species than any of the cultists you've probably met," it said with a warbling chuckle. "They believe in the purity of Ull. I feel like we're being kept back by isolating ourselves from the rest of the galactic quadrant. Most of us would prefer a less isolationist approach."

"We're getting a bit far afield here," Murph said. "So, you claim to not be one of them, but you're working for the cultists. Why wouldn't they just come after Jacob themselves?"

"There aren't that many of them," the Ull said. "They're not leaving their stronghold on Ull that much anymore. They prefer to hand over assignments like this to contractors."

"You're a bounty hunter?" Jacob asked.

"Among other things. I prefer not to take on assassinations since localities tend to frown upon random murders. I mainly make my living smuggling small loads onto Cridal Cooperative and ConFed worlds."

"Watch him a moment, please," Jacob said to 784 while motioning the others to follow him outside the ship.

"Thoughts?" Murph asked.

"The obvious solution is to use this gift that has landed in our laps," Jacob said. "We use him to work backwards to his handler, and then go in from there."

"The problem with that is it seems far too convenient," Murph said. "We were given some vague intel about a specific target that listed this clown as tied to Jansen and her Ull backers, and then he just happens to show up and try to shoot you?"

"I agree with both of you," 707 said. "It is an opportunity to exploit, and it is also too coincidental to believe. However, knowing this was likely a setup for something else can be turned to our advantage."

"Go on," Jacob said.

"It would require some more...aggressive...forms of persuasion. So far, this Ull has been forthcoming with any information we request and speaks in a familiar, almost friendly manner with us. I do not believe he is a common smuggler."

"Ditto," Murph said. "He's too smooth, and he's lulling us with this tale of the hapless smuggler working for the eeeevil cultists. My money is on him being either a direct member of the cult, which we need to find out more about anyway, or he's an Ull intelligence operative trying to infiltrate them."

"Son of a bitch!" Jacob groaned. "I just want to shoot Margaret Jansen and go home, not play another spy game mission."

"If you didn't want to play these games, you shouldn't have joined an intel outfit," Murph said.

"*Joining* might be overstating how I got into Scout Fleet," Jacob said. "This was more akin to a mob deal...an offer I couldn't refuse. Either way, I think we can use this asshole."

"What've you got in mind?" Murph asked.

"You're going to love this." Jacob smiled widely.

"I can promise you I won't," Murph sighed.

2

"They flew here on *this?* They're braver than I thought."

"I don't think brave is the word I'd use," a rumbling voice came out of the dark.

"Just download the nav computer, Twingo," a human voice said. "Crusher, go do something besides distract him."

The dilapidated Eshquarian combat shuttle, christened *Bone-shaker* by her former crew, had definitely seen better days. The hull was buckled and rent in places, mismatched drive components were visible through the access hatches, and the smell of burning plastic hung heavy in the hangar. Her meager armament looked about twenty years out of date, and the life support systems were frighteningly out of spec.

No...Jason Burke wouldn't call the crew of this ship brave. He'd say they were genuinely idiots, his son the chief idiot among them.

Jason and his crew flew their current ship, the *Devil's Fortune*, back to S'Tora as fast as she'd fly to see if there had been anything left behind by Scout Team Obsidian that might clue them in as to where they'd taken the *Phoenix*. Two of his crew, Kage and Doc, had gone ahead to their base along the coast to search the hangar while the rest combed over Obsidian's old ship. So far, he'd come away with nothing but a profound disappointment in his son's decision-making ability.

"You have to admit...this is pretty damn funny," Crusher said. The hulking Galvetic warrior had been nothing but a pain in the ass since Jason had learned Jacob had swiped the *Phoenix*.

"The only thing I'll admit to is I'm giving very serious consideration to leaving you here," Jason said as a Jepsen SX-5 rolled up to the hangar entrance and shut down. A few moments later, Kage and Doc walked out.

"Any luck?" Jason shouted.

"Just what we already knew," Kage said. "Also, some human they called MG drove your Camaro around outside on the landing pad. No clues as to where they were heading, though."

"Okay let's update the list. We go get the *Phoenix*, take Obsidian back to Webb but, first, we kill this MG asshole for touching my car," Jason said before shouting into the *Boneshaker*'s open hatch. "Twingo! Move your blue ass! We don't have all day for you to figure out a simple task."

"Screw you!"

"Go help him, Kage," Jason said. "I want out of here as quickly as possible."

The little Veran, sensing the boss wasn't in the mood for his usual games, scampered through the hatch and up to where Twingo struggled to download the logs from the cobbled-together nav system. Jason knew the ship had originally belonged to one of Saditava Mok's crews before his kid swiped it. He wasn't sure if the ship had been in such bad condition already or if Obsidian's abuse had done most of the damage.

The SX-5 popped and pinged outside as the metal cooled from her latest flight. He looked out at the small attack ship fondly, reminding him of a miniature version of the *Phoenix*. The *Devil's Fortune*, a corvette-class ship from Mok's personal fleet, sat in a high parking orbit while they investigated on the surface.

The ship could be brought down for a planetary landing, but it required special clearance from orbital control and took forever to deorbit and land. The SX-5 could zip down and back before the corvette even began final deceleration burns.

"What the hell is that? I thought you were just going to download the logs?" Crusher said. Jason turned and saw Kage and Twingo coming down the ramp with their arms full of avionics boxes, one of which still had wires dangling from it.

"This is quicker," Twingo said. "This is all encrypted and non-standard stuff, Captain. We can hook it up on the *Devil* and let Kage take a crack at it."

"Whatever. Toss it in the ship," Jason said, impatient to leave.

S'Tora was on the edge of a vast emptiness of space called the Delphine Expanse. The system was just inside the band of space the ConFed technically claimed was their territory but did little to enforce. It was one of the reasons Omega Force had picked the planet to put their base on. There was no permanent ConFed fleet presence over their home, and that was the way they liked it.

As it was so remote and on the edge of ConFed space, they could move back towards the more populated areas of the quadrant and still have plenty of time for Kage to dig into the nav logs and find a place to start. The longer they were on the ground, the further away the *Phoenix* got.

"We've got everything, Captain," Kage said. "We can head back up."

"Are we picking up more whiskey while we're here?" Crusher asked.

"No! Get on the ship!" Jason physically pushed them out of the hangar.

He yanked the ground-power cable out of the *Boneshaker* and closed the hangar once they were all out. The ship was not at all flyable, but there was no point inviting thieves and vandals to pick her over once they left. The ship could actually be salvaged, and it was a model Jason liked, but it would need about a year with a competent engineering crew and a ton of money to get her there.

"We're waiting on you now!" Crusher shouted from the ramp of the SX-5.

"Gonna be a long mission," Jason groaned, jogging to the ship as the engines whined in startup mode.

Captain Marcus Webb, the current commanding officer of NAVSOC, was a dead man walking, and he knew it.

Maybe that was too dramatic.

It would be more accurate to say his career was about to die. The catastrophic failures of too many missions coupled with traitors and rogue operators in his ranks had made him a prime target for his political enemies. They were now saying, and not without justification, that Webb was an ineffective leader and his bungling at NAVSOC put all of humanity at risk. They were already getting the support they needed within UEAS Central Command to approach the civilian oversight and have him removed for cause.

In the meantime, he still had missions to plan and run.

The UES *Kentucky*, one of NAVSOC's advanced command and control ships, was just now re-entering Terran space with the UES *Eagle's Talon*. The latter flew with a skeleton crew after it had been seized from a crew that had gone completely off the reservation and had joined up with the rebellion currently fomenting against the ConFed. Earth absolutely could not be seen taking sides in the conflict, so Scout Fleet had been sent to find the heavy cruiser so Webb's strike teams could recapture it.

Obsidian had been the crew that found the *Talon* but had then decided to engage in an unauthorized mission of their own after Lieutenant Brown thought he'd found a way to suss out where the leader of One World hid. On the surface, it was almost worth it to try. One scout team in exchange for the head of Margaret Jansen made sense from a command level.

Unfortunately, there were other considerations, not the least of which was what Jason Burke would do to him if his only son were killed on a half-baked seek and destroy mission. Another high-profile incident within NAVSOC also wouldn't look great if Brown caused another mess on someone else's planet.

"Captain Webb," a deep voice said from behind him.

"701," Webb said without turning around. "Still here, I see. I take it your task is not yet complete? What other treacheries do you plan to inflict upon me before leaving?"

"I have apologized for the earlier deception," 701 said. The battlesynth moved and came to stand right beside him. Whenever one of them stood close, Webb was uncomfortably aware they could kill him without anyone being able to stop them. "I am remaining on the *Kentucky* to provide you additional tactical power should any of the *Talon*'s crew try anything foolish."

"I appreciate that," Webb said, swallowing his sarcastic retort at the last second. The battlesynths weren't mindless automatons, and he knew them to have a strict honor code and morality. They wouldn't have helped Brown's team escape if they didn't feel it was absolutely the right thing to do. "Will you be moving your colony to Olympus when we get back home?"

"I am unsure what 707 has decided. We like the desert and the isolation on Terranovus, but it is now to become a civilian world. I am not certain we would fit in there."

"We've got a few nice deserts on Olympus," Webb said, referring to Earth's newly acquired planet being tooled up as the secret home of the United Earth Armed Services. "One is more rocky than sandy, so maybe you'd enjoy that more."

"Perhaps," 701 said.

"I'm guessing that's not why you came up here?" Webb asked.

"I always enjoy talking to you, Captain," 701 said diplomatically. "But no, that was not the main reason for my visit. We are worried about retaliation by your government for our interference on the behalf of Lieutenant Brown. Lot 700 has enjoyed your hospitality, but our commitment and oath to the Burke family supersedes any loyalty we have to Earth or the UEAS. If we are no longer welcome, it would be best if we found out now so we could relocate without any...unfortunate misunderstandings."

Webb's blood chilled at that last sentence. Knowing 701 as he did, the meaning was crystal clear. If the UEAS tried to impose sanctions or pursue criminal complaints against Lot 700, they would leave. If they were blocked from leaving, things would get bloody.

Battlesynths had not been treated well by the other species within the quadrant, not even the Pru, who had designed and built them. They were veritable slaves for much of their existence, freed with some reluctance, and still treated with distrust and hostility in most places. If Earth tried something foolish like sanctioning them for exercising their free will, they would not tolerate it.

"I appreciate the heads up," he said. "I don't think it will be a problem. I have omitted much of your group's actions from the report submitted to my superiors. Other than you coming aboard the *Kentucky* in an advisory capacity as experts in ship boarding actions and assisting me in hunting Elton Hollick, you're not mentioned. The people who actually saw you aboard the *Talon* only know you were there not *why* you were there. The official story going up the chain makes no mention of you helping Obsidian run a rogue operation."

"My thanks, Captain. We would—"

"But," Webb went on, "you have two members still with Obsidian, and I no longer have any control over that situation. Jacob Brown sealed his fate when he disobeyed orders to return to base. His men will obviously be in their own amount of trouble as well. I would suggest you make sure 707 and 784 know not to be around them when the fleet inevitably catches up to them."

"I see," 701 said. "I will inform 707 when next I speak to him."

"Aren't you all always connected? Or did I misunderstand that?"

"We have means of communication that aren't widely known," 701 said evasively. "For the duration of their mission, 707 and 784 have isolated themselves from us."

The battlesynths had been highly secretive as to how they seemed able to pass information to each other regardless of distance. Webb assumed it must have been some sort of miniaturized slip-com system built into each of them, but discreet scans of individuals while they were aboard Terran ships detected no localized slip-space fields.

For now, it would remain their little secret. Apparently, the system could also be used to track as well. Otherwise, it made no sense for the other two to have switched off their coms.

"Just pass it on whenever you hear from them," Webb said. "I won't pry into your secrets, but I can't guarantee I can protect you, either. I promise if I catch wind Earth wants to take action against Lot 700, you will be the first person I contact about it before I use any political juice I have left to fight it."

"You are a true ally and friend, Captain Webb," 701 said. "Thank you. Let us hope none of that will be necessary."

"Let's hope," Webb agreed.

3

"Your ship smells like absolute shit. You should be ashamed of yourself."

"Then don't fly with me. I'd prefer not to have one of you jabbering primates on my ship to begin with," Grynn said. Jacob had no idea if that was his first name, last name, *only* name, title, or a made-up word. It was just what the Ull had said when they asked what they should call him.

"I won't be," he said. "I'm just here to make sure you fully understand the nature of our arrangement."

"I understand it just fine," Grynn said, snorting.

"Good," Jacob said, walking off the flightdeck of the Ull's cramped, disgustingly filthy ship. Down on the main deck, the rest of his team finished the rest of their preparations.

"Charges are set," Murph said. "We covered all of the emergency air dumps and put some nasty breaching charges your old man had in the armory on the outer hull in places he probably couldn't find. If he gives the battlesynths any trouble, they can let the air out for him."

"I'm still not in love with this plan," Jacob told 707.

"It is your plan."

"No, my plan had *me* coming along on Smelly's ship," Jacob argued. "I don't like the idea of both of you being on here."

"Given how much more punishment we are able to survive, along with the fact we do not require sleep, this plan *only* makes sense if we are the ones to accompany Grynn," 707 said in his infuriatingly calm voice.

"To be honest, LT, this plan sucks," MG said from an access hatch on the deck. "I mean, your plans aren't always the best, but you really didn't put a lot of effort into this one."

"A lot of effort into this one *what?*" Jacob said.

"A lot of effort into your bullshit, stupid plan...*sir*."

"When I want the opinion of someone who goes by two letters because he can't remember his own name half the time, I'll come get you," Jacob said. "Until then, less mouth, more work."

"He's not wrong," Murph said quietly. "These people are bound to have failsafes, passcodes he can use to quietly tell them he's been compromised."

"I think the *Phoenix* will be the equalizer there. Even if they see her coming, they don't know we're aboard," Jacob said after a moment of thought. "They'll probably be on the lookout for the *Boneshaker*. Mettler rummaged through the files on this ship and confirmed his intel is well out of date. The people after us don't know about the battlesynths or the gunship."

"If you're right, we'll have to go scorched earth when we engage them," Murph said. "You ready for that? You can't risk leaving survivors if we're really going to sneak up on Jansen."

Jacob gave the question the serious consideration he felt it deserved. "I'm all-in," he said finally. "I know I've tried to straddle that line before, but it's come back to bite us in the ass more times than not. I volunteered us for this job. It's up to me to make sure we do it right."

"Now you're getting it," Murph said. "Special Forces is an ugly, dirty business, LT. When I first came here from NIS, I wasn't prepared for the level of violence the Scout Fleet teams saw while deployed to some of these shithole planets. Believe me, it's a dog-eat-dog galaxy. Your mercy will be seen as weakness, and they'll come for you. I'm glad your delusions are getting scrubbed away so fast."

"They were scrubbed away when I lost Taylor," Jacob said quietly.

"You didn't lose him. Hollick took him. But you made that right." Murph punched him on the shoulder and walked away.

Obsidian used to have a dedicated tech on their team named Taylor Levin. On their last mission, Elton Hollick snatched Taylor off the *Boneshaker*, tortured him to death, and then dumped what was left of his body back onto the shuttle as a message to Jacob to back off.

Later on, Jacob tracked Hollick to some out-of-the-way planet and put him down like the rabid dog he was. The Marine shot him in a dirty alley, and then tossed his corpse out the airlock of the ship when they left. No one would ever know the corporeal remains of Elton Hollick, ex-NIS agent and traitor to Earth, had burned up re-entering the atmosphere of a planet called Noelin-2.

"We are almost ready to begin, Lieutenant," 707 said. "It would be a good time for you to head back and get the *Phoenix* ready to fly."

"Sully's done his preflight already," Jacob said, "but I can take a hint. Pack it up, boys. We're Oscar Mike in ten."

"Thank God," MG said as he climbed out of the deck hatch. "It smells like moldy cheese dipped in ball sweat, and then wrapped in Murph's boxers in here."

"Disgusting but accurate," Jacob said. "Is Mettler still on our ship?"

"Yeah, he's standing guard while Sully handles the *Phoenix*," Murph said. "Every time we leave Sully alone, someone sneaks aboard and brains him. Figured we should leave him some protection if for no other reason not wanting our only pilot suffering repeated head trauma."

It had taken less than a full day for them to prep and execute this side of the plan. The *Phoenix* had an impressive amount of hardware between the armory and the engineer's fully equipped workshop, so it took Mettler and the two battlesynths no time at all to rig up the components they installed on Grynn's ship to ensure his compliance.

Jacob's original plan had been to rig all of those to his neural implant somehow so he could trigger them if Grynn tried anything stupid like killing him in his sleep, but 707 had firmly rejected that idea.

Now, the plan had a bit of a complication since, instead of leading Jacob off his ship as his original contract had stipulated, Grynn would need to adlib a bit to get his buyers to expose themselves. It wasn't an insignificant problem, but 707 wouldn't budge. Since the battlesynths were there of their own accord and didn't technically report to him, he had no choice but to give ground on that detail.

"I won't miss this hot-ass planet," MG said as the trio walked the half-klick or so back to where the *Phoenix* was parked. When the ship came into sight, Jacob had to admit his pops had an impressively mean-looking ride. Newer ships coming from the quadrant's major builders had all adopted a blocky, utilitarian look to them and used the nav shields to smooth the airflow out within an atmosphere.

The *Phoenix* was smooth, sleek, and elegantly proportioned. While graceful, she exuded menace even when sitting on the ramp powered down. If even half the stories were to be believed, the ship he borrowed was half the reason for Jason Burke's notoriety.

"When they toss us in Red Cliff, you'll long for this heat and sunshine," Murph said. He referred to the infamous Red Cliff Military Prison Complex. It was named for the color of the sheer bluffs surrounding it and was most noted for temperatures outside similar to Siberia.

"Just a ray of fucking sunshine, huh?" MG asked, tripping Murph with his left foot. "Besides, I'm just some dumb grunt following the orders of my duly appointed superior officer. They'll toss the LT in jail not me."

"He's not wrong." Jacob shrugged. "Our orders always filter through me. I could have easily lied to you guys and dragged you along. Mettler will be in prison, too, though. He actually snuck away from Captain Webb to come out here, so they won't believe his story."

"Maybe they'll let you guys be roommates," MG said. "It'll be just like one really long, boring recon mission."

"I don't think it's that kind of place, MG."

By the time they walked up the ramp, the *Phoenix* hummed with power, prepping for takeoff. Even though all three of them had been injured in the blast of Grynn's concussion grenade, they'd been put back in working order in a matter of hours by the *Phoenix*'s amazing infirmary.

There was advanced machinery in there Mettler had never even heard of but, thankfully, was completely automated. It was a taste of the kind of tech available in the quadrant if you weren't under the constraints of restrictive trade treaties like Earth was with their membership agreement with the Cridal Cooperative.

"That Ull's ship is already off the pad," Mettler yelled from the main deck hatchway. "Sully wants us buttoned up and in orbit within the next thirty minutes."

"Tell him once he gets a green light on the ramp he's clear to lift off," Jacob said, flipping the controls near the back of the cargo hold to raise and lock the rear ramp, as well as close the internal pressure doors.

He took one last look around the hold to make sure no nasty surprises waited for them. The *Phoenix*'s odd AI personality, a program that called itself Cas, had promised to keep an eye on things, but Jacob didn't fully trust it. He wanted to verify with his own eyes that Grynn hadn't been some elaborate distraction to sneak aboard some other assassin or assault team that would drag him out of his rack and kill his team out of convenience.

The repulsors fired just as he climbed the stairs to the main deck. He heard the *Phoenix* pop and groan as her weight shifted from landing gear to the lift-drive. For whatever reason, the starport they were at wouldn't allow them to move off the landing pads using the grav-drive.

Maybe the locals loved the thunderous racket of twenty ships an hour blasting off on repulsor jets. Sully would be required to hover up to an altitude of one hundred meters or so before Departure Control would give him the go-ahead to engage the main drive and give them an orbital vector.

"Well, this is comfortable," he said as he walked onto the bridge, the repulsors vibrating the deck hard enough to make his teeth rattle.

"Stupid local laws," Sully griped. "When they made this regulation, it was probably to keep the big heavy lifters from overflowing to this starport when the main one up north was full. But now, even the big ships have repulsor drives powerful enough to get them in the air. The law is out of date, and all it's doing is making sure nobody who lives in the nearby villages gets any sleep. Ever."

"If I lived here, I would have bombed this starport already," MG said.

"That's the sort of measured, rational response I'd expect from you," Sully said. "Or...you could just move away."

"Why should *I* have to move because of some else's stupid rule?" MG asked.

"Standby for switchover," Sully said.

There was a moment of stomach-dropping vertigo as the grav-drive picked up the weight of the ship just as the repulsors cut out. Now running on her main drive, the *Phoenix* tore away from the starport, climbing hard for their orbital intercept.

"Mesh-out point is about nine hours out once we're clear of orbit," Sully said. "It'll be a long, boring ride until then."

"Cool story," MG said.

"That was my subtle way of saying get the hell off my flightdeck," Sully snapped. "I have to be up here for the full flight since none of you are qualified to fly, and I'll be damned if I'm going to listen to you degenerates the entire time."

"Subtle enough," Jacob said. "Let's go."

"Appreciate it," Sully said. "Stay out of Engineering, too."

"He used to be a lot more fun before we became fugitives," Mettler said as he walked off the bridge.

The screams of the Ull reverberated within the confines of the tiny ship. Grynn cowered in front of the two battlesynths, one with its fists raised to deliver another blow.

"I'm sorry! I'm sorry!"

"We warned you repeatedly that any attempt to damage or neutralize us would result in your harm," 707 said calmly. "This mission still has a high probability of success regardless whether you survive this trip or not."

"I won't try again! I WON'T!" Grynn whimpered. Blood oozed from half a dozen cracks in his torso dermal plates where 707 had smashed him with an armored fist.

Since the ship had meshed-out of the system, they'd dodged three clumsy attempts by the Ull to dispatch them. The first time, he was given a stern warning. The second time, they reduced the temperature within the ship to 275 Kelvin, just above the freezing point of water, and kept it there for almost two hours. Ull are a hardy species but, by the time the air handlers started blowing warm air again, Grynn was lethargic and stumbled about.

This third time, 784 had caught him trying to use the ship's grav-plating to rig a trap for them. Grynn wanted to increase the gravity where they stood to the point it would overcome their ability to resist and trap them on the deck until he could figure out a way to permanently deal with them.

His mistake was in greatly underestimating the level of Gs a battlesynth could operate in. He never did find out. All he knew was it was more than his ship could produce before the plate emitters burned out.

Once they'd detected what he was doing, they played along and pretended to be stuck and immobile. When Grynn approached to gloat, 707 punched him with enough force to send the Ull flying through the open hatchway and into the cargo area. After that, it was just an old-fashioned beatdown with two battlesynths taking turns pummeling the biotic.

It was a level of savagery that 707 rarely indulged in, but his anger boiled over at the thought of young Jacob Brown almost being caught alone on this ship and at the Ull's mercy. While it was laudable the young officer risked himself before his troops, his decision-making ability left a lot to be desired.

"You've broken me too badly to give you much of a fight now," Grynn said, holding onto his sides as the cracks in his dermal plates leaked all over the deck.

"You will be restrained for the remainder of the flight. We will decide later whether your continued existence is still of use to us once we land," 707 said. The icy calm demeanor and casual way he talked about killing Grynn had the desired effect, and the normally pink alien paled by several shades.

"I think I need medical attention," Grynn said.

"That seems likely," 707 agreed, "but you will receive none. Your species is tough. It is highly probable you will survive your injuries with only minor lasting effects."

The two battlesynths dragged the Ull back to the ship's cramped cargo bay and secured him to the bulkhead with the restraints already hanging there. Apparently, Grynn wasn't too concerned with his target's comfort when he ran down a bounty. By the time they'd chained him up and made sure the hold's security system monitored him, the Ull had lapsed into unconsciousness.

"If he dies on us, it will negatively impact the mission outcome," 784 said once they'd closed and locked the hatch to the hold.

"We cannot risk him free movement so he can try increasingly desperate measures to eliminate us," 707 said. "The brutality is regrettably necessary."

"You misunderstand me," 784 said. "I have no concern of the Ull or his comfort. I have yet to meet any from their species I have found agreeable. What I am worried about is his inability to function once we land."

"I have a contingency for that," 707 assured him.

4

"We're coming up on our mesh-in, everybody," Sully called over the intercom.

The *Phoenix* shuddered as she was spit out of slip-space and carried her relative velocity into the Kizarain System. The prime planet was a Tier Three world that declared itself aligned with the ConFed but didn't pay enough in taxes or have enough natural resources to warrant any fleet presence.

Now that the rebellion had drawn blood and looked to be heading for a full civil war as member systems peeled off, the ConFed wasn't sparing ships to aimlessly pop into systems like Kizarain to fly the flag these days.

"How's it look?" Jacob asked as he walked onto the bridge and climbed into the copilot seat.

"Nothing unusual," Sully said. "No ConFed, Cridal, or Saabror ships in the area. Or at least none broadcasting their ident beacons. I'm not picking up Grynn's ship either, so we either made it here early or 707 already went down to the surface."

"Unlikely," Jacob said. "If we're not there, the whole plan is out the window. Let's take a normal approach to the planet and see if they're out there flying silent. This system isn't real big on enforcing the ConFed's declaration laws."

"You got it," Sully said. "What do you want to do if we get to the planet and they're still not here?"

"Just hang out in orbit so we can hit the starport the same time they do. If orbital control complains too much, we can always claim we're working a maintenance issue that's keeping us from deorbiting."

Sully looked doubtful but said nothing. Most planets like Kizarain-2 didn't let you loiter too long in an orbital lane. They tried to get ships in and out as quickly as possible, and a small ship like the *Phoenix*, which wasn't bringing in any needed goods to the planet, wouldn't be tolerated flying in circles for long.

"Grynn's ship just popped up on the screen," Sully said after they'd been flying in the system for almost four hours.

"Now, the party can get started," MG said, rubbing his hands together and smiling at the thought of the potential violence about to unfold.

"Coded message coming in from 784," Mettler said from one of the sensor stations. "They're good to go."

Since they hadn't had time to fully toss Grynn's ship, the decision was made to stay off all the slip-com nodes aboard it since they could be monitored. Once they arrived in the system, the battlesynths sent a short message on an RF-burst transmission on a frequency not normally monitored. They were to just give a go, no-go signal for the mission.

"Sully, do your thing," Jacob said. "Everyone else, down to the armory and get ready. We don't know if we're going to be grabbing an Ull or a human, so be ready for both."

The next phase of the mission was the most stressful for Jacob. He trusted the battlesynths completely, but to not have any idea how their end of the operation was going until the *Phoenix* landed on the planet was nerve-racking. They had an emergency abort signal that could be triggered if shit went totally sideways, but there were no guarantees at this point.

"Your old man has some wild shit in here," MG said as Jacob walked into the armory.

"It isn't just Burke's toys," Murph said, waving to a wall loaded with racks of oversized plasma guns and wicked-looking edge weapons. "Crusher's stuff is all still here, too. If you're going to use anything off that wall, just remember, if you break it, he's not known for his patience or understanding."

"You talk about that dude like he's some sort of monster," MG scoffed. "You ever actually met him?"

"I did," Jacob said. He almost hadn't realized he'd said it aloud. When he saw everyone staring at him, he went on. "I was fourteen. Jason—my dad—had just saved Earth from the Ull invasion, though we all heard differently. Anyway, before he left Earth again, he arranged to see me. Parked this ship right in the middle of a field where the whole crew walked out.

"Crusher is terrifying. He's damn near seven feet tall, and if he weighs less than three hundred and fifty pounds, I'd be shocked. He could rip your arms off without even trying."

"What's he like?" Murph asked. Jacob looked up and saw they all stared at him with rapt attention.

"He's actually pretty funny once you get used to the voice and the fact he talks with his hands so he's always waving those claws in your face," Jacob said.

"I'll just stick to my own gear," MG said, pulling out the transit crate that had all the weapons and equipment they'd taken off their old ship.

"Good choice," Murph said. "Most of Crusher's guns are fit to a Galvetic hand anyway. Your little mitts would barely wrap around the handle."

Jacob just shook his head as they quickly assembled their gear and prepped for the op. The chatter was just nerves. Even after so many harrowing missions and so much time working together, they all still got the jitters before something like this.

Commander Ezra Mosler, Obsidian's original commanding officer, had told Jacob that combat junkies didn't belong in NAVSOC,
and if he didn't get a case of nerves before the shooting started, he
should find another line of work before he got his team and himself
killed.

"Sully, we're all set back here," Jacob said into the intercom panel.

"Sit tight, LT. I'll have you on the ground in about an hour.
Grynn's ship is just starting to deorbit, and we'll follow them in."

The team filed out of the armored hatch into the cargo hold and
sat in webbed seats that folded down from the port bulkhead. Each
sat without speaking, lost in their thoughts and prepping for what
was coming. The mission could be an absolute cakewalk, or it could
be a bloodbath.

Kizarain-2 was the type of world that would allow a certain
amount of violence on the out-of-the-way starports, figuring that
spending the money and effort to try and tame those areas wouldn't
matter anyway since there were always new smugglers and mercenaries coming in.

Usually, if the gunplay was contained to the starport, no civilians
were involved or harmed, and nobody broke out any heavy or
strategic weapons, they would look the other way...for a fee. You
break any of those rules, and law enforcement would blow your ship
up on the ramp, and you'd find yourself subjected to a local legal
system unconcerned with your rights under ConFed law.

The *Phoenix* rocked and bumped gently as she pushed down into
the lower atmosphere and leveled out. Since they deorbited over the
equator, it would be another fifty-minute flight to the industrial starport Grynn claimed was the rendezvous point for the prisoner transfer. The port was in the southern hemisphere in an isolated area that
was mostly featureless, flat grassland.

Given the port was meant to service the planet's industry, it made
little sense to have it so far out in the middle of nowhere. Jacob was
mildly curious about this but hadn't been able to find any sort of
answer on the local Nexus other than it had something to do with a

planetary ordinance that required certain types of cargo to be kept over five hundred kilometers away from any population centers.

"Standby, guys," Sully called down. "Just got word from 784 over the com. He's requesting immediate assistance."

"What the hell kind of assistance can we give two battlesynths?" Mettler asked.

Jacob's reply was cut off as the *Phoenix* rolled and dove for the deck, her engines coming to full power, the vibrations through the deck becoming harsh and pronounced. The ship was an extremely potent weapon...in the right hands. Sully had to concentrate on flying the ship without a copilot, and Cas had made it clear it couldn't operate any offensive or defensive systems to help out.

They were also woefully undertrained on the ship and couldn't yet use her to her full capability. He hoped they weren't rushing into getting blasted out of the sky because they had no idea what the hell they were doing.

"They shot me!"

"If you do not be silent, I will shoot you as well," 707 said.

The battlesynth stood inside the ship's cargo hold, keeping out of sight and waiting to see if more enemy fire came their way. When they'd sent the Ull out of the ship to make contact, a projectile from a long-range weapon hit him in the torso, dropping him.

Rather than rush out to drag him back into the ship, the two battlesynths had let him writhe in agony as they scanned the area to see where the shot had come from. Since they didn't know for certain either way, they decided to operate under the assumption their presence was still unknown.

Grynn had eventually dragged himself back into the ship, now bleeding profusely. The fact there were no follow-up shots after he began moving made 707 wonder if the shot had been a random crime or simply a mistake by an overeager sniper. After pulling himself to the forward bulkhead with no help from either battlesynth, the Ull had taken to lying on the floor and complaining loudly.

"Were you supposed to make contact to let them know you were clear?" 784 asked. When Grynn didn't answer, he walked over and kicked the Ull in the torso. The pain was so great Grynn couldn't even scream. He just made guttural warbling noises.

"The next time, I will not be so gentle."

"There was a code I was supposed to transmit when I made orbit," Grynn said. "I was chained up in the hold, so I obviously never sent it."

"Shall I kill him?" 784 asked.

"Not until we are certain there is no further use of him," 707 said. "Then you may kill him."

"Wait!" Grynn wailed. "I can still help!"

Another projectile, this one fired from a different vantage, slammed into the bulkhead mere centimeters from Grynn's head. The Ull had popped up from behind the crates to talk to 707. From the angle of this shot, it was still likely the battlesynths had remained hidden from view.

"What will be the makeup of the team coming to claim Lieutenant Brown?" 707 asked.

"Who? Oh, the human. There will be two ships, both Aracorian in design, nine soldiers per ship," Grynn said.

707 was highly skeptical the information was accurate, but it was all he had to work with. If there were real soldiers out there, they probably had weaponry that could harm them, especially since they were pinned down.

"Go to the flightdeck and try to locate two Aracorian ships," 707 said to his partner. "Transmit the information to Lieutenant Sullivan and have the *Phoenix* provide air cover."

"Standby," 784 said, diving back through the open hatch into the interior of the ship.

"What ground-defense armament does this vessel have?" 707 demanded.

"None!" Grynn wheezed. "I operate on planets where that's illegal.

I can't have—" A sharp explosion on the outer hull cut him off. The ship rocked on its landing struts, and alarms blared from inside.

"They have just taken out the main drive!" 784 shouted from the flightdeck. "Lieutenant Sullivan is on his way. He is not entirely confident he can operate the *Phoenix* in a combat situation, however."

"Not optimal but unavoidable," 707 said. "Have him target the Aracorian ships to ensure they cannot depart."

"Target package uploaded," Cas said. "This is the extent of my ability to help you. I cannot directly control any of the—"

"Tactical or defensive systems," Sully said. "Yeah, yeah. I got it the first six times you told me."

He wheeled the *Phoenix* about and pushed her nose over, diving for the deck and getting the first of the ships Cas had targeted lined up for a lateral run with the main guns. The armament panel was still a little bit of a mystery as he wasn't sure exactly what each of the icons meant, but he felt certain the six big plasma cannons nestled in the wing roots would be up to the task.

The ship he was after was parked off by itself on the tarmac, so he assumed that would be where the enemy's reserve force was hiding. He angled over slightly, and when the reticle on the targeting display flashed green twice, he squeezed and held the trigger. The gunship shook with the rhythmic *thumps* of the six main guns unleashing hell onto the unsuspecting ship below.

As it turned out, they probably weren't the best choice in weapons for the job. The powerful cannons obliterated the target easily enough. They also ripped up a massive section of the tarmac, took out a fuel truck, blew up a storage building, and blasted the tail section off a ship parked nearby.

"Oh. Oh, shit."

"The main cannons are more suited for ship-to-ship combat in space," Cas informed him. "They're meant to overwhelm the shields of another ship."

"I feel like you could have mentioned that before I opened fire," Sully growled as he pulled the *Phoenix* into a high, vertical turn.

"I was curious to see what would happen," Cas said. "For the last target, I would suggest switching to the chin turret. Second icon from the left."

Sully, feeling sick and hoping he hadn't killed anyone he wasn't supposed to, switched over to the chin turret and just barely felt the ship buffet in the air as it deployed from under the nose. The twin cannons mounted in the turret were significantly smaller, more precise than the main guns, and were able to be trained independently of the ship's orientation.

As the *Phoenix* swung back around, the reticle moved and automatically locked onto the second target, tracking it as Sully pushed the nose over and came back towards the starport.

"This one won't blow the whole damn place up, will it?"

"No," Cas said. "It will incapacitate the ship."

Sully swore under his breath and opened fire again. This time, plasma shots of lesser intensity than before lanced out and peppered the Aracorian ship. He watched as the shots ripped through the port engine nacelle, across the backbone, and into the starboard winglet.

He released the trigger and wrapped into a tight, descending turn so he could deploy his Marines near Grynn's ship. He noted the Ull's vessel burned, one of its engines blown completely off the pylon and laying on the ramp.

"Standby, Brown...we're coming in hot!"

Once he leveled the ship out over the drop zone, Sully lowered the rear ramp and descended so the edge of the ramp was only half a meter off the tarmac and held a steady hover. He watched on the monitor as all four of the Marines ran out the back and sprinted for the Ull ship.

He rotated the *Phoenix* to provide them cover before raising the ramp and lifting away from the fray, heading out over the open plains. He took a few more shots at the remaining ship with the chin turret for good measure, the blasts all hitting the flight deck canopy. One looked like it might have gotten through.

"Now, let's hope they wrap that up quick," he said. "The locals will probably have a response inbound."

"Monitoring local emergency channels now," Cas said. "The explosion has been reported but has not been linked to an attack."

"That's something, I guess."

"Go, go, go!!"

The *Phoenix* thundered off towards the open grassland, hitting one of the enemy ships one more time, as Jacob and his team ran for the Ull ship. At the far end of the ramp, there were two or three ships burning and emergency vehicles screaming across the tarmac to respond.

"Sitrep!"

"They had sniper cover, likely in the far craft Lieutenant Sullivan destroyed and shot Grynn as he emerged from the ship. They fired to damage the engines so we could not leave, but have so far made no other aggressive moves," 707 said.

"We're sure they're in that Aracorian ship?" Jacob asked.

"Reasonably so, but no direct recon," 707 said.

"Then let's get over there," Jacob said. "Mettler, you stay here with Grynn—"

"He is dead," 784 said. "The cumulative injuries were too much, it appears."

"Okay," Jacob said. "Mettler, you're back with us. I want you and Murph to go straight down that row across from here and come in behind them. MG and I will split that angle and approach while keeping that small shuttle for cover. 707 and 784 will move at it head-on. If it looks like they're going to open fire with the ship's weapons, bail out."

"Acknowledged," 707 said.

Jacob took one glance at the Ull, who was gray-colored in death, before taking off with MG while the other two-man teams split off for their targets. Obsidian had worked together long enough to know, once they reached the objective, they would try to take live prisoners to question but take no chances if it came to a firefight.

Jacob would rather lose a lead than lose a teammate. He drilled it into his people that, in these situations, they needed to defend themselves and each other as the first priority. If that changed, he'd let them know specifically.

"*Still no request for support from the field operations center, but we're only monitoring public channels,*" Sully said over their headsets.

"Copy," Jacob said, running up to the shuttle he intended to use as cover. "Keep clear until we're ready for pickup."

"*LT, the canopy on their ship was blown out,*" Murph said on the team channel. "*Lots of smoke coming out.*"

"Move further around and—"

"*We have been engaged,*" 707 said calmly. "*Four Ull and three humans.*"

"This is definitely our party then," Jacob said. "Drop the Ull, try and bag the humans. Where are they now?" As he said it, the distinct bark of battlesynth arm cannons sounded, along with the sporadic zip of Terran plasma arms, as well as something that actually sounded like regular, old-fashioned gunfire.

"*Trying to defend the cargo hold of their ship,*" 784 answered. "*They are fortifying and appear to be waiting for rescue. Perhaps they do not know their other ship was destroyed.*"

"I doubt it," Jacob said. "Sully! Keep an eye out for anybody else coming into this area faster than normal traffic. These assholes may have called for a dustoff."

"*Copy.*"

"Converge," Jacob ordered. "Battlesynths, try and draw their fire, but don't risk taking a direct hit."

"*Acknowledged.*"

Jacob was about to pull two stun grenades off his harness to try and surprise the target, but just as the battlesynths started their diversion, the enemy broke cover. The Ull, incredibly, rushed the two battlesynths while the three humans took off towards the starport terminal, apparently hoping the local authorities would shelter them.

The Ull seemed confident in the heavy armament they carried, completely unaware their numerical advantage would mean nothing against the battlesynths.

"Shit!" Murph said, raising his weapon and drawing a bead on the running humans, but they'd already gotten too close to the now-panicked civilians to risk a shot.

Without thinking, Jacob took off after them at a dead sprint. His teammates already knew about his secret, so he poured on the speed. The soles of his boots heated up as he accelerated, and he dropped his primary weapon to let his arms move free for balance.

The first human, apparently confident in their lead, looked back with a smirk that morphed to disbelief, then fear as he saw Jacob closing on them at nearly fifty-three kilometers per hour. While Murph had been worried about collateral damage, these clowns showed no such restraint.

When the leader opened fire, most of the shots went harmlessly wide, but two smacked into Jacob's right shoulder. The first round deflected off his body armor, but the second found the seam between the chest plate and the pauldron. The impact spun him and threw him off his trajectory, but his speed was such that he still closed the distance between himself and the trio.

He tried to draw his sidearm, but his right arm dangled uselessly, so he lowered his shoulder and slammed into the left-most human, still traveling at nearly twenty-five kilometers per hour.

The impact was horrendous.

The guy he hit had been standing flat-footed and stopped, so he absorbed most of the kinetic energy. Bones snapped, and he was sent flying into his friends, taking them out. Jacob tripped on the leader, went airborne, and slammed into the tarmac on his right shoulder. The impact sent waves of agony spiking through him and blurred his vision, but he remained conscious as he rolled over and tried to get to his sidearm with his left hand.

Two of the trio he'd been chasing were down for the count, but the one furthest away climbed to his feet, blood running down his face. He pulled a plasma sidearm and stumbled over to where Jacob struggled to get to his knees.

"You're fucking dead," he spat out, blood running down his chin. Jacob tried to gather his strength for one last lunge when his would-be killer's head exploded.

"I got ya, LT!" he heard MG's voice, sounding like it was miles away.

"You've got a lot of inbound," Sully said. "Probably less than fifteen minutes. I'm on my way for pickup."

"Is anybody hurt?" Jacob asked as Murph propped him up.

"You," he said.

"Besides me."

"Nope. Mettler and the battlesynths are raiding their ship, MG is restraining the two living dickheads, and the headless horseman here won't be of much use to us," Murph said. "This place is getting hot. All the ships blasting off out of here should give us some cover, but we need to move. Can you walk?"

"Yeah, yeah, I'm good," Jacob said, climbing up on shaky legs.

"MG and I can carry these two," Murph said, handing Jacob's dropped weapon back to him. "Shit, you're leaking like a sieve. You sure you can make it back to the ship?"

"Let's go," Jacob said, stumbling towards the burning Aracorian ship. Murph hadn't been kidding about everybody fleeing. Ships blasted off at full power every few seconds, shaking the ground and causing a ton of confusion.

By the time the *Phoenix* roared into view and came in for a hover near the damaged Aracorian ship, Jacob was barely standing. He watched in a fog as the two battlesynths dragged three large crates up, and Mettler ran over with what looked like an avionics box with cut cables hanging from it. Both human prisoners were secured after some argument about only taking one of them, and Jacob was gently led up the ramp.

"We rigged the ship to blow," Mettler said. "Sully! We're all in! Let's go!"

"Not a moment too soon," the pilot said over the intercom.

The engines vibrated through the deck as the *Phoenix* carried them away from the death and carnage they'd caused. The last Jacob remembered was being taken to the infirmary and having his gear and clothes cut off before Mettler turned loose the automated systems to begin repairs. The darkness closed in on him before the ship had even climbed out of the atmosphere.

5

"That's definitely her. Whoever is flying was a little exuberant with the main cannons."

Jason Burke stared at the repeating video clip that showed the *Phoenix*—*his* ship—attacking two Aracorian gunboats painted up in Guild colors. That could be problematic. Omega Force wasn't a member of any of the mercenary guilds that populated the outer regions near the quadrant border, but they were in good standing with most of them. The *Phoenix* attacking two of their ships would likely raise some uncomfortable questions depending on what they were doing on Kizarain-2.

Or the ships could have been painted in Boack Guild livery as a ruse. Those merc crews all tended to stay out along the edge of ConFed space where the fleet wouldn't bother them. The Kizarain System was pretty far from their usual stomping grounds. The fact they were newer Aracorian-built ships was also a bit incongruous. Nobody out along the border flew such new, expensive ships.

"Using the mains to light up a starport like that...either your boy's crew is inexperienced or they're sending a hell of a message to someone," Twingo said. He was the crew's chief engineer and the first biotic alien Jason had met when he'd left Earth. The pair had been inseparable since.

"Let's go with stupid," Crusher said, leaning over and watching the footage. "They stole a ship they have no idea how to operate, and now they've taken it into combat. Although...there is something to be said for your son's scorched earth style of overkill. It beats your hand wringing and constant whining about collateral damage any day."

"Nobody asked you," Jason told the hulking warrior. "And go hover somewhere else. Your hot breath on the back of my neck is getting on my nerves."

"All I'm saying is we have more important shit to do," Crusher said. "I know you love that ship, but we're in the middle of an open rebellion against a super power, and we still have no idea where Lucky is or how to help him. Tracking your son—who doesn't even like you, by the way—across the galaxy while ignoring everything else seems like a waste of time. Let your people deal with him."

"As...unartful...as he put it, he does have a point, Captain," Doc said. "We're spread pretty thin right now."

"I know," Jason sighed. "It can't be helped, though. Kage, you seriously have no way to track her?"

"I made sure that even *I* can't find her," the crew's code slicer said, shrugging all four of his arms dramatically. "That's what you asked me to do. Normally, we could still ping one of the slip-com nodes and at least try to get a message to whoever has her, but they've deactivated them all. My guess is they slapped a couple of their own in to keep us from doing just that. There were two nodes missing from that deathtrap they flew to S'Tora."

"So, what are we going to do?" Twingo asked.

"Get us to Kizarain-2," Jason said after a moment. "We need to look at the carnage left behind and talk to the locals before whoever owned those ships gets there to clean up."

Crusher just groaned and walked off the bridge while Doc punched in the new destination into the ship's nav interface.

"Looks like it's only a fifteen-hour flight at max power," he said.

"Let's do it," Jason said. A moment later, the *Devil's Fortune* meshed-out, still two steps behind Jacob and his team. His crew was right. They didn't have a lot of time to waste chasing Scout Team Obsidian all over the quadrant. He was being honest about their need to recover the *Phoenix,* but that was partially just a convenient excuse to mollify his crew. What was really driving him at the moment was an icy fear his son had gotten in far over his head and was about to tangle with some *very* dangerous people.

Jason had never been burdened with an overabundance of paternal instincts, hell he'd not even known about Jacob until the boy was already a teenager, but something drove him now to be there for him and make sure Jacob didn't face dangers he'd underestimated alone.

"I'm surprised this ship doesn't have a brig," Murph said. "Given the shady shit your pops is into. No offense."

"None taken," Jacob said. "The reason they didn't waste the space on a brig is because they rarely take prisoners. They favor a more absolute approach to problem-solving. Cas said starboard berthing can be secured, but I think Kage and Crusher sleep in there usually. Feels strange tossing these assholes into someone's quarters."

"Fine. We'll leave them chained in the cargo hold for now. It is starting to get a little ripe in there, though."

"We can hose it out later."

The *Phoenix* sat in a high orbit around a moon of the seventh planet in the Kizarain System. They'd been a little late on the mad dash out of the area, and by the time they'd gotten out of the planet's atmosphere, the local enforcers had shown up. At first, Jacob thought it was no-shit ConFed warships coming in, but the ship's computer identified them as decommissioned crafts sold as surplus to a private fleet that hired itself out to poor systems. They kept the ships in ConFed Expeditionary Fleet livery to give the illusion they were there in a governmental capacity.

Sully could have easily outrun them and meshed-out of the system before they'd had a chance in hell of landing a shot, but Jacob was curious to see how this might play out. They were pretty sure the group they just hit had called for backup, but since none arrived before they left, they had to assume it was coming in from outside the system.

They picked a nice quiet spot and shut down the main drive and nav beacons to see who showed up and how they reacted to the security ships flitting about, pretending they were ConFed.

"So far, they're not talking," MG said, coming up from the short corridor that led to the cargo hold. "They're too young to be part of Jansen's original group of traitors. These have to be new recruits."

"How the hell are they getting them off Earth or Terranovus?" Jacob asked. "Free travel off either planet isn't a thing yet and, for the most part, Fleet knows where its people are."

"We need to ID them before we can even start to unravel where they fit in," Murph said. "I hate to suggest this, but I think you need to reach out to Captain Webb and see if he'll run them through facial recognition. I could maybe try some NIS contacts if that's a bust."

"That's not my favorite idea," Jacob said. "If we make direct contact, he's going to have a much stronger position when it comes to ordering us back to Terran space. As of right now, we're operating in a bit of a gray area where we're outside of our orders but not technically disobeying them."

"It's cute you think that," Murph said. "Look, this mission was your idea. You're either all in or you're not, and we pack it in and go home to face the music. We don't have forever to pull this off. Eventually, Omega Force *will* catch up to us to get their ship back."

Jacob hated he sometimes felt like a child being lectured by Murph. He hated it even more when the NIS agent was right. They had a limited window of opportunity to try and exploit a vulnerability in One World's network. If they dragged their feet too long, all of that was for naught, and they'd be looking at either a court-martial or deserting altogether and heading out to the frontier systems.

"Get me some high-res scans I can upload to Webb," he said

finally. "I'll reach out to one of his secret slip-com nodes. I really don't want to put him at risk if Fleet Ops finds out he's communicating with us. In the meantime, I'm going to get Sully to get us back into slip-space and heading towards the Orion Arm. I have a feeling whatever we find will lead us there."

"You've got some balls contacting me at this address, *Lieutenant*. Can I assume you're reaching out to negotiate your surrender?"

"I'm afraid not, sir," Jacob said. Captain Webb had always intimidated him before. For some reason, he didn't feel that now. "We have apprehended two One World operatives, both human, who are too young to have been with Jansen's original crew. I'd like to upload biometric data and facial scans and see if you're able to get a match. We no longer have access to NAVSOC's databases, obviously."

Webb's mouth opened and closed twice, but no sound came out. His eyes bulged, and his neck turned an interesting shade of purple. He stared at Jacob as if the Marine had just grown a second head.

"You cannot be serious," he finally managed to get out. "You're not serious about this request, are you, *Lieutenant?*"

"Yes, sir."

"*Yes, sir?!* That's all you have to fucking say to me?!"

"Yes, sir."

"Do you realize the damage you morons have caused? Half a dozen careers flushed down the shitter because you've decided you know better than all the flag officers at Fleet Ops and the people at NIS about how to deal with One World. Are you so arrogant to think you're going to win this little war all on your own?"

"If I get her, sure," Jacob said. "If not, I'll probably be killed trying, and there won't be much lost in the effort. If I'm not killed, I'll be prosecuted and tossed into Red Cliff for the remainder of my natural life, or executed as an enemy of the state. Either way, the risk seems worth the reward. One World has killed two of my friends, and I'm barely out of the Academy. No offense, sir, but all the flag officers and administrators at NIS have managed to do jack shit about it this entire time."

"Sometimes, I can't stand you, Brown. You and your entire family," Webb said. "You know your father knows what you're up to? He knows you took that ship, and he's coming for you. Do you think he'll pull his punches because you're his kid? After the way you've treated him all these years?"

"I'm hoping he won't risk damaging his ship," Jacob said. He hadn't meant it to sound flippant, but Webb's comment stung him more than he wanted to let on.

"What pisses me off about this isn't your actions, it's your arrogance. If Ezra Mosler had gone off the grid to chase down a high-value target, I'd know he weighed the risks carefully because he was an experienced, skilled operator," Webb said, speaking calmly but still looking ready to pop a blood vessel. "The fact you think you—you...a first lieutenant nobody—knows better than all of the hardened, dedicated people at NAVSOC is a slap in their faces. You think you know all the angles after a couple of hairy missions? You don't. And now, you've taken the careers of four other people down the tubes with you."

"I understand where you're coming from, sir," Jacob said carefully. "But that doesn't change the fact Obsidian was put in a position to have a real shot at cutting the head off the snake. Whether that was by dumb luck or not, we still felt compelled to go after it. If you don't want to be involved, I understand, and I'll see you when we come back to turn ourselves in."

"Like I said...arrogant." Webb sneered. "Don't you presume to tell me what I don't want to be involved in."

"I didn't mean that—"

"Shut up," Webb snapped. "Send me the scans and just keep your bullshit to yourself. You can be reached at this node? I notice it's from your old stolen ship and not one of the *Phoenix*'s known addresses."

"Yes, sir. This node is always monitored."

"This won't take long." Webb killed the channel without warning.

The conversation had been better than Jacob had expected. It was also infinitely worse. While Webb had quickly decided to assist them with NAVSOC's resources, it hadn't been without a price. Some of the things he'd said had cut Jacob to his core. One worrisome aspect was that Webb, who knew his father better than he did, seemed convinced Burke would come at him guns blazing to reclaim his ship.

Jacob had assumed, given his father's past overtures, this would be smoothed over quickly. It shamed him to now realize that what he intended was to exploit his father's desire for a relationship to get something he wanted, namely access to a powerful ship.

He also didn't take Webb's accusation of hubris lightly. Invoking Ezra Mosler's name had been a low blow, but Jacob once again found himself having difficulty crafting a counter-argument that didn't sound pathetic even to himself. Had he become arrogant and reckless after his short string of successful missions? Why did he think he could do what all of NAVSOC and the NIS couldn't after years of continuous effort.

"How did it go?" Murph asked. Jacob hadn't heard him slip into the cramped com room just behind the bridge.

"It could have gone better," he said. "But I think he's going to help us."

"Webb will bluster and rant but, in the end, he'll see we have a good shot at taking Jansen down and give us what we need," Murph said. The confidence in his voice helped bolster Jacob's floundering spirit.

A moment later, the slip-com node chimed, and an incoming channel request popped up on the monitor. Jacob looked at Murph, who nodded in return. He accepted the request and sat back, ready for another bombardment. Instead, it was the cool, calm professional Jacob was used to staring back at him.

"This is pretty big," he said. "Both of those prisoners show as active members of the UEAS. They're listed as intel officers assigned to Fleet Ops, but the files are all blacked out even at my clearance level. What I can see of their service record does not indicate any detached duty, AWOL status, or any other unusual flags that could explain how they abandoned their post and joined a terrorist faction. How the hell they were even on Kizarain-2 is a bit of a mystery. NAVSOC and NIS are the only two organizations authorized for covert operations, and they don't belong to either of us. On the books, these two are just data analysts."

"I've never seen analysts ready to throw down like that," Murph said. "These guys came out blazing."

"Obviously, something is not what it appears to be," Webb said. "This brings up some unpleasant possibilities."

"Indeed," Murph said. Jacob had his own theories about why this was especially bad, but he decided it would be better to sit and learn than pipe up and risk Webb's wrath again. "You have their complete dossiers in the data file you just transmitted?"

"Surface level stuff that won't flag at Fleet Ops that I accessed it," Webb said. "If I dig deeper, someone up top will know. For the time being, I think it's best if we don't advertise we're onto something. Right now, I've got Obsidian listed as MIA after the *Eagle's Talon* fiasco. I added a note stating your ship had been heavily damaged and you'd dropped out of com contact but, so far, there was no reason to believe you were dead.

"Before you get too excited...that's for the official record. My private files detail how you morons have gone off the reservation. I'm keeping it low-key until you complete your mission or get yourselves killed, but if you come back that deception won't save your asses. You'll be at the mercy of military justice."

"I'm NIS, so I'll just be tossed into a prison cell at a black site or killed outright, sir," Murph said. He didn't even sound that bothered by it.

"True enough," Webb said. "Anyway, try to use that to get some answers from these guys. I'd suggest letting Agent Murphy take point on the questioning. It would also probably help your case if you kept them alive and didn't torture them to death and toss them out the airlock...not that they don't deserve it."

"Not our style, sir," Jacob said. "Although, I have a feeling the two battlesynths tuned-up the Ull bounty hunter pretty hard before we met these guys."

"That's their business," Webb said. "You may be criminals right now, but you still represent Scout Fleet and NAVSOC. Behave accordingly."

"Yes, sir," Murph and Jacob parroted each other.

"I haven't heard from your father for a while, but you need to assume he's hot on your trail. He likes to play up the bumbling rube act for all it's worth, but he has an uncanny ability to turn up where and when he's least wanted," Webb said. "Underestimate him at your peril."

"Understood, sir."

"I want you to consider one thing before I sign off," Webb said, leaning into the camera. "You need to consider coming back in. The longer you stay out, the less likely this will have any sort of positive outcome for any of us. You may be a moron, but I'd hate to see you snuffed out or rotting in a prison for the rest of your life. If you call this off now, maybe we can just let it slide with stripping your commission and booting you out of the service in disgrace."

"We'll talk it over again, sir," Jacob promised, knowing what the answer would be already. His team was all-in. They wanted revenge, and they wanted to make a difference. Eliminating the leadership of One World accomplished both.

"Do that," Webb said, killing the channel.

"He does make some good points," Murph said.

"And?"

"And nothing. We've already talked this to death. We'll either dig Jansen out of her spider hole or we'll die trying. No half-measures will do it this time."

"How do you want to handle the two we captured?" Jacob asked.

"I haven't done this in a while, but they didn't seem like they'll be tough to crack," Murph said. "Of course, it's also just as probable they don't know anything, so prepare to be disappointed. I think we should pin our hopes on whatever Mettler and 784 were able to pull off the ship."

"Let me know what you need and when you want to get started," Jacob said. "In the meantime, I'm going to get some sleep."

6

"Rise and shine, asshole."

"Oh, God! What the hell is that?"

"A little bit of goodness from the gray water bilge," Murph said, putting the putrid-smelling bucket down he'd used to dump the dark brown, filthy sludge over the head of one of their prisoners.

The gray water bilge was two large collection tanks in the belly of the ship where the environmental system dumped any extra moisture it pulled from the air. The system would reclaim, filter, and reuse any water it could, but the rest of what it took from the air was left in the tanks until a purge and clean cycle. It was disgusting, to put it mildly.

After a while, the tanks concentrated all of the airborne filth that accumulated from biological beings sharing a cramped space for extended periods into something that was best avoided. It was bad enough that Murph wore gloves despite the tanks being periodically irradiated to kill off anything that could be infectious.

The prisoner, a young man who looked to be in his twenties and spoke with an American accent, promptly threw up all over himself, unable to move his head far enough to the side to hit the deck.

"Well, the good news is puking on yourself was actually a bit of an improvement," Murph said, sitting in the chair he'd brought over. "The bad news is you're about to find out that being covered in that shit is going to be the best part of your day."

"You gonna torture me?"

"If you have to put a word on it, Specialist Mitchel Stanley Easterbrook, then sure, we can call it torture," Murph said. When he used Easterbrook's real name, the intel specialist flinched visibly. "In the NIS, we had a clever euphemism for it but, in the end, the result is the same. Don't tell me what I want to know, and I'll make you wish you'd sucked on your pistol instead of letting us take you alive."

"NIS? What are you doing here with these Marines?" Mitchel asked.

"I'm not sure you appreciate the one-way flow of information that's expected during these situations," Murph said. He pulled out a length of wire and one of the knives from Crusher's collection in the armory. "You don't get to ask questions. Are you ready to begin?"

"Wait! Wait a damn minute! You haven't even asked any questions!"

"Ah," Murph said. "To be honest, I doubt I'll get much out of you. I'm just hoping your screams will convince your buddy on the other side of the cargo bay that I mean business, and then he'll be the one to give me what I want."

Easterbrook sweated profusely and gasped in short, hitching breaths. Murph looked at him closely, hefting the knife in his hand as if trying to decide where to start. The truth was, the kid really didn't have the bearing or look of someone who knew much. That could just be due to really good training, but if he'd had that sort of training, he'd know NIS agents don't actually torture people. It's too unreliable. There were some gray areas but, for the most part, the agency preferred a hands-off approach to interrogations if possible.

"Hey, man...let's be reasonable here."

"Reasonable? Look, champ, you're a traitor to Earth and humanity in general. You think my superiors are going to care if I practice my knife working skills on you?" Murph asked.

"I'm not a traitor! I'm following orders!" Easterbrook squealed. "I swear!"

"How can you have legal orders to betray the UEAS and work with a known terrorist faction like One World?" Murph laughed.

"What the hell are you talking about?" Easterbrook asked, looking genuinely confused. "One World? I take my orders from the Office of Special Operations. I transferred over to them from Fleet Ops."

"You're flying on two Aracorian ships with members of a species that tried to invade Earth once," Murph said. "You seriously think I'm buying your bullshit?"

"I just do what I'm told," Easterbrook said. "My boss said to meet up with the Ull, fly with them, and supervise the apprehension of some human smuggler named Jacob Brown. Nobody said shit about Marines and what the fuck ever those killbots you had with you were. We just assumed he was some civilian out here causing trouble."

"Our friends are called battlesynths, and they're a sentient species. If you have any sense of self-preservation, you'll never call them bots or androids where they can hear you," Murph said. "Now, back to this ridiculous story you've spun. I don't suppose you have any way to prove this?"

"My orders were on my tablet. It would have been on my rack in berthing."

"I'll see if it was secured." Murph stood. "I figure I owe you at least a cursory check before things turn nasty. But if you're lying to me, I'll cut your balls off and stuff them in your mouth just so I don't have to hear your screaming when the *real* pain starts."

"I swear!" Easterbrook's voice broke.

"We'll see." Murph shoved the bag back over his head before leaving the cargo hold.

"Well?" Jacob asked as he walked into the galley.

"Damned if I don't believe him," Murph said. "I also don't think this guy is any sort of trained operative. His fear response was no act. He almost passed out when I mentioned cutting bits off him. Did we take any human-built tablets off that ship?"

"There were a few. Mettler and 784 have them in engineering,"

Jacob said. He looked up and noticed the agent's expression. "What's wrong?"

"If he's telling the truth, we have bigger problems than we thought," Murph said. "He claims he's not working for One World. He says he has orders from what might be an office within Fleet Ops that put him on a special mission with those Ull to grab you. Nothing about us, nothing about you being in the military...just grab a human named Jacob Brown."

"But they're definitely doing it at the behest of One World," Jacob argued.

"Which means the problem within the UEAS goes well beyond some sympathizers and saboteurs. It means certain commands are fully cooperating with Jansen and using their resources to help her further her goals. It also means Grynn could have been a setup. They might know we've compromised their com system and they're using that to feed us false intel to herd us where they want."

"This makes no sense why a UEAS unit is involved directly." Jacob frowned, working through all the angles in his head. Maybe this is what Webb had been trying to tell him when he said he was too young and inexperienced to fully understand the complexities of a mission like this. How did a clandestine office within Fleet Ops figure into One World's operation? Damnit.

"It does, assuming certain things, none of which bode well for us," Murph said slowly. "Let's go ahead and give the technical team a little more time, and then go at them again."

"Sounds good. Probably should turn the temperature back up out there and maybe spray the bilge slime off Easterbrook," Jacob said.

"Cas, can the cleaning bots in the cargo hold take care of the human chained to the bulkhead and covered in shit?" Murph asked.

"I will make the necessary adjustments to their program," Cas said. "It won't be comfortable, but he will be unharmed."

"Good enough for me," Jacob said.

"He's a chip off the old violent, borderline-sociopathic block, isn't he?"

"I know you think you're funny, but I'm giving serious thoughts to killing you," Jason said to his code slicer.

"Which only just proves my point," Kage said.

The pair of them, along with Twingo and Crusher, had come down to the surface of Kizarain-2 in their SX-5 to inspect the aftermath of Scout Team Obsidian's fight at an isolated starport firsthand. The spot where their inexperienced pilot turned the *Phoenix*'s main guns onto a parked ship was impressive. The cannons had ripped the paved surface up, and whatever bits of tarmac that weren't vaporized were flung kilometers out into the plains. There was no sign at all of the ship.

The remains of the second Aracorian ship sat near the terminal complex. Talking to the internal security people—after an obscene number of credits to bribe them to let the four of them inspect the site—it appeared Jacob and his friends did the right thing and tried to blow it up before leaving, but whoever had set the charge had made a crucial mistake. They had placed it in the cargo bay of the small ship and left the ramp down and the armored hatch to the rest of the interior closed.

When the device detonated, the energy had a place to escape, and it turned the yawning bay opening into a rocket nozzle. Rather than blow up the ship, they'd just sent it spinning around on the tarmac.

It had still taken heavy damage to the aft end, and the Kizarainian crews had already cut away the ruined engineering section, but the flightdeck and crew quarters were intact. After yet another hefty bribe to another official, Kage and Twingo were allowed into the wreckage to do their own inspection.

Jason had told the officials he was part of the Aracorian Federated Shipyards rapid-response team, and they were there to make sure the incident hadn't been caused by a malfunction of their craft. The Kizarainians knew they were lying, but Jason's untraceable credit chits meant they didn't care.

"Your kid is an idiot," Kage declared as he climbed back out of the wreckage. "Or, if not him, his friends are idiots. They actually cut avionics boxes out of the racks and took the whole damn thing with them instead of just the backup data cores."

"I doubt they've had much experience with these types of ships," Jason said, not taking the bait. "What'd you find?"

"It's not a guild ship, but they made it look like one and even put the Boack crest on the sides to complete the illusion," Twingo said.

"Low-risk strategy to warn off any would-be pirates," Jason said. "Boack Guild would blow them out of the sky for trying to imitate them, but they never come this far into the interior. What else?"

"The backup data cores had been damaged, so the locals just left them in place," Kage said. "I powered up the console and determined there was *another* backup somewhere in the ship. No idea where, but I was able to do a transfer and pull everything off before I wiped it. I'll analyze the data on the *Devil*."

"Good thinking," Jason said. "We won't be able to stay much longer without coughing up another ten thousand credits or so."

"This is coming out of your personal funds and not the treasury, right?" Crusher asked.

"Mostly," Jason said evasively. "I'm definitely paying for the bribes."

"What about the fuel and munitions for the *Devil* and the SX-5?" Kage asked.

"We can figure that all out later." Jason waved them off. The arguments about money were mostly on principle since each member of Omega Force had done pretty well for themselves, but they still fought over the collective accounts like jackals. The crew worked on a profit share model so if one of them blew a ton of money on a personal side-job, the others didn't take too kindly to it.

"You suck," Kage said, walking off to talk to Twingo.

"Well, that was uncalled for," Jason said.

Crusher was about to respond, but he snapped his head towards the terminal and narrowed his eyes. Jason didn't waste time asking him what he heard or staring dumbly at the building. He knew when his friend was joking and when he wasn't.

"Get to the ship! Now!" he yelled at Twingo and Kage, sprinting for the SX-5 just as the first explosion ripped into the terminal building.

Jason spun and saw the explosion had been a breaching charge on one of the doors leading into the main terminal. After the attack by Obsidian, the whole place had been locked down tight and was being watched from orbit so, apparently, someone decided a ground attack would be the best way to go. Now, all he had to do was figure out if the attack was targeting them or something to do with the ship they'd been poking around on.

He made it to the SX-5 just as another charge finished off the heavy alloy door. Crusher came stomping up the ramp just behind him. Kage and Twingo were already on the flightdeck prepping her for takeoff, but Jason hated to waste an opportunity like this. The bad guys so rarely cooperated and came to you.

"Bring the drive up but keep the marker lights off!" he called from the small cargo bay.

"What are you thinking?" Crusher asked.

"Let's see who's come calling," Jason said, disengaging the locks on the hidden false-deck panels and opening up a smuggler's cavity crammed with a veritable arsenal. Jason grabbed one of his personal favorites, a carbine-style railgun with selectable velocity settings, and tossed Crusher a heavy plasma rifle. After snagging a couple of grenades, he lowered the deck panel and moved carefully to the ramp.

The SX-5 had been parked so the left wing pointed towards the terminal. It was possible the assault team didn't know they were there and would ignore the ship as belonging to the Kizarainians. They'd still been trying to blow the security doors open by the time he and Crusher made it inside the ship.

"I wonder if the locals will send backup," Crusher rumbled.

"Let's hope not. I'd like to get a look at who these clowns are." Jason leaned forward a bit more and saw a five-person tactical team moving quickly across the tarmac. Sure enough, they were going right to the damaged Aracorian ship.

"Wanna pop 'em?"

"Let's wait," Jason said. "If all they wanted to do was blow the ship up, they could have lobbed mortar shells from twenty klicks away and not risked a guided munition, much less a tac-team. They're after something."

"You notice anything...special...about them?" Crusher asked.

"Yes, I saw they're human," Jason said. "Hopefully, we're not about to fuck up one of Webb's teams."

"I'm good either way," Crusher said. "I can't stand humans." Jason just rolled his eyes.

"Let's go. They all went into the ship," he said.

The pair moved quickly, running to the hulk of the Aracorian ship. Jason felt exposed as they moved right in front of the bridge canopy. If anybody was on the flightdeck, they wouldn't be able to miss them. He kept his head on a swivel as they ran. Just because they only saw five humans didn't mean that's all there were. He was also worried about any Ull they might have with them if they were a team from One World.

"—I know what the fuck it looks like! I'm telling you, it ain't here. Just a bunch of cut wires!"

"Well look for the backups, damn it!"

Jason and Crusher looked at each other and shrugged. The frenzied conversation inside made it pretty easy to piece together what was happening. Whoever owned the ship came for their secret stuff, but Jacob had chopped it out with an ax and taken the whole damn unit with him.

Now, they crawled around searching for the backup cores even Kage hadn't been able to physically locate. It didn't matter if they found them since the Veran had wiped them clean.

The pair of mercs moved around to the jagged, charred cavity that used to be a cargo bay and slipped inside. They'd posted a single sentry, some poor kid who gaped at Jason instead of raising an alarm. Crusher punched him hard enough to snap his head back and knock him clean out. The guard crumpled into a pile like someone had just flicked off a switch.

"They should have sent a damn engineer with us this time,"

someone said from inside the ship. "I have no idea what half this shit even does. What does the backup data core look like?"

"It's about the size of a shoebox," Jason said, stepping through the hatch. "Most of that will be armored casing, though. The data core is only about the size of an old cassette tape. You kids old enough to even remember what the hell those were?"

"Who the hell are you?" one demanded, going for his weapon.

"I wouldn't," Crusher said, moving out of the shadows. He had his plasma rifle trained on the four of them.

"So, you with Jansen's crew? That One World bullshit?" Jason asked.

"I asked who the—"

"Dude, *look* at him," another whispered. "And he's standing there with a Galvetic warrior. Who do you think it is?"

"There's no way that's him. That guy has to be like sixty by now."

"I'm standing right here, idiots," Jason said. "Who do you think I am? You know what, let's save some time. My name is Jason Burke. My friend here goes by Crusher because he's immature and his real name is hard to pronounce. I feel like you've heard of us."

"Hey, man...we were just sent to do a job," the leader said, now sounding like he wanted to negotiate.

"Sure, sure," Jason said. "But it's a dangerous job. You know that. For instance, you just attacked a civilian starport terminal in order to recover something your bosses think is important, and now you're probably going to be killed by a couple of mercs in the process. It's all part of the job, see?"

"What I mean is—"

"You mean to ask what can you do to live through this encounter? To be honest, probably nothing," Jason said. "You're out here representing humanity, blowing up shit on other people's planets and generally giving us a bad name—"

"Uh, Captain."

"Shut up! I know it's hypocritical," Jason snapped at Crusher. "My point is that Margret Jansen is sanctioning violence on other worlds.

That can cause blowback. Plus, getting rid of a few more One World assholes would be doing everyone a favor."

"Uh, who the hell is Margret Jansen?" the leader asked. "We work for Captain Aster Rizzo. I'm Lieutenant Esposito."

"You're UEAS?" Jason asked, frowning. "You're here on official order from your chain of command?"

"Yes," Esposito said. "This is one of our ships, and we were sent to recover the flight data recorder and com buffers."

"What outfit are you with?"

"Office of Special Operations," Esposito said. "We're a clandestine service that—"

"Yeah, yeah...got it," Jason said. "For being clandestine, you're sure quick to give up the information to save your own ass."

"That's because he's lying," Crusher said. "Let's waste these rats and get going. We don't want to be here when the locals show up to find out why this place was attacked again."

"I'm not lying! We were just supposed to get in and out with the hardware!"

"Why were your ships attacking a NAVSOC Scout Fleet team?" Jason asked, trying a different tactic. If the kid was lying, he was one of the best Jason had ever seen. "And why would they send someone so obviously out of their depth to mount a raid on an alien planet Earth has no diplomatic ties with?"

"I'm a com specialist, they're the operators," Esposito said, pointing at his companions. "Since I'm the only officer on the mission, I've been given operational command."

"This true?" Jason asked one of the others.

"Yeah. We're all just dumb grunts, so they had to send a lieutenant desk jockey to lead us."

"We'll kill him first so you can watch," Jason promised.

"Thanks. I actually appreciate that," the operator said, still glaring at Esposito.

"No problem," Jason said. "So, you're not part of Jansen's One World group? You're not moles or embeds in the UEAS?"

"I'm really not sure what you're talking about," Esposito said, now a lot more cautious in what he said. Apparently, his team's excitement at the prospect of watching him die had unnerved him.

"This is getting strange," Jason said to Crusher. "What do you think?"

"We already have the thing they're looking for. Let's just get the hell out of here and let Kage do his thing," Crusher said, then looked at the operator Jason had talked to. "You want us to pop him for you? Give you plausible deniability?"

"I...guess not." He actually looked like he had been considering while Esposito stared at him, mouth hanging open. "He's an idiot, but he's an okay officer. You used to be an enlisted puke, too, right, Burke?"

"Yeah, but I was Air Force. Our enlisted are at least as smart as a Navy lieutenant," Jason said. "I'm guessing you've been briefed on us before?"

"We were told we might encounter you by chance. Some light background on who you were, along with key members of your crew."

"What's your name?"

"Simmons."

"Well, Simmons, I'm going to go ahead and leave you alive this time," Jason said. "Tell your superiors it is a really, *really* stupid idea painting up your ships to pretend you're in one of the frontier guilds. If the Boack had caught you in this thing, they'd have skinned you alive, ate you, and then backtracked you to Terranovus to kill and eat whoever sent you. They're not to be fucked with."

"Got it. Anything else?"

"You know why this team was sent in the first place? Like I said, they were here ambushing a NAVSOC team."

"I honestly hadn't heard anything about that, but it doesn't surprise me," Simmons said, ignoring Esposito's strangled cry and warning looks. "Rumor is, NAVSOC is on the way out. Scout Fleet has shit the bed one too many times, and Earth is propping up at least two new clandestine forces I know about, one of them being us."

"That is enough, Specialist!" Esposito said.

"Sir, you don't think it's prudent to let him know that other human teams might be out here on official orders so they don't get killed?" Simmons asked. "Or did you want to be the only one to divulge classified information, sir?"

"Who's at the top of this...Office of Special Operations? Jesus, you guys need a cooler name for that. Sounds like a team of corporate lawyers or something," Jason said.

"It's pretty compartmentalized," Simmons said carefully. "I don't have any idea who is in charge, and I think that's not an accident."

"Got it," Jason said. "Well, it's been fun. If you're going to blow the ship up, do it right this time. Hopefully, the Kizarainians you killed won't cause any trouble for Earth."

"They're not dead. Knocked out," Simmons said.

"Right on." Jason nodded. "Speaking of knocked out, you may want to check on your guy out there in the cargo bay."

"I'm more confused now than when we got here," Crusher said as they walked back to their ship.

"Normally, I would never let that sort of opening slide, but I'm right there with you. I feel like we're missing a couple of big pieces of the puzzle," Jason said.

"What now?"

"Let Kage get to work on that data he stole and try to get in touch with Marcus Webb. If nothing else, I owe him a heads-up that he's about to be burned."

7

"How's it coming?"

"Good...I guess," Mettler said, slouching into one of the bridge station seats. "784 has everything torn apart in engineering and was pretty insistent I was in the way."

"You're a good medic and the closest thing we have to a tech, but he probably has a point," Jacob said. "He's an expert and has a few hundred years of experience."

Jacob took his turn on watch duty while Sully grabbed some much-needed sleep. The pilot had been awake for almost two full days by the time they'd meshed-out of the Kizarain System. Pulling watch while in slip-space was a breeze. Just sit in the seat and hope no alarms go off.

The *Phoenix* had an interesting feature in that a moving starfield, a representation of the space they actually flew through, was projected onto the canopy. It was quite beautiful and a damn sight better than looking at blacked-out windows or ugly alloy shields.

"It's crazy working with these battlesynths," Mettler said. "They're so ancient and have seen so much yet, in many ways, they're almost childlike. I mean that in a non-insulting way, of course."

"I get you," Jacob said. "The one that ran with my dad for all those years, Lucky, was the same way when I met him. I was told then it's a quirk of their kind, but not to mistake that implied innocence for gullibility or stupidity."

"I heard from 707 that Lucky used to be one of them. As in, he's from their actual unit. How did he end up with your dad?"

"Long story," Jacob said. "Short version is that when my dad got himself abducted and almost sold into slavery, Lucky had been stored in a crate brought aboard this ship. When Jason and Crusher escaped, and then opened the box, there he was. They reactivated him, and he decided to stick with them. To be honest, my mom told me more stories about him than my dad did."

"Really?" Mettler turned, now clearly intrigued. Jacob wanted to stop talking right then, but his mouth opened seemingly of its own accord, and the words poured out.

"Yeah. Remember in school we learned about that alien attack? The first one?" he asked. "My dad came back—in this very ship—to stop it, ended up having to rescue mom from a group of angry locals who knew she was connected to him somehow, and she stayed aboard the *Phoenix* while they ran around trying to stop that crazy synth.

"She would tell me stories about their adventure and, as a kid, I just thought she was a really good storyteller. It wasn't until I was older, and after she was already gone, that I understood it had all been true. She told me about Lucky, Crusher, Twingo, and the rest of them. How they'd looked after her and how what dad was doing out here was important. I didn't meet Jason Burke until I was fourteen. By then, the genetic tweaks he'd passed on to me had only just started making themselves known. I wasn't very gracious to my dad the first time I met him. I don't think stealing his ship is going to help in making amends."

"Wow...I thought I had a fucked-up family," MG said. Jacob looked and saw the weaponeer leaning against the hatchway. "Why did you keep all that to yourself all this time?"

"Partially because it was important to hide my connection to Jason, hence me using my mom's last name," Jacob said. "Mostly because I was pissed off at him for leaving my mom, and then not being there when she died. I guess now I understand him a little better."

"Before we all start getting weepy and singing "Cats in the Cradle," you might want to know that 784 has had a breakthrough," MG said. Angel "MG" Marcos was as hardcore as they came. Any hint of sharing feelings made him uncomfortable. "He says he's compiled the entire core, and now all he has to do is decrypt it."

"That sounds like that'll be the hard part," Mettler said.

"He doesn't think so." MG shrugged. "Oh, and 707 knocked Murph flat the fuck out. He's in the cargo bay bleeding."

"What?!" Jacob jumped out of the pilot's seat. "Why?"

"No idea."

"You're utterly fucking useless, as usual," Jacob said, pushing by him and running off the command deck. "Mettler, watch the ship."

When Jacob ran into the cargo bay, he was greeted by an odd sight. Murph lay on the deck, bleeding, and 707 stood in the middle of the hold.

"What the hell is going on in here?" he demanded.

"Sergeant Murphy thought it would be a good idea to let the prisoners walk around and stretch their legs," 707 said. "I am assisting."

"I suppose I could have been a bit more specific," Jacob said, struggling to remain calm. "Why is my senior team member on the deck bleeding."

"I warned him what would happen if he called me Tin Man again," 707 said. "It is not helpful to make threats you do not intend to follow through with."

"The big metal guy whapped him so fast we didn't even see his hand move!" Specialist Easterbrook said. He stood back by the rear pressure doors with his hands in the air.

"Where's your partner?" he asked, looking around the bay for their second prisoner.

"Right here! Don't shoot!"

"Get your dumbass where I can see you," Jacob said. "I'll deal with you soon enough, Specialist First Class Carl Witter."

"I'm just trying to stay out of the line of fire here," Carl said, also raising his hands.

"Please, make sure they behave themselves or chain them back to the bulkhead," Jacob told 707. "I'm taking Murph to the infirmary, and then we need to have a talk about boundaries. You volunteered to be here, but I can't have you assaulting my team because of something said."

707 said nothing. He just stared at Jacob with that unreadable expression battlesynths had. Jacob ignored him as he picked Murph up and slung him over his shoulder so he could take him to the infirmary. On the way back into the ship's interior, he wondered if he would need to dump the battlesynths off somewhere and let them get a ride back home.

From what he knew of the species, they had high levels of restraint and weren't prone to emotional outbursts or random violence. 707 was the leader of his group, so it would stand to reason he'd be the most controlled.

"Put him on the bed in there, and I'll get to him," Mettler said from the top of the stairs that led to the command deck. "What happened?"

"Looks like he mouthed off to 707 and got backhanded," Jacob said. "Tell MG to get his ass down to the cargo bay and supervise the prisoners. You handle Murph, and I'll go wake Sully up so I can go see what 784 has for us."

Sully was predictably grumpy about being woke up so shortly after he'd gone to sleep, but he got up and trudged up to the bridge anyway. With his team having so many quirks and anti-social tendencies, Jacob was always appreciative of Lieutenant Sullivan's quiet professionalism.

He always worked on solutions while MG and Mettler usually

took existing problems and poured fuel on them, laughing maniacally while the flames burned the building they stood in.

"What have you got for me?" Jacob asked. 784 sat at a workbench in engineering, the sight startling the human at first. "You're sitting in a chair?"

"Trying something new," 784 said. "Also, the engineer on this ship is quite short, so the monitors are all positioned for a lower viewing angle."

"Yeah, Twingo," Jacob said. "I was taller than him when I was a kid."

"The decryption software on this ship is far more advanced than I would expect to find given your father runs a crew of mercenaries not a branch of military intelligence," 784 said, pointing to one of the monitors. "But it is already cutting into the data we secured and producing actionable intel."

Jacob pulled over another seat and looked through what the computer had pulled out and organized so far. It looked like Easterbrook was telling the truth, and they were still active members of the UEAS. Whatever this Office of Special Operations was, their orders originated from Earth, not Olympus.

That meant this division might technically sit under Fleet Ops on an organizational chart, but they were a political entity taking orders from the civilian oversight. The only reason you want to do that is because you bypass NAVSOC and cut NIS out completely.

Unfortunately, no specific names were tied to the issued orders. Point of origin was clear, though, since all of Earth's governmental slip-com nodes followed a specific addressing scheme. The orders pulling this team, designated Troubleshooter Baker, off a previous assignment and putting them on an acquire-and-capture mission after Jacob came from the United States, Washington DC specifically.

"Do we have a reverse look-up chart for these slip-com nodes?" he asked.

"No," 784 said. "My suggestion would be, once we have more data pulled from this file, you forward it to NAVSOC and let Captain Webb handle that aspect."

"That's probably the only— Ah! Here we go. Jansen is mentioned by name in this one," Jacob said. He read through it, then read it again. "Well, this doesn't make any damn sense."

The message was a memorandum regarding ongoing operations in the Orion Arm, and they referenced Jansen specifically, but the context was odd.

Jansen retirement request pending. Ull unaware. Please advise.

The message was from someone within the Office of Special Operations to a contact in Washington DC and, ostensibly, the US government. Like most covert communications, it wasn't verbose to the point of helping someone fill in the blanks.

Was Margaret leaving One World? She was getting up there in years, but One World didn't seem like the type of outfit you *retired* from. Did she get a pension and a gold watch?

It seemed obvious whoever was the recipient on Earth had some connection to One World, but they already suspected the faction had deep roots within the governmental offices. The date on the message showed the message was sent three months ago.

Was Jansen even still in charge of the group, or had someone else taken over? Hopefully, more would be pulled out of the haul from the ship they raided that would point them in the right direction.

"Keep at it, please," he told 784. "This is all good stuff, but I'd like a little more before sending it to Webb."

"I will do so," 784 said.

"By the way, 707 just assaulted one of my Marines down in the cargo bay...is that something he's prone to?" Jacob asked. 784's head snapped over so quickly it startled him.

"It most certainly is not. What exactly happened?"

Jacob filled him in with the details as he knew them from what MG and 707 had told him. When he was done, the other battlesynth sat impassively for a moment, seeming to be lost in thought.

"I have never known him to be reactionary to something as petty as verbal insults," 784 said carefully. "Our kind have endured them for many centuries. I will speak to him."

"Please do," Jacob said. "In addition to an injured member of an already undermanned team, I can't have these internal squabbles popping up all the time. I appreciate the help offered but, if it comes down to it, I'll have to let you off somewhere so you can head on back home."

"I understand, Lieutenant," 784 said. Jacob stood, sensing the battlesynth was now uncomfortable with his presence.

"I'll be on the bridge if you need me," he said, leaving engineering. He debated going into the cargo bay and talking to 707 himself about what happened but, in the end, decided to leave it to 784 to handle for now.

8

"This is an unexpected pleasure, Marcus, but I'm guessing this isn't a social call."

"Michael," Webb said, nodding to the holographic likeness of NIS Director Michael Welford. The pair had a strong personal friendship forged when they fought alongside Jason Burke and his crew against Margaret Jansen's forces when she first tried to take control of Earth.

Since Webb had been assigned as the head of NAVSOC, the pair had made sure to keep their personal and professional contact separate, an unspoken rule he was now breaking by directly briefing the NIS Director about an ongoing operation. "I know we said we'd never do this—"

"But you're about to drag business into one of these calls. I can only assume it's for good reason. What've you got?"

Slip-com nodes had been the de facto standard for superluminal communication in the quadrant for over a thousand years. Improvements had been made, of course, but the system was essentially the same as it had always been. Earth researchers decided slip-com just didn't suit their purposes, so they developed an all-new system they called Hyperlink.

The ultra-high bandwidth superluminal system was nearly instantaneous—slip-com still had some perceptible lag—and allowed for luxuries like the broadcasting of a full-size holographic representation as Director Welford was doing now.

"What do you know about the Office of Special Operations?" Webb asked, getting right to it.

"Loaded question, that," Welford said. "Your people tangle with some of theirs?"

"In a manner of speaking," Webb said. "There was a fight between a group claiming to be them and one of my NAVSOC units."

"Holy shit," Welford said, rubbing his eyes. "This is more than just a general inquiry, Marcus. And your team? Which was it?"

"Obsidian."

"This just gets better and better. You mean the team your official report states is MIA right now? *That* Obsidian?" Welford asked.

"There are reasons for them being off the grid you don't want to know," Webb said. "Plausible deniability. I will say most of Obsidian is still alive and still on the job."

"What do you want from me? And am I right in assuming this is off the record?" Welford asked.

"Way off," Webb confirmed. "I need to know who these OSO clowns are. Who's in charge of that outfit, and how does it fit into the UEAS command tree?"

"On paper, it's just an administrative office tasked with post-action analysis of Fleet engagements," Welford said. "They're not in your chain of command. Not even the Joint Chiefs have any authority over what they do."

"Unofficially?" Webb asked.

"Unofficially, they're an unsanctioned black ops unit that handles all the dirty work the government wants done but can't task the military with," Welford said. "Given you know all the underhanded stuff NAVSOC is tasked with, imagine what these guys are up to. They're dangerous, unaccountable, and given far too much leeway for my tastes."

"Still not hearing a name, Michael."

"It's because I don't have one to give you." Welford shrugged. "Nobody within NIS knows who is actually running the show, and we can't make an official inquiry because the group officially doesn't exist."

"This is a problem," Webb sighed. "So, I have a Scout Fleet team holding two members of a quasi-legal paramilitary unit, and I can't even get a name to ask how they want their people back."

"You want my honest opinion?" Welford asked.

"Always."

"Tell Brown to kill them and toss them out the airlock, and then forget you ever even heard of the Office of Special Operations."

"Jesus, Michael," Webb said, genuinely shocked.

"I'm serious," Welford said. "You don't want your people on their radar. They'll kill every member of Obsidian for even knowing they exist. It sounds like they're on to you already if they were sent to ambush your boys."

"How the hell is this even legal? This had to have been approved by either Geneva or Washington," Webb said. "What's their mandate? Just a black ops kill squad, or do they operate within any sort of charter?"

"From what I hear, it's more of a domestic policy group," Welford said uncomfortably.

"So, they're an assassination group," Webb said. "Let me take a wild guess...they used Jansen's One World faction as an excuse to get something like this started."

"Never let a crisis like this go to waste. You know how they are," Welford said. "Fighting One World's incursions has allowed the bureaucrats to divert funds, get approvals for groups like the OSO, and amass power never meant for them. They're unelected and unaccountable. Say what they will about NAVSOC and the NIS, but we operate under strict rules and are accountable to the oversight committees and, ultimately, the voting public."

"As interesting as that all is, it doesn't help me in my current predicament," Webb said. "Assuming I'm not quite ready to just kill and toss these two, what are your suggestions?"

"Take them off Obsidian's hands and pass them up the chain," Welford said. "Eventually, someone in Fleet will know how to get to the people they belong to. In the meantime, they can sit in Red Cliff for safe keeping."

"They probably won't be all that safe in Red Cliff," Webb said. "They'd almost certainly be the victims of *random* prison violence or killed trying to escape less than a week after being there."

"Bring them to Olympus and turn them over to NIS," Welford offered. "We have our own detention center that isn't staffed with Marines who would let them get shanked in the lunch line. You have any way to get them back from Obsidian?"

"I'll take the *Kentucky* out and arrange a swap," Webb said. "Brown will be skeptical, so I'll have to arrange some sort of blind drop. It's not like this ship could catch the *Phoenix* anyway."

"Excuse me?" Welford frowned. "The *Phoenix* as in...*the Phoenix*?"

"My overeager young Lieutenant stole the damn thing from his dad's hangar while Omega Force is riding around on one of Mok's corvettes," Webb said. "So, if the OSO operatives don't kill him, his dad might."

"This is an impressive mess he's made in such a short amount of time," Welford said. "Contact me when or if you get your hands on those two captives. The more I think about it, the more I think I'd like to have my people take a turn questioning them."

"I'll try to arrange it," Webb promised. "Webb out."

He killed the channel and watched as Welford's holographic likeness froze, then faded away. The news from Welford was worse than he'd feared. He'd hoped the OSO was just some vaguely named spec ops group within the UEAS's control. But from what his friend just told him—and he had no doubt Welford knew much more than he was telling—this was some sort of independent hit squad under the control of the political structure on Earth.

That meant Brown's reckless mission to grab Jansen could be a bit more complicated if the OSO was helping her. Did that mean there was a traitor within that organization too? Or were they being directed by a political power higher up? If they were there to try and grab Brown, then it was a safe bet Jansen knew he was coming.

Their advantage from going through Elton Hollick's old files will have been nullified. Jansen hadn't eluded capture this long by being sloppy, and she would most definitely rotate her encryption schemes, dump her schedule, and probably purge her personal security in case one of them informed on her.

Realistically, Obsidian's self-ordered mission was over. They were now operating based on a set of conditions that no longer existed, and the risk just climbed well past acceptable levels. It was no longer a sneak in and out raid and, even if they found her, she'd be ready for them. But he knew Brown well enough at this point to know that the kid wouldn't see it that way until it was almost too late. He was a victim of early success, and now he was under the wrongful impression these missions just fell together at the end if you just believed hard enough.

The first time he was lucky because Hollick and the Ull didn't understand what made him unique and underestimated him. The second time, he succeeded because the battlesynths of Lot 700 had decided to intercede on his behalf. There would be no third miracle for him, and Webb feared this would be the mission that got him. Unfortunately, he'd also take an irreplaceable scout team of seasoned Marines with him.

"Ensign Weathers, get your ass in here," he said into the intercom. A moment later, his new aide walked in.

"Yes, sir," he said, already with tablet out ready to take down whatever his boss said.

"We need to put together a care package for our wayward scout team. We're going to be doing an exchange with them for two prisoners—*very* high-profile—so make sure the master at arms knows to have the brig ready and his people briefed."

"Normal speedball drop, sir?"

"More extensive than that," Webb said after a moment of thought.

"These guys have been in the wild for some months now, lost two ships out from under them, and are running on the edge. Have them raid the armory and supply sections to put together two X5 transit cases loaded with everything they might want."

"I'll get on it now, sir," Weathers said. "Does this need to be sanitized?"

"No more than usual," Webb said. Normally, Scout Fleet teams used equipment that could never be traced back to Earth if it was left behind or captured. These sanitation protocols were strictly adhered to in the early days of NAVSOC but had become more relaxed as more and more human small arms were shipped out to Earth's Cridal trading partners and found their way into circulation throughout the quadrant.

Once Weathers was out of the office, Webb composed a message for Lieutenant Brown. Deciding against having a text-only message sent through NAVSOC's com system, he activated an isolated, private slip-com node in his office to talk to them directly.

"Yes, sir," Brown said as the connection resolved.

"Where's Murph?" Webb asked, not looking up from his computer.

"Ah...indisposed, sir," Brown said. "He's handling something in the infirmary."

"Then you'll need to remember all of this. I'm going to give you just a few more feet of rope to hang yourself with, but only because you've apparently stumbled across something important. At this point, it seems clear Jansen is on to you, so I don't think you're going to get a shot at her, but she seems to be willing to spend resources to get you."

"Bait, sir?" Brown asked.

"Very good, Lieutenant. I don't know why everyone thinks you're an idiot," Webb said, finally looking up. "Since Jansen seems to be willing to activate some pretty deep connections on Earth to get you, we're going to keep you in play a bit longer and see what else she has up her sleeve. In the meantime, I'm arranging a supply drop for you in exchange for the two prisoners in your hold. I'm going to hand them over to the NIS director and let his people go to work on them. Got it?"

"Drop location and time, sir?"

"Can you make Camderan-2 within three days?" Webb asked. Brown looked off-camera, apparently plugging the information into a computer terminal.

"Easily," he said. "This ship has been there a few times. Looks like Omega Force was involved in a nasty engagement there, but the *Phoenix* is still cleared to land. Who is Crisstof Dalton? Sounds like a human name."

"It isn't. That's all you need to know about that."

"Oh, shit! Is this some relation to Seeladas Dalton?" Brown asked, his eyes widening as he kept reading whatever was on his screen about the Dalton clan.

"What the hell did I just say?" Webb asked. "Drop it. If you want to pry old war stories from your dad when he comes for his ship, that's between you two, but if you have any sense at all, you'll not mention that name around anyone connected to the Cridal."

"Got it. We'll change course and speed as soon as I get this information to Sully," Brown said. "Anything else, sir?" Webb looked at his young officer for a long moment without speaking.

"Nothing I've said has even penetrated that skull, has it? You still think you have a shot to take down Jansen," he said finally. "Let me leave you with one parting thought, Lieutenant. Whether you bring in Jansen's head or not is immaterial. You and your team will be brought up on desertion charges, and you'll have to plead your case to the Tribunal. I can't, and won't, intervene on your behalf. My responsibility is to humanity, the UEAS, and NAVSOC. In that order."

"You've made our situation perfectly clear, Captain," Brown said. "We've all discussed it and, since we're going to burn no matter what we do, we all prefer to go down swinging at least."

"As long as you're all agreeing to be stupid, I guess that makes it okay." Webb rolled his eyes. "Clichés like 'going down swinging' won't save the lives of your teammates, Lieutenant. The *Kentucky* will be in orbit over Camderan-2 if you decide to do the right thing and come back in. If you do, I'll let your dad know where he can pick up his ship. Otherwise, I'm going to squeeze a bit more usefulness out of you, and then your fate will be sealed, one way or the other."

"Understood, sir. *Phoenix* out."

The screen went blank, and Webb switched off his own slip-com node, leaning back and staring the ceiling. He'd intended to push on Brown to get him to see wisdom and come in on his own, but it looked like all he'd done was make the kid more determined than ever to buck the system and take on One World alone.

"Damnit!" he said to nobody in particular.

Given how poorly NAVSOC missions had gone lately he knew his time in command was probably short. As soon as the UEAS Oversight Council got around to voting for his replacement, he'd be sent packing. Probably back to Earth, where he'd be closely watched until he qualified for retirement, and then he'd be squeezed out. The ships and locations may have been a lot more exotic, but the bureaucracy was just like the old Navy he remembered from back home.

"Webb to bridge," he said into the intercom.

"Go for bridge, Captain."

"Please, set course for Camderan-2. We need to be there within the next couple of days."

"Aye, sir. We'll let you know once we're underway."

9

"It looks like they were definitely after your kid specifically and not his team."

"What makes you say that?" Jason asked, leaning over Kage's shoulder to peer at the monitor.

"Quit hovering and I'll tell you. Go on." The human grumbled but stepped back, crossing his arms. Kage looked to make sure he was staying there before continuing. "Breaking the encryption on the files was relatively easy. It's the human-specific context making it tough to go through. What we've managed to find is that Jacob Brown is referred to by this One World as *EB*.

"The ship we pulled that data from had been tasked to apprehend and secure EB, and then signal for a rendezvous. The rest of Scout Team Obsidian is referred to as collateral damage. It looks like this crew was going to grab your son, kill his team, and then hand him off to some interested party."

"EB," Jason repeated. "Maybe some acronym with the last letter meaning Brown? So, the real question is, who are these assholes? If they're not with the United Earth Navy, who are they working for?"

"Don't know, don't care," Kage said. "I'm just mining the useful stuff out of this data dump."

"You're not irreplaceable. You know that, right?" Jason asked.

"You'd actually fire me?"

"No, I'm going to toss you out of the airlock. It would be morally reprehensible to just fire you and have you inflict your bullshit on some other poor crew."

"I honestly don't know why I stay and put up with this sort of abuse," Kage muttered, turning back to the terminal and bringing up a few new images. Two were navigation charts. "It looks like this crew operated mainly out of two places, at least according to their nav data. Recognize the first system?"

"Sol System?" Jason frowned. "What the hell? That doesn't make sense. Sol-4...so they're flying to someplace on Mars quite a bit. What's the other place they've been hitting?"

"It's a planet called Koliss-2," Kage said. "Tier Three world pretty far down the Orion Arm towards your home system."

"Who owns it?" Jason asked.

"The database said it's been a ConFed planet since the Third Wave Expansion a few hundred years back, but there's nothing listed about it in the export control registry," Kage said. "That's a bit strange. The ConFed doesn't hang onto planets that don't produce something for them."

"Maybe," Jason said. "Some backwater Tier Three world may have an official affiliation with the ConFed, but you can bet they have no representation in the Council, and the fleet sure as hell isn't sending any warships out to fly the flag or respond to distress calls. Can you access the orbital control database on Koliss-2?"

"Not from here," Kage said. "We'd need to be in orbit and tied into the system. This isn't a Core World that uploads their records to the public Nexus. Why?"

"I'd be interested to see how many known Ull vessels are flying to and from there." Jason rubbed his scalp. "If we're still assuming One World is being sponsored by a faction of Ull extremists, then we need to figure any place these human sympathizers are operating from will also have some of those gangly fucks roaming around."

"Please, don't ask me to fly out there in the SX-5 to check it out," Kage begged. Jason pretended to consider it while the Veran became noticeably uncomfortable, shifting in his seat and fidgeting at the thought of a long slip-space flight in the Spartan strike craft that sat in the hangar bay of the *Devil's Fortune*.

"Let's all go out there," Jason finally said, causing Kage to wilt with relief. "If we run into any big game that's aware of our equipment, I'd rather have the *Devil*'s guns backing us up."

"I'll start prepping the intrusion package to get us into the orbital control's system when we arrive," Kage said.

"Where the hell is Cas?" Jason asked, just realizing he hadn't seen the small, floating probe that housed the erratic AI personality in some days.

"Down in the cargo bay still trying to recompile what's left of the Archive," Kage said. "Apparently, it takes a lot of cycles, and it can't afford the bandwidth to float around and annoy people at the same time."

The Archive was a massive database with an interactive AI integrated into it that was the last legacy of a long-extinct hyper-advanced species from well beyond the ConFed's borders. It was a repository for all of their accumulated knowledge. A wondrous and terrible thing that held the potential to transform the quadrant...or destroy it.

The Cas AI had been a part of an access system to one of their abandoned superweapons floating around in space, a machine capable of destroying planets and destabilizing stars. Jason had inadvertently gotten Cas stuck in his neural implant when he was using it to store the Archive in a compressed, inert state. Even after getting it out and putting it into its own mobile body, the aggravating AI had still clung to him like a lost puppy.

Now, Cas tried to repair the Archive, which was damaged during Omega Force's last mission in service to the current open rebellion against the ConFed. The dilemma Jason had was whether or not the Archive was something that should be repaired at all.

It was easily the most dangerous object in the quadrant and contained knowledge that could tip the balance of power dramatically and rewrite the political structure practically overnight. He didn't trust anybody with that sort of power, not even his own people. *Especially* not his own people, the more he thought about it.

On top of his estranged son stealing his beloved gunship and an ultra-powerful, all-knowing AI on the fritz, Jason had another, more pressing problem. He was missing someone from his crew and was desperate to get him back. Omega Force's battlesynth member, Lucky, had undergone a sort of metamorphosis after being severely damaged, and then brought back to life in a new body.

Jason wasn't entirely sure what his friend had become, but he knew it was something very dangerous. They needed to find Lucky for not only his own safety but for that of anyone he came in contact with. The corvette-class ship he borrowed wasn't well-suited for the task of trying to track down a single target out in the frontier regions where Lucky was rumored to be. He needed the *Phoenix*, which meant he couldn't even begin his search for Lucky until he got her back from his son.

Even though he was secretly impressed with Jacob's grit for stealing the ship in the first place, his timing for a stunt like this could not have been worse.

"Move!"

Jacob marched the two prisoners ahead of him towards the starport's maintenance terminal as he'd agreed upon with Captain Webb. He didn't fully trust he wasn't about to be taken into custody, so he'd had Sully drop him, the prisoners, and the two battlesynths off and take the *Phoenix* to a small regional airfield almost three hundred kilometers south of the starport.

If Webb wanted to grab him, there was little he could do to stop it. He wouldn't risk harming any Marines or spacers just doing their job of apprehending an AWOL Scout Fleet team.

"Where are we?" Easterbrook asked.

"Camderan-2," Jacob said. During the flight out to the planet, the Obsidian team had become less combative towards the OSO guys. The spec ops community was small, and even though one of the teams had been sent out to neutralize another, there was still a sense of comradery that outsiders wouldn't quite understand. The OSO crew had just been doing their job, the same as Obsidian had when they tracked down and boarded a Navy cruiser and arrested her captain.

The crew Obsidian had captured seemed to be low-level operators, not particularly well-trained or experienced, that genuinely didn't know anything of value. The data they pulled off the ship had some interesting stuff, but nothing that helped them crack that final layer of network security protecting Margaret Jansen and her inner circle.

"Does that ship you're flying use our navigation database? The one provided by Fleet Ops?" Easterbrook asked.

The question was odd enough that Jacob thought about it before answering. Just because he didn't consider the two OSO punks to technically be his enemies, he also didn't trust them any farther than he could throw them.

"It's not a Terran ship," Jacob said. "We had to steal it after we lost our ride in the Reaches."

"No shit? You guys are some real badasses," Easterbrook said without a hint of mockery in his voice. "I...can't give you much. I don't know what's actually going on, but I know enough to see we weren't given the whole story. If you compare the UEAS nav database to the alien one you have in that ship, you might find a few interesting things."

"Why are you giving me that much?" Jacob asked suspiciously.

"Assuming this is anything more than a little misdirection on your part."

"Look, bro...I'm about to be sent to an NIS black site where I'll probably never see the light of day on any world, never go back home, never see my parents again. All of that makes me think the OSO isn't quite on the level I was led to believe when I was recruited."

Easterbrook paused and looked out at the horizon to the west where Camderan Major rose over the mountains.

"I'm not violating my oath by telling you this. Not technically. I guess I'm hoping when this all shakes out maybe you'll mention to someone higher up we were cooperative, and they don't just let us die in some hole on Terranovus."

Jacob felt for the guy. Unless he was a much better actor than Jacob gave him credit for, it looked like he was going to burn for being a pawn used by a powerful faction. An expendable resource given just enough information to do the job but not enough to expose the higher-ups no matter how much Director Welford's people worked on them.

"Chances are good I'll be rotting in the next hole over from you, but if I get the chance—and your info pans out—I'll make sure my boss knows you helped," Jacob promised. "So, you've really never heard of One World?"

"Just rumors when I was in college. I was recruited into the OSO directly from there, and we're pretty isolated," Easterbrook said, his guard going back up. "I'd forgotten about it until you said something about it while I was chained to the wall of your ship."

Jacob wondered at what sort of training Easterbrook had. He called a bulkhead a *wall*, so that indicated he didn't have any formal naval training. The civilian agencies flew their own ships so maybe his training was specialized in other ways. He did find it a bit insulting that One World sent such amateurs after him after he'd blown Hollick's arm off and ruined one of Jansen's plans on his first outing.

"Stop here," he said. He pulled his com unit, connected to the local Nexus, and sent a short message to Murph aboard the *Phoenix* to let him know he was in position. 707 and 784 had taken up posts that allowed them to remain hidden but still cover Jacob if needed.

He'd yet to get to the bottom of why 707 had attacked one of his guys, but Murph seemed none the worse for wear. In fact, the sergeant actually laughed about the incident when he finally came to and wouldn't let Jacob know exactly what had happened in the hold. MG, as usual, was very little help in trying to get to the truth of the matter.

Kentucky *in orbit. Shuttle inbound to your position.*

The message from Murph arrived only a few moments before the Sherpa-class light-duty shuttle touched down on the tarmac. Jacob tensed as its engines spooled down and the rear ramp dropped. He still expected a team of Marines to come boiling out of the small ship to overwhelm and detain him but, instead, it was just two spacers in blue overalls dragging a couple of black plastic crates. Behind them, Captain Webb himself stepped off the ramp and walked directly towards Jacob and his prisoners.

"Lieutenant," he said once he was within earshot. "I assume the rest of your team is hidden and covering me?"

"No, sir," Jacob said. "The *Phoenix* is parked at an airfield some kilometers away. The two battlesynths are here, but they're only to intervene if a non-UEAS force arrived. If you arrest me now, they've agreed to sit tight, and then find their way home. Obsidian will then return the *Phoenix* to S'Tora and return to Earth in our ship. If it manages to make it back, they'll surrender to you as well."

"Well aren't you just so reasonable." Webb sneered. "Don't think that because you have my balls in a vice with these OSO clowns that I'm not tempted to just drag you in on principle."

"Yes, sir," Jacob said, refusing to rise to the bait. He could tell Webb was genuinely hurt at Jacob's actions, and he understood why. Win or lose, Jacob had probably ended Webb's career. Jacob was committed now, however. If he was screwed no matter what he does, he might as well try to see it to the end. When the hell had he become so fucking idealistic? He hadn't even wanted to be a Marine when he went into the academy.

"I'll take these two off your hands," Webb said, apparently done lecturing. "The two crates are for you. No tricks, trackers, or anything other than just some equipment and data you might find useful." The captain turned and waved to one of the Marines who had come out of the shuttle and taken up a guard position.

"Sir!" the Marine barked as he ran up to them.

"These two are coming with us. Search and restrain them in the shuttle, but no games. I don't want them banged up until we know who the hell they belong to."

"Aye-aye, sir," the Marine said, turning to the OSO detainees. "Gentlemen, if you'd follow me, please." Easterbrook turned to Jacob and nodded.

"Remember what I said."

"You two buddies now?" Webb asked once they were out of earshot.

"Hardly, but I saw no reason to be enemies after you'd agreed to take them," Jacob said. "He did tell me something I'll probably need your help looking into, sir. He said I should compare the Fleet's navigational database with the one aboard the *Phoenix*."

"What the hell for? Did he say why?" Webb asked.

"Wouldn't divulge that. Just said I should do it," Jacob said. "Could be just a skilled intel operative fucking with us. Might be something more. We haven't had a copy of the updated UEAS nav charts since we left the *Corsair*."

"I'll get you the latest charts," Webb said. "The *Phoenix* has plenty of computing power to do the comparison, but I'd guess you could focus on the Orion Arm first. Anything he's wanting you to find would probably be something out past Breaker's World, but not quite to Pinnacle Station. That's where most of the Ull activity is, anyway."

"Got it."

"After this, you'll be on your own," Webb said. "There's no way to hide these prisoners once they go to Welford. The NIS has just as many leaks as NAVSOC, and once they're turned over, One World will know we're on to them. I'll try to keep it hidden as long as I can, but for your own protection, you won't have access to Scout Fleet or NAVSOC resources."

"Understood, sir," Jacob said. "If we can't pull this off, I'll pull the plug. I won't waste the lives of my men."

"Glad to hear it," Webb said. "If by some miracle you make it back to Terranovus, maybe it will just be you in Red Cliff and not your entire team. It sickens me that I have to play the political game and disavow you, but that's the deal, shitty as it is."

"I knew the score when I made this decision, sir," Jacob said. "Having them send hit squads after me from governmental black organizations they've apparently infiltrated only affirms I was right. Once we finish breaking into their com network, we should be able to drop the hammer."

"Just...be careful," Webb finished. "Also—and I'm just tossing this idea out there—if you get into a real bind, there is someone you can call who could come in and haul your ass out of the fire."

"I can't imagine that conversation would go well." Jacob just shook his head. "Not well at all." Webb just shrugged.

"Keep it in mind. If nothing else, Burke will probably swoop in just to make sure the *Phoenix* is okay."

True to his word, Webb packed up his Marines, the prisoners, and his spacers, and left in the shuttle a few minutes after leaving Jacob standing on the ramp, pondering what to do next. As the Sherpa zipped off to the east to pick up its orbital ascent vector, 707 and 784 broke concealment and came up beside him.

"Do you trust Captain Webb enough to take the equipment aboard the *Phoenix*?" 784 asked.

"I do," Jacob said. "There's no need for games. I volunteered to surrender myself and my team if he asked me to. Once I agreed to meet him here, I wasn't exactly a missing, rogue element. Not really. Now, we're operating on semi-legal orders while still needing to answer for deserting in the first place. It's the type of legal gray area the military justice system loves."

"I see."

"As for you," Jacob turned to look at 707, "what's the idea attacking a member of my crew and injuring him so badly he had to be pumped full of medical nanobots?"

"I simply did what he asked," 707 said.

"As detailed and helpful as that is, you're going to need to give me a little more," Jacob said after it was clear 707 wasn't going to add anything more.

"Sergeant Murphy insisted I needed to have a *real name*, as he put it. When I refused, he wagered he could last five minutes against either of us in a sparring match. He said that if he did, I would have to let him call me Tin Man."

"So, you knocked the shit out of him?" Jacob asked, exasperated.

"Not at first. For the first two attempts, I simply kept him from injuring himself."

"This will go a lot faster if you just tell me how he got hurt."

"I did not anticipate that Sergeant Marcos would shove Sergeant Murphy in the back just as I raised my hand to block another ineffectual attack," 707 said. "Sergeant Murphy tripped on a deck tie-down and ran his face into my closed fist. I regret I did not anticipate that Sergeant Marcos would use the distraction to try and injure his comrade."

"Marines 101...trust nobody, especially not your friends," Jacob said, beginning to see what actually happened now. The most infuriating part is that, after causing the problem, MG had been the one to run onto the bridge to tell him a bullshit version of it. "I'll deal with MG later. Just, please, try not to injure any more people on our team."

"I will try," 707 said. "Shall I call for an extraction?"

"Go ahead," Jacob said. "784, do you think you can scan these crates? I trust Webb, but I doubt he packed these himself."

"Of course," 784 said and walked towards the two black speedball crates.

The hardened cases were meant to be tossed out the back of a shuttle or gunboat to resupply ground forces engaged and running out of essentials. Webb had sent him two of the largest size Fleet used, so he'd not skimped on the gear.

784 had barely started on the second speedball crate when the

deep roar of the *Phoenix*'s engines were heard as Sully brought the gunship down from the traffic pattern. Jacob shielded his eyes as the gear cycled and the repulsors fired to cushion the landing. When the ramp dropped, the two battlesynths grabbed the crates and pulled them into the ship without help despite each likely weighing nearly a quarter of a ton.

"We're in, Sully," Jacob said into the intercom. "Close her up and get us out of here."

"*We have a destination?*" the pilot asked.

"Just get us up into orbit and lost in the traffic. Try to avoid the *Kentucky* if she's still up there."

"*Will do.*"

The ramp rose and boomed shut as the inner pressure doors slid into place. While his crew secured their new cargo, Murph and MG helping the battlesynths, Jacob ran up to the bridge. He walked in on time to see Sully swing them out to the east and push the throttles up, sending the gunship rocketing away from the starport.

Despite everything Captain Webb had just told him about his slim odds of success, guaranteed court-martial, probable incarceration, and complete lack of support from his command, Jacob still felt...hopeful.

There was an odd positivity hovering about him as the *Phoenix* pitched her nose and pulled hard for space. He couldn't explain it, but he felt like something was about to break their way and they might even be able to close this last mission out as a success before Obsidian was disbanded completely.

10

"Our patience is at an end. You will deliver the jump drive or we will expel you."

Margret Jansen leaned back, a smirk on her face as she eyed the two Ull that had stormed into her office. More and more, Ricardo Avelar noticed his boss adopted an adversarial posture the moment their Ull sponsors walked into a room. He wasn't sure if it was a defensive strategy, or if Jansen, living up to her legend, actually did have such an upper hand that she saw them as nothing more than a minor nuisance.

Avelar had been brought on to serve as Jansen's aide and fixer after Elton Hollick had simply vanished, but so far she'd been making him serve a kind of probationary period. He knew Hollick had been working more than a few side angles, and he figured the ex-NIS agent had been spooked, knowing Jansen planned to *retire* him upon his return from yet another failed mission.

Hollick probably had more than a few rabbit holes around the quadrant, but Avelar would bet money he had fled to the Kaspian Reaches, specifically the planet Niceen-3. Once they finalized this last deal, he was certain Jansen would send him to hunt Hollick down and tie off that loose end.

"You're still banging on about that?" Jansen laughed. "Haven't recent events told you the quadrant is moving past you and there are much larger things at stake? You think this trinket of Traveler technology will still make you a player in a game that doesn't even exist anymore?"

"Your constant word games are tedious, human." The Ull's name was Agonym, and Avelar knew him to be particularly disagreeable.

Jansen's demeanor and reactions seemed to be a deliberate strategy to maximize the Ull's ire. Even though he'd just come out from Earth, Avelar had made sure to develop his own relationships with their Ull partners separate from his work as Jansen's right-hand. Agonym was someone he felt would be particularly useful.

"I'm not playing games, Ull," Jansen said. "You want something that's the most guarded secret on Earth, yet you'll commit no resources to allow me to get it. I have no fleet. It was wasted because you failed to hold off Seeledas Dalton's forces long enough for me to secure Earth, thus allowing me to just hand you the jump drive. The government controlling the wreckage was spooked after our aborted invasion, and they've hidden it someplace my operatives have yet to uncover. My point, however, remains. You're obsessing over something that hardly matters now. You know the ConFed is about to fall, right?"

"Nonsense. There are small, underwhelming rebellions that come up every few hundred years. The Pillar Worlds tolerate it for a while, and then move their *real* power out to smash it," Agonym declared.

"There is no real power in the Pillar Worlds anymore," Jansen said, still smiling as if amused at some inside joke only she got. "The Council has been run by an outsider for some time, someone who comes from well beyond our quadrant. The Grand Adjudicators all work for it and, so far, there's been no response to an attack on Miressa Prime itself. You're telling me the Pillar Worlds used to tolerate attacks on their capital world in the past?"

Avelar frowned at that, not caring that the Ull could see him. The arrogant species never bothered to learn what human expressions or inflections meant anyway. What bothered him was Jansen not only seemed to have access to intel above and beyond what One World's planners had, but she was tossing it out to the Ull like it meant nothing.

At this point, his instincts screamed for him to step in and stop the meeting, or at least pause it to rein in Jansen's game playing, but he'd seen what happened to Elton Hollick when he'd tried to control Jansen. After having a hand blown off, he'd been humiliated, beaten, cast aside, and was now hiding in some bolt hole somewhere wondering where it all went wrong.

"This circular conversation and your antics have bored me beyond belief, human," Agonym said, standing to his full height. His words were all bluster. Avelar could tell Jansen had rattled him.

"Then see yourself out, *Ull*," Jansen said, still smiling but now showing her teeth. Agonym stood for a moment, staring at her, before turning and leaving the room with his underlings in tow.

"That was a dangerous game, ma'am," Avelar said once the door shut.

"Hardly," Jansen scoffed. "Our days of groveling for the Ull's assistance are about at an end, and they know it."

Avelar said nothing. He knew what bait looked like when dangled in front of him. What he didn't know was why Jansen seemed to be playing the same sorts of games with him, someone who was supposed to be her trusted right-hand, as she did with her adversaries like the Ull.

"Nothing to say, Ricardo?" she asked. "My estimation of you has gone up a touch. Your predecessor liked to mine for intel for his personal gain, much to his detriment."

"I assume if you want me to know something, you'll tell me," Avelar said. "I've no interest in repeating the mistakes Hollick made, nor do I have ambitions of striking out on my own. I'm here for the mission."

"That you can so convincingly lie to my face is impressive," Jansen said, laughing again. "Come, we have much to do. Agonym will be on a slip-com call with the Ull home world right now, trying to verify what I've given him. They'll be able to confirm just enough to spook them, and then they'll send him crawling back to us for proof of the rest. The real fun is just beginning."

"Fun?"

"You'll see," she said. "First, tell me how our acquisition project is going. Any word from the field?"

"There has been a...complication," Avelar said. "The target managed to overpower the first team. When we sent in a sanitation crew, they were also hit. A merc crew our files say is called Omega Force—"

"What?!" Jansen spun so fast that Avelar had to sidestep quickly to keep from running into her. "They're sure? And they're still alive?"

"The crew was left largely unharmed, minor injuries only. The team lead said they had positive identification on who it was. The merc crew questioned them a bit, then left," Avelar said.

"Shit!" Jansen fumed. "If Burke is on the scent now, we don't have much time to try and grab our target."

"I'm afraid I'm a little lost, ma'am," Avelar admitted.

"We've been trying to get our hands on a Marine lieutenant named Jacob Brown. He's part of Webb's Scout Fleet," Jansen said. "He started as a simple nuisance, even managed to screw up Hollick's op to recover the Zadra Intel Network, as well as blow the moron's hand off in the process. Later, we found out through our contacts on Earth that Brown's recruitment had been highly irregular, as was his assignment into Scout Fleet in the first place.

"The more we dug into Brown's past, the more questions were raised. It eventually led us to an obscure note embedded into the personal logs of a Commander Ezra Mosler—and I hope you can appreciate just how deep our organization had to dig to discover all this—indicating an interesting connection between this Brown and a group of battlesynth refugees called Lot 700."

"The group living on Terranovus?" Avelar asked.

"Exactly," Jansen said, seeming pleased he was keeping up. "Apparently, Mosler enjoyed a friendly relationship with one of them named Battle Unit 707—not the most creative group with their names, apparently—and when 707 learned young Lieutenant Brown was coming into NAVSOC and being placed in Mosler's care, the battlesynth told him all of Lot 700 would go to war to protect Jacob Brown because they owed his family something that loosely translates to a blood debt, or whatever the machine equivalent is."

"A group of ultra-secret refugees from the planet Khepri, a planet no human has even been to, somehow owes the Brown family a blood debt?" Avelar asked skeptically. "Ma'am, that makes no—"

"Not the Brown family," Jansen said. "Jacob goes by his mother's last name not his father's. His father ended up being quite the shock as well. Your sanitation team just met him."

"This Burke guy you spoke of?" Avelar asked.

"How you know about Lot 700 but not Jason Burke is a genuine mystery." Jansen rolled her eyes. "I'm not explaining the whole thing to you. Go read up on Jason Burke and his crew of sociopaths, and you'd better be proficient in them the next time we talk."

"If you feel it will be relevant," Avelar said.

"More than you know. If Burke's in the game, this just got a lot more interesting," Jansen said. "We may need to eliminate him as he complicates the reason we want Brown in the first place."

"You want to gain control of Lot 700 through Brown," Avelar guessed. "Ma'am, from what I've read of battlesynths, they're just as likely to kill us all as do what you ask because you're holding Brown hostage."

"There are ways around all small problems like that," Jansen said, her odd smile pasted back on. Putting aside her answer made no sense, it reminded Avelar of the uneasy feeling he'd had watching her entire interaction with the Ull.

"I'll be read-in before we speak again," he promised her. "In the meantime, I still need to manage the clean-up and figure out what happened to our first acquisition team."

"You do that." Jansen waved him away.

As Avelar walked off, he tried to sort the entire episode in his head. He'd looked over multiple psychological profiles and had watched hours of footage on Margaret Jansen before he ever left Earth. There was definitely something...off. Were the years of hiding on alien planets and being hunted by no less than four military organizations finally wearing her down?

There was little he could do at the moment other than what she asked of him, but he filed away the odd behavior as something to look into. If the head of One World was cracking under the strain, there were people back home who would need to know about it.

Before he'd been flown out to Jansen's base in one of the Office of Special Operations clandestine ships, he'd been completely briefed on the thing the Ull wanted, the only thing that kept them locked into this uneasy alliance with One World. It was an ancient bit of machinery from a wrecked ship they called the Traveler Jump Drive.

It was an entirely different method of superluminal flight than the ubiquitous slip-drives the entire quadrant employed. It essentially allowed a ship to instantaneously *jump* across space-time, the only theoretical limitation being the availability of power. The drive had been used by the ships an enigmatic cult of eco-terrorists Earth's intel community called the Travelers. Avelar wasn't sure if that was the name they used for themselves or if it was just a codename.

When the Ull had found out about the jump drive, they'd leveraged their assistance to Earth to get their hands on it. When Earth, specifically the United States, got cold feet, the Ull made a side deal with Margaret Jansen. At the time, she was the appointed administrator of the Terranovus Colony Project. She was supposed to prepare Earth's new planet for human colonists.

Instead, she used the Ull's technical assistance to build a war fleet she intended to use to install herself as Earth's ruler, and then would hand the jump drive over to the Ull. What happened instead was the Cridal Cooperative showed up to stop her, Earth entered into a trade agreement with Seeladas Dalton, and Margaret Jansen fled into exile.

Now that Jansen had re-established a power base, the Ull still wanted their prize. But there was a new problem. The *Traveler* wreckage had been moved and hidden multiple times since Jansen knew where it was. The old storage location, a deep vault located at the Groom Lake Test Facility in Nevada, was empty. Nobody seemed to know where the hell the jump drive components had been moved to, and One World was spending considerable resources trying to find out.

The appearance of Omega Force was a wrinkle Avelar hadn't counted on. Avelar was very much aware of who Jason Burke was and what he'd been up to the last couple of decades. All of the operatives within his organization had extensive briefings on all the known humans who were off-world without the approval of the government. Burke was one of them. Carolyn Whitney, also known as the Viper, was another.

Avelar also knew Jansen had a personal history with Burke, so he pretended to be ignorant to see just how deep that animosity ran. She'd kept her reactions buttoned-up, but her initial outburst at knowing Omega Force had engaged their forces told him all he needed to know.

If he was going to succeed where Elton Hollick failed, he would need to understand all the dynamics at play and their nuances. The biggest mistake his predecessor made was in assuming Margaret Jansen could be manipulated or controlled so easily. Avelar had met Hollick some years ago, and the man's ego was immense. He always thought he was the smartest person in the room and wasn't shy about letting that disdain slip out around the edges of his urbane demeanor.

While Hollick was exceptionally smart, highly trained, and experienced, he also had the fatal habit of underestimating everyone he came against. Case in point was how he lost his hand to some rookie jarhead lieutenant on a mission that should have been a cakewalk.

The situation was becoming more complicated but manageable.

11

"The speedball crates were clean. Lot of decent gear in there, as well as some new clothes, all fitted to our sizes."

"Good," Jacob said absently as MG stood in the hatchway of the *Phoenix*'s cramped com room. "Why don't you go grab a shower first, and then change into some of those clothes?"

"You saying I stink?"

"Worse than usual, yeah. Any other cool toys in the kits?"

"Weapons. They even tossed in some older cartridge-style firearms like they still use on Earth. Real high-end stuff, too," MG said. "Comes in handy since the gunpowder guns don't typically show up on most weapon scans at starports."

"Get all that broken down and stored in the armory. I don't want loose weapons aboard in case we end up with any more prisoners," Jacob said. "Have Mettler help you, and ask Murph to come up here."

"Will do."

As promised, Jacob had received a complete copy of the UEN Navigational Database from the *Kentucky* before she meshed-out on her way back to Terran space. It hadn't taken him long to set up the computer to begin a point-by-point comparison of the charts the UEN used and the extensive database in the *Phoenix*.

He'd instructed it to concentrate on the small sliver of space between where Earth resided in the Orion Arm and towards the galactic center in a narrow cone he hoped would encompass Ull-controlled space as Easterbrook had mentioned. Of course, it was equally likely the OSO puke sent him on a wild goose chase out of spite.

"What's up?" Murph asked.

"The computer is about done with its first pass. It should catch all the big discrepancies before drilling down into every little space rock cataloged in the database," Jacob said. "Figured you'd want to see this."

On cue, the computer beeped softly and displayed the summary report from the first-pass analysis. It was a short report.

"So, on the charts everyone else in the quadrant uses, there's a star system here with a habitable planet," Murph said. "On the official UEAS charts, there's open space and multiple warnings of a gravitational anomaly that must be given a wide berth. Interesting."

"Interesting and suspicious," Jacob said. "The Koliss System. The *Phoenix* shows it as an unremarkable Tier Three world, but it does fall within what we assume to be the Ull's operational area."

At his words, the holographic display on the tabletop computer fired up and showed a representation of that region of space, highlighting both the Koliss System, as well as the Ull System. Jacob assumed Cas must be listening in and providing the help as it saw fit. For some reason, the strange AI personality had stopped talking to them altogether but still appeared to be active.

"So, why would Earth not want any Terran ships traveling to some unimportant planet like Koliss-2?" Murph asked. "There are no particular risks associated here according to this ship's nav data. Hell, Breaker's World is a lot more dangerous sounding than this place, and we travel there routinely."

"I think NAVSOC is actually operating an outpost on Breaker's World now," Jacob said. "Not even really a classified outpost, either.

But there could be something else at play with this Koliss thing. Don't we get our nav database updates from the Cridal?"

"Ah," Murph said, nodding. "You're thinking this has nothing to do with any games by Earth and the UEAS and it's the Cridal hiding something there."

"Maybe," Jacob said. "The fact that OSO guy was the one telling me to look here tells me it's probably something to do with our people."

"There's something else bothering me," Murph said, rubbing his face and sitting down. "We used the data we stole from Hollick to reach out to one of his Ull contacts supposed to be an information broker, right?"

"Right."

"So, how did we end up getting attacked by Ull *and* human fighters?"

"I just assumed the bastard played both ends and took our money, then went and told One World he'd been approached by one of Hollick's associates," Jacob said. "But that is a little too convenient now that I think about it. You think Webb is right? We're blown, and Jansen's people know we're coming?"

"I think we have to consider it," Murph said. "Someone on Earth *definitely* knows we're out here if they sent those OSO lackeys after us, but don't forget they were traveling with Ull agents as well."

"Meaning there are One World sympathizers within the government who have the same freedom of movement NAVSOC teams do," Jacob said.

"Most likely scenario." Murph nodded. "So, what do you want to do?"

"We have to go to Koliss-2 and see what might be there," Jacob said. "We don't have any other leads right now, and an entire system being hidden in the official nav data is a pretty big red flag that something shady is going on there."

"No argument here," Murph said. "I'll send the course data up to the bridge if you want to go wake Sully and tell him we're ready to hit it."

"Poor bastard hasn't slept more than five hours at a time since this mission started, and I think he's been concussed at least twice," Jacob said. "I almost feel bad he'll be prosecuted and put in prison after this."

"He might be looking forward to the break, to be honest," Murph said. "He didn't have a much easier time even when Mosler ran Obsidian. The commander barely slept and didn't like to fly the Corsair so, anytime he got a wild hair up his ass to head somewhere, he'd drag Sully out of the rack."

"I don't feel so bad now," Jacob said. "I'll go get him, and we'll get the hell out of here. I'm starting to feel like this mission is dragging on, and the longer we go without being able to pin down Jansen, the less likely we'll be able to pull this off at all."

"Welcome to Koliss-2," Sully said as the *Phoenix* popped into real-space deep in the Koliss System.

"How do you want to skin this pig?" Murph asked.

"What the hell does that even mean?" MG asked. "And what was that accent?"

"I'm just keeping in practice," Murph said. "Trying different vernaculars and cadences. It's called tradecraft."

"So, you're practicing to be the only six-foot-five black dude who talks like someone from the hills in West Virginia?" MG asked. "I don't pretend to be a spy or anything, but I think you might still stand out."

"The point of the exercise is to develop a character on the fly," Murph said. "If I'm talking into a slip-com channel, they won't know what I look like."

"I can't believe you're actually bothering trying to explain this to him," Mettler said.

"I feel like maybe if he's exposed to new ideas enough he won't be so myopic and single-minded in his life's pursuit of blowing things up and trying to trick women into sleeping with him," Murph said.

"I never pegged you for such an optimist," Jacob said.

"And you never answered the question. What are we looking for down there?" Murph asked. Jacob opened his mouth, and then closed it.

He had no idea.

One thing that was sometimes lost as a matter of perspective was scale. They flew around observing ship movements and tracked targets to specific star systems or planets, but once you dug down that far, there was only so much you could do with a small crew. Planets were huge, with billions (sometimes trillions) of beings with unique topography, weather, and political conditions. You could spend fifty years searching a planet and never find what you were looking for.

He watched the planet rotate slowly on the main display as the *Phoenix*'s forward optics magnified it on the main canopy for their benefit. The computer also displayed any pertinent data it thought the crew might want like basic atmospheric composition, different temperate zones, as well as extreme weather conditions, and any special warnings regarding local customs or politics.

From what Jacob could see, there weren't any special considerations when it came to landing the *Phoenix* or carrying personal arms up to area denial weapons. That usually translated as bring all the small arms you want but no explosives, mortars, or missiles.

"Sully, how long will they let us loiter in orbit?" Jacob asked.

"I don't think they give a shit what we do up here as long as we're not interfering with local commerce or shooting at each other," Sully said. "They only care about that second part due to debris clogging the orbital lanes needed for the local commerce I mentioned. What do you have in mind?"

"Does this thing have any sensors that can passively scan the surface?" Jacob asked.

"I think I get where you're going with this," Murph said. "You want to survey from orbit to see if anything jumps out. It has to be something obvious, otherwise, the tip from that OSO puke wouldn't mean anything, and he clearly wanted you to find it...unless this is all just a con job."

"Pretty much," Jacob said. "There has to be something we can spot quickly and easily. If there wasn't, it wouldn't make much sense to doctor the nav charts to hide this system to begin with."

"I think I found what you're looking for," Mettler said. "This ship has something called the passive surface surveyor array. It's in the belly and looks like it takes multispectral sweeps of a planet's surface from orbit."

"That sensor array is not designed to pick out minute details, but you should be able to program the computer to search for any obvious anomalies," a familiar voice said from the overhead speakers.

"Welcome back, Cas," Jacob said. "You've been awfully quiet lately."

"As I said when we met, I am not the full Cas matrix. The more I am active on this system, the more the *Phoenix*'s main computer tries to purge me. It sees me as an errant, malicious bit of programming it's trying to get rid of. I will be of what help I can for as long as I can, but I fear our time together is coming to an end. It has been a pleasure to help you on your mission."

"Drama queen," Murph muttered.

"Uh...yeah, it was a pleasure here, too," Jacob said. "So, anyway, can you get the specs for this passive array to Sully so he can position the ship?"

"Of course," Cas said. There was a soft *beep* to let them know it was now offline again. Jacob frowned, wondering if that was it and the AI had been zapped from the *Phoenix*'s main computer core.

"Got it," Sully said. "The good news is that it sees at a decently wide angle so we won't have to make five thousand orbits to get a complete picture. We can hit most of the landmasses except for the polar regions without needing to change orbits."

"Let's get started right away," Jacob said. "I'm no longer certain this ship is as good a camouflage as we first assumed."

Jacob and Sully were the only two who remained on the bridge as the *Phoenix* was programmed into a specific orbital track to allow the passive survey array maximum coverage. Once he'd gotten the hang of the interface, which mercifully could be switched over to English thanks to his father, Jacob was able to start programming in some basic search parameters.

Almost immediately, the computer plucked items of interest from the clutter and put them aside for a closer scan on the next pass. By the thirtieth orbit around the planet, they had twenty-seven targets on the surface the computer thought they would like to take a closer look at.

As the ship searched, something unexpected happened. The *Phoenix* had been to Earth a few times, as well as Terranovus, and she had a human owner. The ship was quite familiar with human engineering and architecture and was able to take Jacob's clumsy search algorithm and figure out he was specifically looking for any signs of human activity on the planet. They didn't have long to wait once the *Phoenix* adjusted her orbit and scanned the northern hemisphere.

"Holy shit!" Jacob said, almost falling out of his seat. "Murph! Get up here!"

"Intercom isn't voice-activated," Sully said, yawning. He seemed completely unimpressed with the Marine's enthusiasm at what he'd found.

"I still heard him," Murph said, walking onto the bridge. "I was in that little conference room thingy back there. It's nice and quiet. What do we have?"

"Take a look," Jacob moved aside and gestured at the sensor station monitor. Murph took one look, and his eyebrows shot up.

"That's on *this* planet?"

"Right below us," Jacob confirmed.

"I'd say this has to be it. Easterbrook was right if he assumed it'd be easy to find," Murph said. "I'll get the other's prepped to go. I guess we're heading there now?"

"As soon as Sully gets clearance," Jacob said.

Murph left the bridge, and Sully prepped the *Phoenix* for atmospheric entry while Jacob took a closer look at the imagery the sensors had grabbed. Below them, well outside of one of Koliss-2's medium-sized cities, was a base with what looked like ten landing cradles for large vessels. Eight were empty, two had hulls that the computer couldn't identify, but two were easily identified as Columbia-class starships.

These human-designed, pre-UEAS ships were the mainstay of Margaret Jansen's fleet she came to Earth with over a decade earlier to try and install herself as the ruler of the planet, answerable only to her Ull partners.

The ships were considered primitive by today's Navy standards, and most of the hulls had been destroyed by the Cridal counterattack, but Jansen had managed to flee with enough they would pop up every so often. What made this pair interesting was that the computer analysis also indicated the base was abandoned.

Multiple passes showed no movement or other signs of activity like heat blooms coming from any of the buildings. Jacob pulled up the specs on the Columbia-class ship to familiarize himself before they landed. He was surprised to see them on the ground as they weren't known to be capable of entering an atmosphere or landing, even with the assist of a grav-beam and landing cradle.

"We'll be on the ground in twenty minutes," Sully said. "I'm taking us in over the base to see if someone at least comes out to look, and then we'll land on the northwest pad near that cluster of small buildings."

"Sounds good," Jacob said, rubbing his hands together at the thought of finding a secret One World base still intact. This was the type of lead he wanted. Now, he just had to stay positive and hope there was something useful down there.

12

The *Phoenix* thundered over the landscape, her engines roaring at full power as Sully buzzed the base before yanking the big gunship into a vertical climb.

"Holy shit! I can see why your old man loves this ship so much," he grunted to Jacob.

They'd decided that trying to sneak in might be a bad idea if they stumbled upon a sizable force still on the base. Instead, Sully fired up the four monstrous plasma-thrust engines the *Phoenix* boasted, put the grav-drive in standby, and blew the windows out of the buildings as he made enough noise to ensure anybody in the facility would come outside to see what the hell was happening.

"No scans detected, no thermal signatures," Jacob said as the pilot pushed the *Phoenix* over and lined up for another pass. If a security force had remained behind, they should have at least tried to ping the ship's ident beacon to see who they were.

"I'll overfly it one more time, and then put her down over there," Sully said, smiling widely as he slammed the throttle back up, eliciting an explosive bellow from the ship as she raced back down towards the base. "You sure you want to land and not have me just drop you off?"

"I need you on the team," Jacob said. "We have to inspect those hulls, and you're the most qualified."

"Do I get a gun?"

"Sure," Jacob said. "Just don't shoot anyone by accident, but if you do, make sure it's MG."

Sully reengaged the grav-drive and killed the main engines. The rumbling plasma thrusters settled with a few pops and bangs as he wrapped the gunship into a tight right-hand turn to bring them back on approach. It was mid-morning over the base currently, with few clouds in the light blue sky so they'd have excellent conditions for a recon mission.

Once the *Phoenix* settled onto her landing gear with a soft groan, Jacob unstrapped and went down to see how the rest of the team was doing. Sully quickly placed all the ship's primary flight systems in standby and followed behind.

They stopped by the armory so Jacob could issue him one of the standard Navy sidearms and plasma carbines the pilot would be familiar with and moved out into the cargo hold where the rest of the team milled around near the pressure doors.

"Open her up," Jacob said. "Let's get started."

When the ramp dropped, Jacob braced himself for whatever stench this planet would have. He took an experimental sniff and found the dry, warm air had just a hint of... Was that lavender?

"Oh, man!" MG said. "This place smells great! After stepping out onto so many planets that smelled like Beelzebub's asshole, we finally got one that literally smells like flowers!"

"This actually is pretty nice," Murph said. "And nobody is shooting at us yet, so this isn't half-bad."

"Let's inspect those landing cradles first," Jacob said. "I want Sully to do a walk-around, and then he can babysit the *Phoenix* while we check the admin buildings. If there was anything left behind worth a damn, it'll likely be in there."

The walk across the tarmac and around the large building they'd landed next to was pleasant. If it wasn't for the fact they were all armed to the teeth, Jacob could have almost forgotten they were on a dangerous mission. Once they rounded the building and walked into the shallow depression where the ships rested, they realized something right away. The ten slots they'd viewed from orbit weren't for landing. They were heavy construction cradles.

"This is a covert shipyard," Murph said, sounding awestruck. "How in the hell did they get something like this set up on an alien planet? Who funded it?"

"I would say the Ull helped, but this is all obviously Terran construction techniques," Jacob said, looking around. "These dry docks are identical to the decommissioned set on Terranovus."

"It also explains the discrepancy as to how Jansen fielded so many ships," Murph said. "We could never figure it out, but a medium yard with space for ten more hulls at a time makes it all line up nicely."

"Why was it just abandoned?" Mettler asked. "There are tools lying around in the pits, I see a power cart... Oh, and four starship hulls."

He was right. The place looked like it had been hastily abandoned, and the ships resting in the cradle slings weren't being repaired, they were being built. The two Columbia-class ships were missing their subluminal drive pods, and one of them was missing most of the outer hull plating along the prow. The other two ships, while unknown, also looked unmistakably human in origin.

"Were these two the start of a new class of ship Jansen was building?" Jacob asked. "That's an insanely ambitious undertaking for someone on limited resources and being hunted."

"They might be an unknown class, but they're not modern," Sully said. "They look to be about the same vintage as those Columbia hulls, but there are some improvements to the design. Either way, they're still much smaller and more fragile-looking than even our light cruisers are today. Which do you want to look at first?"

"Let's go see if that power cart has any juice left in it and turn one of these bastards on," MG said. "See what happens." Jacob wanted to tell him to leave the heavy thinking to the experts, but he actually thought his weaponeer had a solid idea.

"I mean, he's not wrong," Murph said, also seeming to want to punch holes in MG's suggestion.

"I will try to start the generator," 784 said. "If something goes wrong, I have the best chance of surviving."

"No arguments there," Murph said.

The power cart was a *cart* only in the sense it was technically portable. In truth, it was the size of two semi-trailers and had to be moved with a high-power tug. The trailer was a small, portable fusion power station the Navy used when suitable ground power wasn't available.

Jacob could only guess as to why a base of this size needed the units unless the utility power available on Korliss-2 wasn't compatible and One World never got around to having a converter or central powerplant installed. On a base like this, it would be used to apply power to the ships until their fusion powerplants were fired up.

They watched as 784 fired his footpad repulsors and arced down into the pit, walking up and inspecting the machine for several minutes before dragging the thick power cable over and connecting it to the interface on the ship. The Columbia-class ships were just shy of two hundred meters long and only sixty meters at their widest point. Most of that space was taken up by the bulky reactors used back then.

The interiors were Spartan and bordered on crude compared to what the Navy flew around in now. Jacob looked over the ungainly ship and shook his head, admiring the bravery of the crews who willingly spend months on end inside one of them. It had to be worse than submarine duty in a seagoing navy.

"A fun bit of trivia...our own Captain Webb served aboard one of these," Murph said. "He was a US Navy SEAL back then, and he was assigned to the USS *Coronado* on a mission to hunt down and kill a rogue human element in space, a mercenary named Jason Burke."

"Cute." Jacob rolled his eyes.

"I'm only partially joking," Murph said. "It was Margaret Jansen who put Webb's kill-team together and sent them after your pops. Director Welford was on Terranovus at the time and tried to stop Jansen because he'd had some dealings with Burke before and knew the team was headed into a meat grinder, but Jansen was adamant the mission had to happen."

"Why did she want Burke dead so badly?" Mettler asked.

"Loose ends, as far as I was ever told. Burke was a wildcard in her plan, and she didn't like that he was out there, uncontrolled and unpredictable," Murph said. "Jansen had found out he had ties to Crisstof Dalton, and the Ull warned her the eldest living Dalton kid —Seeledas—would be able to marshal a fleet that could stomp a hole in their ass if she came to Earth. Ironically, she'd have done no such thing if Jansen hadn't dragged Burke into the whole mess by going after him. He'd have never known what she was up to or that Earth was about to be conquered from within."

Jacob frowned but said nothing. The story of his father's time in space was a lot more complicated than the disparaging tale of a selfish adrenaline junkie he'd told himself as a kid. His ruminations were cut short by a high-pitched screeching coming from the power cart below them. He made a mental note to ask Murph to brief him later on the Dalton family since the NIS agent seemed to have detailed knowledge.

Everyone tensed up to run, but 784 walked around the machine as if he hadn't a care in the world, so they stood fast. After a few more minutes, the sound faded, and the marker lights of the ship's hull blinked.

"Well, there's at least a power mux system installed with some of the more basic control systems," Sully said, pointing at the lights. "Don't get your hopes up for much else. I can't imagine any computer cores or classified com gear would have been left behind. Actually, without the reactor cluster being installed, the computers were probably never even brought aboard."

"Still worth a look," Jacob said. "After that, we'll try one of those unknown classes, and then we'll start the building search. It doesn't look like any of these other hulls are power-ready."

Once 784 rejoined them, the team walked the edge of the pit to the gangway that extended down to the port boarding hatch. As they expected, the hatch was dogged but not locked. With a little bit of battlesynth brawn, the latches gave way with the groan of metal-on-metal contact from the unmaintained mechanism.

"Interior lights are all up. That's a bonus," Jacob said, peering into the ship.

"Where to first, LT?" MG asked.

"Let's go forward to the bridge, and then work our way back," Jacob said. "707, you want to take point with your sensors?"

"Of course," 707 said. There was a sharp pop/whine as 707 switched to full combat mode, his arm cannons deploying, and his eyes glowing a brilliant crimson.

Once he'd made it ten meters in, the rest of the team followed in a loose column. The old human starship was so cramped the main corridor off to the side of the boarding hatch was only barely wide enough for two people to walk side-by-side.

The bridge of the ship wasn't located in the superstructure as it would be on most ships of that size. Instead, it was up towards the prow, buried beneath two decks and hull armor. The tower-like superstructure on a Columbia-class ship was crammed full of tachyon-emitting sensors, communications gear, high-power radar arrays, and other equipment that pumped out radiation humans would want to avoid exposure to. The bridge and CIC were kept more towards the middle of the ship where the crews were more protected.

The rooms and alcoves they passed were stuffed with uninstalled parts, tools, and even a pair of work boots. Access panels hung open, with loose wiring piling out of them and schematics taped to bulkheads all over. The documentation was all in English, so the work crews at the secret base were human and most likely from the United States.

"You smell that?" MG asked.

"Just the conformal coating on the electronics burning in," Mettler said. "That's normal."

"How the hell would you know? You're not an engineer."

"I'm also not an absolute fucking moron. You'd think if you have a job riding on spaceships you'd bother to learn something about them."

"Knock it off," Jacob said over his shoulder.

"The bridge is clear," 707 said over the team channel.

"Copy," Jacob said. "We're on the way up. 784 and MG, I want you to stay here in the main corridor and keep an eye on the hatchway. Everyone else with me."

There were some sounds of a scuffle behind him as MG flicked Mettler in the ear as the medic walked by, who then shoved the weaponeer into the bulkhead. Before Jacob needed to intervene, 784 grabbed both and forcefully separated them. Jacob rolled his eyes and kept walking.

"What a mess," Murph said as they walked onto the bridge. Cables snaked out of openings in the panels where wire harnesses had been pulled in and left unterminated. Some of the control panels and displays sat on the deck, further highlighting the base had apparently been hastily abandoned some years ago.

"We will likely need 784 to investigate further, but it appears none of the central computer cores have been brought aboard. All the equipment functioning right now is for discrete systems with their own controllers," 707 said.

"We'll need to have him—"

"Welcome!" The voice came from the bridge speakers and startled everyone except the battlesynth. "From the images I saw earlier when you were milling about outside, I'm assuming you're one of Marcus Webb's Scout Fleet teams."

"And you would be?" Jacob asked.

"That's not particularly important right now," the voice said. "What is important is we don't have a lot of time to talk. When you landed on the base, you triggered a security response. Lucky for you, the locals we hired to watch the facility aren't an ambitious lot."

"So, you're part of One World," Jacob said.

"Your understanding of the problem is horrifically limited, but for the sake of brevity...sure, I'm with One World. Can I assume this is

Team Obsidian and I'm speaking to either Lieutenant Jacob Brown or Special Agent Alonso Murphy?"

"This is Brown. Murphy is standing here with me," Jacob said, shrugging at Murph. He didn't have a lot to gain by withholding that information when they had already tripped a security alert.

"So, you're the one I have to thank," the voice said with a chuckle. "When you embarrassed Elton Hollick by screwing up his simple retrieval mission, he fell out of favor with leadership and made room for my advancement. Poor Hollick has yet to return, so I assume he's hiding somewhere, trying to figure out what to do."

Jacob raised an eyebrow at that. Either they were being manipulated, or One World wasn't aware Hollick had been killed. That could be turned to their advantage later.

"He's a slippery one," Jacob said. "I'm guessing this isn't a social call, so what do you want?"

"I'm impressed you managed to track down the Koliss base. As you can see, you're about ten years too late for that to matter, but you've gotten deeper than any of the others Webb has sent after us. "

"It looks like you guys left in a hurry," Murph said.

"It was before my time, but from what I understand, there was a recruitment shortfall, and we needed the personnel back, and the hulls you see were for ships already obsolete and not needed. Koliss-2 was a good location, and they'd sunk so much into getting that base up and running they decided to keep it. The locals have been watching after it until we can decide how best to use it.

"The reason I activated the remote link on the Solstice when our operations center detected you aboard her is to tell you there's more to this than you can possibly understand. You're tilting at windmills, my friends. Go home, take your lumps with the UEAS justice system, and live to fight another day."

"So, this is just an altruistic effort?" Jacob asked. "Because you're so very concerned about our wellbeing?"

"Wasting talent is pointless," the voice said. "I doubt we'd ever try to directly recruit you. Webb makes sure his operators are all diehard patriots and flag wavers, but that doesn't mean you still don't serve a purpose even if you don't realize it. Having you snuffed out by Jansen's Ull thugs or killed by your own people when NAVSOC finally gets around to bringing you in would be a monumental waste of potential."

Jacob looked at his mission clock, seeing how long the conversation had been running. Whoever was talking to them seemed to be having an earnest conversation and not just stalling for time, but Jacob still didn't want to get caught up in a firefight with the locals if he could avoid it.

He waved to get Mettler's attention, and then used hand signals to tell him to start getting ready to pull out. 707 had taken the time to dig into the panels on the bridge and had apparently found a few things of interest, ripping them out and handing them to Sully. The pilot stuffed them into his pack while he continued his search.

"I'm still not getting a good sense of what you want from us right now other than to show off you're tracking us," Jacob said.

"Who said I wanted anything? To be honest, I just happened to be in the operations center when you tripped our security," the voice said. "It seemed like a good opportunity to see what you might know and have a little talk while nobody else from either side is listening. I have no doubt we'll speak again soon."

"You sound confident in that."

"I'm confident you'll be able to defeat the yokels we hired to guard the base. I'm also confident you won't stop just because you didn't find anything there of value," the voice said. "You're tenacious because you think there's redemption at the end of the road if you succeed. As I said, your ambition will only be rewarded with disappointment."

"You're looking to the future," Murph said. "To a post-Margaret Jansen organization. You're probably high enough up you would stand to benefit greatly if we end up snagging her. In fact, you're likely hoping we can, but you're smart enough to not offer us any tangible support in case we're captured and questioned. This brings up some interesting possibilities."

"Indeed it does, Agent Murphy. Or is it Sergeant Murphy now?

You've been on loan to the Corps so long the NIS may have forgotten about you. Either way, that's a discussion for another time. Farewell."

"Channel is closed," 707 said. He stood by one of the com stations and monitored the slip-com node.

"Don't suppose there was any useful tracking information to be had from the system he was using?" Jacob asked.

"Node identifier was masked, and he was not routing through any of the commercial networks," 707 said. "It was a private node, direct point-to-point channel."

"Figures," Jacob said. "Okay, let's move. I'd like to avoid the locals if at all possible."

The team quickly moved back down the main corridor to the junction that would take them back out to the port entry hatch. Jacob wished he had a full day or more to carefully comb over the derelict hulls and buildings on the base, but he'd clumsily put his ship down right in the middle of a monitored area.

He half-thought the voice's threat of a local security force might have been bullshit, but as the conversation went on, he felt like whoever was talking to them had no real motivation to screw with them.

13

"What is that place?"

"No idea," Kage said. "From what I'm seeing, it looks abandoned. All four of those hulls are definitely from your people and have been there a while."

The *Devil's Fortune* had arrived in orbit over Koliss-2, and it didn't take the ship's impressive sensor suite and powerful computers long to sift through the data and find what looked to be either a small shipyard or heavy maintenance facility with a few obsolete hulls in the pits. Two of the hulls looked to be of the same type of ship Webb had flown out when they tried to kill him, but Jason had never seen the other two.

"Anything else interesting?" he asked.

"Oh...maybe," Kage said, manipulating the image so it zoomed in on a bit of open tarmac near one of the large buildings. Sitting on the ground was the familiar shape of his DL7 gunship, the *Phoenix*.

"That little bastard!" Jason hissed.

"Oh, *now* he's a bastard? When I called him that, you almost shot me," Crusher said from where he lounged at a sensor station, not even pretending to be helping. Jason just turned to glare at him but said nothing.

"Can we access her now that we have line of sight?" he asked Kage.

"Security is still airtight," Kage said. "You, and only you, will need to actually put your hands on her for a full biometric reading so you can reset the protocols and regain access."

"Cas! Where the hell are you?" Jason yelled. The small, hovering recon probe that Cas's AI matrix inhabited floated onto the bridge.

"You needed something?" it asked.

"I need you up here. You and Doc will handle the *Devil* while Twingo takes me, Crusher, and Kage down to retrieve the *Phoenix*," Jason said.

"And if your son is still aboard her when you arrive?" Cas asked.

"Then junior and I are going to have a little talk," Jason growled.

"Who the hell are these guys?" Kage asked, pointing at the main display. Jason looked and saw seven ground vehicles approaching from the opposite side of the base from where the *Phoenix* was parked. They were still nearly three kilometers from the shipyard pits but definitely inside the perimeter of the base.

"Probably locals who claimed the base once the humans left," Jason said. "Keep an eye on them. We'll put down between the two large manufacturing areas there and split the difference between them and the *Phoenix*."

"Let's move," Crusher said. "We don't have too long before that group gets organized and set into a defensive position or moves out to attack. Let's go get the ship and get the hell out of there."

"Incoming!"

At MG's shouted warning, Jacob and the others picked up the pace, running for the exit. The weaponeer and 784 stood just inside, looking up. Just as they approached the pair, some sort of aircraft

overflew the base, engines rumbling. Assuming it must be the local
contractors the voice on the slip-com had told him about, he poked
his head out to see what size an aircraft they brought.

"What the hell?" he muttered. "Does that look like a miniature
version of the *Phoenix*?" 707 also looked.

"Similar," he said. "It appears to be one of the new Jepsen ships
since the company was reopened. Possibly from the SX-series. That is
not the type of ship a local defense force would be flying."

"So, who are these clowns, and where are the security guys we
were threatened with?" Mettler asked.

Jacob stepped onto the gangway to get a better view of the small
Jepsen as it flared and dropped out of view behind one of the large
support buildings. Not even half a minute later, the ship rose sharply
back into the air, turned away from the base, and shot off into the
distance.

"Shit," he said. "That could only have been an insertion for a strike
team."

"Agreed," 707 said. "It seems unlikely we are their target. They
would have had to track us to Koliss-2, and they have had ample
opportunity to hit us or the ship since we have landed."

"Maybe there's something here they want and this is just a wild
coincidence of timing," Mettler said. The others just turned and gave
him unfriendly looks. "Yeah, I realized how stupid that sounded after
I said it."

"We have to get back to the *Phoenix* no matter what," Jacob said. "If
they inserted a team behind those assembly buildings, we should
move around the edge of these docks and make a sprint for the ship."

"Tactically unsound," 707 said. "We still do not know the direction
or composition of the local security contractors."

"We can only deal with the threat we know of," Jacob said. "I have
no idea who these guys are, so I have to assume they're a higher risk
than the security teams our friend on the com seemed to think were
no big deal."

The sound of distant weapons fire made everyone snap their

heads up. 707 focused his eyes on a point in the distance that, to Jacob, just looked like a part of the landscape.

"Multiple ground vehicles," the battlesynth said. "They appear to be converted civilian vehicles and not purpose-built for military use. They are firing at something behind the second row of buildings."

"What are they shooting at?" Murph asked just as the screech of a hypersonic projectile reached them and one of the vehicles on the horizon exploded. The rest of the security force scattered, trying to find some defensible position.

"What the hell?!" MG yelled. "That strike team brought a damn railgun to the party?"

"We need to move immediately," 707 said. "There are only a few groups in the quadrant who prefer that type of weapon, and we want to encounter neither of them."

"Let's go!" Jacob said. "We'll cut through that last building while they're engaged with the locals."

"That was...excessive," Kage said. Crusher held his ears and glared at Jason.

"This is the new model the Legions made for me. Has a little more ass than the old ones. Bigger projectile, too."

"Still stupidly loud for the stupid person shooting it," Crusher snarled.

"It's not *that* loud," Jason said, smiling at the carnage his new railgun carbine caused. A single max-velocity shot had turned one of the technicals that had been closing on them inside out.

"The rest of the locals are scattering," Cas said over their tactical channel from where it watched from the *Devil's Fortune.* "They appear to be a low threat now. There is another team moving from one of the Columbia-class derelicts towards the *Phoenix.* There are two battlesynths with them."

"That'd be Obsidian," Jason said. "Which way are they heading?"

"Looks like they're cutting through the large building behind you. The one closest to the *Phoenix*'s landing site."

"Cas, keep an eye on the locals," Jason said. "They'll reorganize or call for reinforcements soon enough. We're going to go intercept these Scout Fleet clowns and get the ship back."

"All these damn hallways look the same!" MG griped as the team moved through the office section of the huge building they found themselves in.

"Just keep moving that way," Jacob said, pointing.

He'd anticipated the building would just basically be a large, empty space from the way it appeared on the outside. It had clearly been a pre-assembly building for large sections of the ships that would then be moved out to the construction pits as needed. Once they'd entered, however, they found that, at some point, the interior had been converted into office and living space.

There were modular buildings stacked and interconnected within the cavernous bay of the larger building, creating a confusing nightmare for the team to get through. At least the lights were on so they weren't running around blindly.

As they ran, a sharp explosion shook the structure, debris raining down on them in the narrow corridor they were in. Two more hit in quick succession, and it became obvious that whatever was being lobbed in was substantially more than small-arms fire.

"Mortar attack," 707 said. "They are punching through the roof and detonating inside the building. They know we have entered this space."

"Move, move, move!" Jacob shouted, marshaling his people forward. "707, protect Sully! Without him, nobody is leaving!"

The battlesynth moved in close to the pilot, ready to shield Sully with his body if needed. 784 also assisted while Mettler brought up the rear of that group. They moved off quickly, with 707 confidently leading them through the labyrinth.

"If a mortar round hits the ship while she's on the ground with the shields down, we're fucked!" Murph said.

"Let's go!" Jacob shouted as another muffled explosion shook the building.

They ran after the others, letting them get some distance so an unfortunate lucky shot wouldn't kill the whole team. They didn't get far before the corridor up ahead imploded, collapsing and bringing at least two stories worth of debris with it.

Jacob kicked open the nearest door to his left and dove through as the hall filled with dust and debris. He heard the door slam closed behind him, and when he looked back, he saw both his teammates had made it through with him, MG already covered in a layer of dust.

"I'm sure most of the shit covering me right now is loaded with cancer-causing agents," he griped, brushing himself off in Murph's direction.

"We'll need to get around that mess," Jacob said. "Hopefully, they don't leave without us."

"Yeah, I should have made sure I was in the group with our only pilot," MG said.

"Sounds like the mortars have stopped," Murph said.

"Great, that means they're on the way down to clear the building out," Jacob said.

"And they probably know their way around," MG said.

They moved quickly through several long hallways that seemed to be identical, each having twenty-eight doors lining the sides. Some of them were opened, and Jacob could see they were set up like your standard permanent party barracks with two racks and wall lockers in each. Apparently, One World had plans for this base that included housing an entire garrison, and it had been a decision hastily implemented.

They had just made it out of the living area and into a large, open bay that looked like it might have been a mustering hall when Murph skidded to a halt.

"Stop!" he hissed. "Did you hear that?"

"What?" Jacob whispered.

"I thought I heard a...growl?"

Before Jacob could accuse his teammate of wasting their time, the door at the far end of the room slammed open, and a shadowy figure stepped through. Jacob went to raise his weapon but stopped as the figure walked slowly towards them with its hands out, unarmed.

"I believe you have something of mine, junior," the familiar voice from a dozen years ago said.

Jason Burke stepped into the light.

A million conflicting emotions coursed through Jacob as his father walked towards him. The man looked like he hadn't aged but a month since last he'd seen him. Still wearing the same military-style clothes, still with that lopsided, sarcastic smirk on his smug face.

"Hello...Dad," he managed to get out.

"Oh, shit," Murph muttered. "We have to have this happen *now?*"

"Get going," Jacob said to his teammates. "Get to the ship, get out of here. Don't wait for me. Go! I'll catch up somehow."

To their credit, his crew recognized when something like a long-brewing family cold war was about to go hot. It wasn't the time to hang around. Their standard procedure would be for Sully to exfil the team, and then loiter once he was in a safe place. After that, they would try to reacquire their missing team members before declaring them lost.

Burke just watched them run out a side door with a bemused smile on his face and shook his head.

"So...how've you been, kid?" he asked.

The casual, offhand manner Burke asked the question settled Jacob's roiling emotions. Replacing all of the conflicted feelings at seeing his father was white hot rage. All of the anger and hatred for the man surged to the surface, as did the hurt of seeing his mother pine away for the loser for the remainder of her life.

"How have I been? That's all you have to say to me, you worthless fuck?" Jacob practically shouted. By now, they'd closed the distance to within a meter of each other. Burke just rolled his eyes and sighed.

"I suppose it was too much to think you might have grown up a little in these years, Jacob," he said. "I'm done defending myself to you. You know the truth. You choose to believe the childish stories you made up about me instead. Then, when you get in a bind, you come and steal from me to save your ass, and I'm supposed to feel bad about this?"

"Fuck you!" Jacob snarled, Burke's words cutting deep and ratcheting up his anger even higher. He tossed aside his primary weapon and stepped closer to his father. Burke just smiled again, leaning in a bit.

That was the last straw. Jacob would show this bastard he wasn't the same scared kid he'd walked away from a dozen years ago. He moved with all the power and speed his improved genetics had gifted him and came at his father with a savage right hand, the type of punch he would never throw at another human for fear of killing them.

He tapped into the anger and pain of his youth, his hatred for the man who had fathered him and put it all into the punch. Just before he expected the hit to impact the side of Burke's jaw, his hand was pushed off course.

Burke had brought a forearm up and slid the blow aside, moving so fast Jacob hadn't even seen it. His momentum spun him around and sent him sprawling to the floor. He rolled over and bounced to his feet, pissed and embarrassed at letting his emotions control him to throw such a sloppy, telegraphed punch. He came in again, more controlled, and watching his opponent before striking again with the right.

This time, Burke caught his hand in midair, again moving so quickly Jacob barely had time to react. His father, never looking like he was putting any real effort into it, bent the wrist back until Jacob had no choice but to follow it or risk injury. Before he could even think about bringing his other hand into play, Burke punched him in the chest with a quick jab that sent him sprawling to the floor, gasping.

"You and I have a real problem, kid, but don't think I'm going to let you take free shots at me to work your issues out," Burke said, looking bored. "I've been doing this a lot longer, and I've been trained by the best. You can't hurt me unless I let you."

"What do you want, asshole?" Jacob spat.

"What the hell do you think I want, genius? I want the *Phoenix* back." Burke walked up and kicked him in the ribs, sending him flying across the floor. If Jacob hadn't had his body armor on, they would have snapped. "I have a missing crewmember I need to track down. Every fucking day I've wasted trying to find where my sniveling little shit of a son took my ship is one more day they get farther away. Your selfishness and immaturity were your problems. Now, you've made them *my* problems."

"I—" Jacob stopped, not sure how to process what was happening. He had known he probably couldn't hurt someone as extensively modified as Burke. In truth, he had actually expected his father to just stand there and take the punishment from him. Having him attack back, and then turn the entire situation around so Jacob looked like the complete asshole wasn't what he'd envisioned when he'd fantasized about this meeting so many times in his head. "Who is missing? It's not Twingo is it?"

"No," Burke said, his posture relaxing a bit. "It's Lucky."

"I heard Lucky was dead."

"It's complicated. He's not dead, but he's not... Either way, he needs my help. The places I have to go mean I need the *Phoenix* back," Burke said.

Jacob's next sentence was cut off as a savage, bellowing roar echoed through the open corridors. Burke turned to him and smiled.

"Looks like your buddies are getting to meet another one of my crew. Hope they have their wills filled out."

Jacob just swallowed. He knew exactly who MG and Murph faced.

14

"Shit! We should go back for the LT," MG panted.

"We're not getting in the middle of *that* family squabble," Murph said. "You know the drill. We back off, and then wait to get Brown after he makes contact...and that's even if Sully is waiting for us in the first place. The ship is at risk while on the ground, so he may have already left the area."

"Cheery thought," MG said.

They ran through a short corridor that dumped into another open space, this one with tables folded along one wall and a buffet counter along the other. The disused mess hall was brightly-lit and had multiple exits, two of which went the way the two Obsidian members wanted to go.

"Which one?" Murph asked.

"You mean you don't know, Mr. Agent?"

"I've never been here before, you moron. Just pick one of those two doors and— What was that?"

"I think it was that same growl from before," MG whispered.

Just as he was about to lift his weapon, the ceiling tiles near where they stood caved in, and something heavy slammed onto the floor. Half the lights in the hall went out completely and the others started blinking, creating an almost zero-visibility condition.

MG's weapon was ripped from his hands, the sling snapping off his tactical harness, and he was flung across the room. Murph peered through the dust just as his weapon was jerked away. His sling held on, however, and he followed it across the floor.

MG, still not getting a good look at whatever had disarmed them, tried to draw his sidearm only to have his hand enveloped by a huge clawed one with dark skin. The pressure exerted broke two fingers immediately, so he swung wildly with his left fist to try and get the damn thing to disengage.

The deep chuckle he heard chilled his blood. It was toying with him. He saw Murph climb up on shaky legs and pull up his weapon, only to see the barrel was bent at a ninety-degree angle. MG looked up, groping for his knife with his left hand, and saw a pair of yellow eyes staring down at him.

"Oh, shit!" Murph shouted. "MG! It's Crusher! Get away from him!"

"Not really my choice right now," MG grunted, the pain in his right hand excruciating.

Murph pulled his knife and moved in quickly, going for a target on Crusher's lower back. The big Galvetic warrior turned his head just as Murph committed to his charge. Crusher spun, grabbing MG with his free hand and throwing the weaponeer at his teammate.

Murph, stunned by the speed and power of the monster, didn't have time to lower his knife before MG slammed into him. They both went down in a heap while Crusher let out another rumbling chuckle.

"You just stabbed me in the ass, you idiot!"

Before Murph could apologize or even pull the knife out, Crusher leapt across the room and slammed into the floor right in front of them, letting loose a bestial roar that triggered every primitive flight instinct both humans had. Crusher straightened and reached behind him, drawing two long, curved blades from sheaths that crisscrossed his back. He smiled hugely and dragged the blades against each other with a rasping sound that sent shivers up Murph's spine.

"You didn't put up much of a fight," the beast rumbled. "Pity. So, which of you wants to die first?"

"He does," MG said, waving towards Murph.

"Crusher! Knock it off," a voice came from one of the side doors.

Murph and MG looked over and saw Jacob walk in with the guy he'd identified as Jason Burke. Murph had known Burke had aged minimally during his time out in space, but it was still jarring to see him looking like Jacob's very slightly older brother rather than his father.

"Just having a little fun," Crusher said, putting his knives away.

"Fun?" Burke asked. "You stabbed this man in the ass!"

"His buddy did that." Crusher pointed at Murph. "No idea why. Seemed weird to me, too."

"Not to be a whiner about this, but I'm pretty sure I need medical attention," MG said.

"Crusher, you're carrying him," Burke said.

"Why me?"

"Because I don't believe for a second his friend just up and stabbed him and you had nothing to do with it. Let's go. Kage is on his way to the ship, and Doc called in saying we have inbound. The locals have called in air support."

"We'll take him," Jacob said firmly when Crusher bent to pick up MG. The warrior shrugged and walked off. Burke was almost to the far door by the time they got MG on Jacob's shoulders and started off.

"There's no excessive bleeding, and you can still feel your feet, so we're leaving the blade in until we get to the infirmary," Jacob told MG. "I don't want to pull it and have you bleed out on me or end up destroying a nerve bundle."

"So, what happened back there?" Murph asked.

"I'll fill you in later," Jacob said. "Short version is I wouldn't have even been able to hold him up long enough for you guys to get to the ship, so the only way we're getting off this planet is with them."

"He that tough?"

"I never even landed a hit. He threw me around like a toy, and then told me Crusher was already tracking you two," Jacob said. "I made a deal after that. I take it things didn't go well?"

"I'd read the file on him, but that son of a bitch is terrifying," Murph said. "Same thing as you. He tossed us around a little bit, took MG's weapon, broke mine in half, and then threatened to carve us up when your dad walked in and called him off."

"He *probably* wouldn't have actually done it," Jacob said. "From what I remember of him as a kid, he likes to fuck with people like that. He and Kage are not to be trusted. Ever."

"This isn't going to be a fun trip, is it?" Murph asked.

"I have a feeling we're going to be missing the *Boneshaker* pretty soon, even though it tried to kill us on multiple occasions."

"Why are you down here?" Jason demanded.

"There are two battlesynths up there I'm not sure aren't going to shoot when I go up the ramp," Kage said. "I figured this would be a good job for you." Jason just scowled at him.

"707! Get your metal ass out here!" Jason yelled up the ramp. The battlesynth walked up to the edge a moment later. It always hurt Jason when he saw 707. Out of all the members of Lot 700, he looked the most similar to Lucky's old body.

"Yes?" 707 asked.

"Are you actually going to bar me from boarding and reclaiming my own ship?" Jason asked. "Keep in mind, I'm not real fucking thrilled right now you helped the kid steal her in the first place." 707 managed to look genuinely confused.

"We are doing no such thing, Captain. Your code slicer came up, saw us, and ran back down the ramp without a word," 707 said. "You are free, of course, to board your vessel."

"That sounds about right," Jason said, glaring at Kage. "Okay, everyone aboard. Move it! Take this guy to the infirmary and get the knife pulled out of his ass cheek. Once we're clear, we'll talk about who is going where and in what."

They all ran up the ramp, and Jason couldn't help but get a bit emotional. He hadn't seen the old girl in some time, and despite the luxury and capability of the *Devil's Fortune*, he'd still missed the *Phoenix*.

He and Kage raced through the main deck while the others scattered to help the wounded Scout Team operator to the infirmary. When he walked onto the bridge, the same lanky bastard he'd seen on the security feed stealing the ship in the first place made ready to drop into the pilot seat.

"Who the fuck are you?" Jason demanded.

"Uh...I'm Lieutenant Ryan Sullivan," he said. "Who are you?"

"I'm the guy who owns this ship, which includes that seat you were about to climb into," Jason said. "Now, move!"

To his credit, Lieutenant Sullivan didn't waste a lot of time arguing with the pissed-off, heavily-armed person making demands of him. Jason slipped into the pilot seat and waited while the *Phoenix* recognized him and reconfigured the station to his personal preferences. Over in the copilot seat, Kage did the same, complaining loudly about whoever had been in his seat screwing things up.

"Welcome back, Captain Burke," a familiar voice said.

"*You,*" Jason hissed. "What the hell are you doing here?"

"Technically, I'm not here," Cas replied. "I am merely a—"

"Shut up, don't care, don't have time for your bullshit right now," Jason said. "I'll deal with you later. Kage, you have the uplink to the *Devil* live yet?"

"You're good to go," Kage said. "Cleared for engine start, too."

"Doc, you got me?" Jason asked, flipping the main drive to 'RUN' mode and waiting as the reactor ramped up and fed power to the grav-emitters in the wings.

"We have you," Doc said. "Inbound targets are less than five minutes out. They were vectored in from an airfield fairly far away, but they're definitely on a direct line and have been communicating with the ground forces you already engaged."

"And what are those jackasses doing?"

"They've set up a security perimeter around one of the buildings on the other side of the construction cradles," Doc said.

"Did they now?" Jason said. "Interesting."

"What's interesting?" Crusher asked.

"We need to splash these inbounds, take out the ground forces, and then take a look in a building on the other side of this base," Jason said. Crusher looked at the downlink data from the *Devil's Fortune*, seeing the troops moving to protect a building they had never been near.

"Pretty amateur move telegraphing the building is important," Crusher said. "That guy who got stabbed by his buddy is strapped down in the infirmary. They pulled the knife out, and now the nanobots are doing their thing."

"They were stabbing each other?" Kage asked. "Damn. Your son's team sounds a lot like this one. I wonder what the common factor could be here."

"Shut up," Jason said. "Standby for uplift and get the weapons online. Why is she listing like this?"

"Emitters are *way* out of alignment. Twingo is going to flip out," Kage said. "You're degraded on the port side by... Wow, almost twenty-two percent. Overall misalignment is near eleven percent at nominal output."

"We've been without an engineer for—" Sullivan started.

"Nobody was talking to you!" Crusher snarled, leaning down to yell in his face. Sullivan paled noticeably but did a damn admirable job of not averting his gaze. Or pissing himself. "Ha! I like this one." Crusher slapped the naval officer on the shoulder, and then went to go sit at one of the forward stations.

"I can't maneuver with her wallowing about like this," Jason said. "Setting grav-drive to null and bringing up the mains. Guess we're doing this old school. Start working with Doc and Twingo to get targeting solutions on our inbounds and the ground forces. If we need to, we'll hit them from orbit with the *Devil*'s guns."

"Orbital bombardment," Kage said. "Well, that won't start a reported incident with the ConFed or anything."

"We'll be gone well before those douchebags show up," Jason said, grabbing the controls as the *Phoenix* surged and lurched to her right on the unsteady grav-drive. "Assuming we don't crash, of course."

"I never assume we won't crash," Crusher said.

Jason looked over and saw the four main engines had gone from 'PRE-HEAT' to 'STANDBY.' He smiled and flipped them into 'RUN' and was rewarded with the resounding *boom* and a sharp kick in the seat as the plasma engines lit off.

"Here we go," Jason said. "Start calling out intercept vectors."

He shoved the throttle up, and the *Phoenix* snarled as she leapt forward, racing over the ground as millions of pounds of thrust pushed her through the dense lower atmosphere.

"I've actually missed this," Crusher said. "Mok's corvette makes it too easy."

Jason let the *Phoenix* run along the ground, reveling in the feeling of being back aboard his ship again. He took a deep breath and reached out with his neural implant, allowing it to fully integrate with the ship. There was a split-second of vertigo before his brain accepted the new inputs, and he was able to *see* with the ship's sensors rather than have to look down at his displays.

It was a sensation that was impossible to describe, and a skill that had taken him years to master, but when he and the *Phoenix* merged like this, he felt damn near invincible.

"Crusher, get back and get a team together," he said. "We'll splash these inbounds, and then you need to get in and out of that building to see what they might be hiding. Don't take any unnecessary risks. This isn't even our mission. If it smells funny, abort, and I'll come get you."

"Sounds fun," Crusher said, leaping from his seat and leaving the bridge.

The *Phoenix* also had access to the *Devil's Fortune* and her sensor suite through the downlink Kage had initiated, so the corvette's vantage looking down on the incoming targets gave Jason their exact location while the gunship still hugged the terrain. Through his neural link, he locked onto all six targets and assigned weapons groups to each one.

Most would be hit with a missile called a Pixie, a small, versatile munition Twingo and Kage designed from scratch to handle soft targets like the small inbound aircraft. The missiles carried simple high-explosive warheads so they could be safely used within a planet's atmosphere, unlike their nuclear-tipped ship busters.

The two ships leading the formation he would handle with the *Phoenix*'s main guns, the six large plasma cannons housed in the leading edges of the wing roots. The tricky part about using the main guns was they weren't able to be aimed independently of the ship's orientation.

Wherever the *Phoenix* pointed was where the shots were going to go, no small challenge in a planet's atmosphere where the ship's attitude and orientation were controlled as much by aerodynamic forces as the engines and thrusters.

"You're lined up nicely for those first two," Kage said. "I'll take control of the missiles and let them loose when we're optimal."

"Thanks," Jason said. "Doc, go ahead and soften the ground targets. Take out their technicals, but don't damage the building."

"*I'm on it,*" Doc said over the open channel.

Jason concentrated on what he was about to do as the distance between him and their targets rapidly closed. At the last possible minute, he cut the throttle and raised the nose, wrapping the *Phoenix* into a hard left-hand turn to bleed off speed and give him the angle he wanted: a lateral run that would let him rake the sides of the inbound aircraft.

As he expected, they tried to scatter when the big gunship rose out of the ground clutter, but it was too late. The aircraft were converted civilian models now carrying the extra weight of weapons and loaded down with reinforcements for the ground force.

The pilots did the most obvious thing and tried to climb out and clear the engagement, but their craft didn't have the power to elude the *Phoenix*. Using the neural link, Jason lined up his first shot and squeezed the trigger. Red plasma lanced out from the six cannons, leaving white streaks through the humid air in their passing.

The target exploded when one of the shots slammed into its left engine. Jason received status updates on the eight missiles Kage launched at the remaining four targets as he pulled into the turn even harder to chase the last one. Right when he was almost lined up, the enemy pilot rolled hard to the right, cut power, and dove for the ground. The unexpected move caused Jason to overshoot and put him completely out of position for a follow-up shot.

"This one has a little skill," he grunted, slamming the throttle forward and yanking the *Phoenix* into a hard climb, looking down and *through* the ship with the neural link feeding data to his optical processors.

The fleeing pilot wisely traded altitude for airspeed and wasn't making any huge course changes, hoping to hide in the same ground clutter Jason had on his approach. He pulled back on the stick and let the *Phoenix* come all the way over onto her back before rolling wings-level and coming around to re-engage.

"You're coming up on a populated region soon," Kage warned. "Better stop playing and smoke this guy."

"Shit," Jason said, pushing the power all the way up. The gunship rocketed towards the helpless aircraft and, as he lined up to squeeze the trigger, he almost felt a pang of sympathy for the pilot. But just as he opened fire, the aircraft juked to the left so hard all of Jason's shots did nothing but tear up the forest below.

"You want some help?" Kage asked.

"Quiet!" Jason snapped.

He kept the throttle buried and continued his powered dive towards the target. Soon, they pushed near three times the speed of sound, and the computer complained about the heating on the leading edges. A second later, it automatically retracted the main guns and closed the hatches to protect the cannons. The small aircraft appeared to be topped out at high-subsonic speed, the flutter of its stubby wings visible as the *Phoenix* thundered towards it.

They overflew the aircraft at a range of less than five hundred feet.

The downwash from the *Phoenix*'s wings sent it into a violent tumble, where it crashed into the trees, sending up an impressive fireball. Jason cut the power and pulled his ship into a gentle, banking climb to the right. He disengaged his neural link and checked all the warnings the ship had spit out. Nothing permanent damaged.

"You're rusty," Kage said. "I'm almost embarrassed to have witnessed that."

"Yeah, it wasn't my best moment," Jason admitted. "Let's get ready to toss Crusher out the back and see what he finds."

"If only you meant that literally," Kage said.

15

"What the hell is that?" Jacob asked, pointing at the hole in the cargo bay deck filled with a wavering blue light.

"You've never used this the whole time you've had the ship?" Crusher asked. "You're going to love it." Then he grabbed a shocked Murph and threw him into the blue maw.

"Hey!" Jacob shouted just as 707 and 784 walked up and jumped in right after Murph. Crusher winked at him and followed the two battlesynths. Shrugging, Jacob stepped off the edge after them.

He expected to fall or be atomized or...something. Instead, Jacob was pleasantly surprised the blue beam zipped him to the ground, slowing him before he touched so all he had to do was walk out of it. As soon as he did, the ear-shattering roar of the *Phoenix* throttling up and leaving the area drowned out whatever Crusher was saying to them.

"Noisy bastard," Crusher growled once the sound had receded. "As I was saying, the *Devil* already softened them up. All the technicals are gone, a lot of their troops are dead, and the rest have retreated into the building. There's only one door we can see, so we'll need to breach someplace else. Thermographic scan indicates there's a corridor running along the southeast wall we can get through without too much trouble. You two want to do the honors?"

"It would be best if we did," 707 said. "Our cutting lasers should be of sufficient power to get through the wall and will be a bit subtler than the breaching charges you are so fond of."

"I like to announce my arrival," Crusher said with a smile. "Okay, let's get to it."

"Wait!" Murph protested. "That's your whole plan?"

"We have operators from three different units who have never worked together before," Crusher said. "It's best if we don't overcomplicate this."

"Do we even know how many troops might be remaining?" Murph asked Jacob as they ran after the others.

"I don't even know how many there were to start with," Jacob said. "I was just grabbed by the big guy and told to get my weapons."

"I feel like this could go very poorly."

They ran around the back of the building they'd been dropped off by, past the construction cradles and half-finished ships and, finally, to the side of the building sporting the new scorch marks from the orbital hits. In total, it ended up being just over two kilometers. The pace set by the battlesynths and the Galvetic warrior was brutal, even for someone with Jacob's gifts. Murph looked like he was going to cough out a lung.

As he gasped and held his side, 707 and 784 were already at work burning a hole through the outer wall while Crusher kept an eye towards one corner and pointed for Jacob to take the other. Every so often, Crusher glanced at the roof even though the team still on the ship in orbit was keeping an eye on the building.

It took no time at all to burn through the outer wall of the prefabbed structure. The smoke from the burning composite cleared out in the gentle breeze, and they looked into a well-lit hallway as generic as any other Jacob had seen in government buildings.

Crusher indicated to the battlesynths he would take point, and they would all move forward as a team. He pointed at Murph and signaled he'd bring up the rear, not bothering to hide his disgust with the Marine's weakness. Jacob felt for him. They'd been going for damn near a full day, and Murph hadn't eaten or rested much during the entire operation. Now, he had some of the galaxy's most badass soldiers sneering at him because he couldn't keep up.

Still...better Murph than him.

The hallway ran the length of the building and came out as Crusher had hoped, right by the main entrance and the security station. But there weren't as many troops guarding the door as they'd expected. There were only two, which the big warrior dispatched with his bare hands, not even wasting the effort to pull a blade. Jacob knew Crusher tipped the scales at well over three hundred pounds, but he moved with the speed and fluidity of someone a third that size.

"Shit," Jacob said. "Where are the rest?"

"Could that have been everyone?" Crusher asked. "Ground team to *Devil*, how many tangoes did you get?"

"*Estimated twelve inside the vehicles, along with another nine nearby,*" Doc's voice came over the team channel. "*We picked up at least seven making it inside.*"

"I just killed two, so that leaves five," Crusher said.

"*I'd have bet good money you couldn't have done that math in your head,*" Kage's voice broke in.

"How about a little professionalism in front of the new people, you four-armed, bug-eyed shit lizard," Crusher said.

"*You have ten minutes, Crusher, and then we're pulling out,*" Jason said. "*Get to it.*"

"We're moving through the main entrance into the interior," Crusher said. "The humans on the team will look for anything that seems worth guarding. The battlesynths, and I will provide cover. Let's move."

They didn't have to wait long to find resistance. The moment 707 walked through the main security door, they started taking enemy fire. The battlesynths were all but impervious to most small arms fire, so they waded into the fray and engaged with their arm cannons.

Crusher motioned for Jacob and Murph to hang back while the pair did their job.

The local security contractors had already had a rough day after being attacked by some random asshole with a railgun, hit from a starship in orbit, and now trying to fend off two battlesynths in close quarters. It was safe to say their heart just wasn't in it, and the last two surrendered after three more were slaughtered. They tossed all their weapons and sank to the ground, hands on their heads.

"Do we require both alive?" 707 asked. Crusher walked in and looked the pathetic survivors over, seeming to really think it over.

"For now," he finally said. "What were you idiots guarding in here?"

"This was our pre-arranged fallback point," one said in Jenovian Standard. "We were to come back here and secure this building, then wait for reinforcements and air support. They never told us what was in here."

"You're willing to die guarding something, and you don't even know what it is?" Murph asked.

"That's what this job is all about," the alien said. "Our clan runs security for seven different installations on Koliss-2. This was the easiest after the humans left. We came here thinking we were just dealing with trespassers again. Local youths like to explore the old ship hulls."

"Why this building?" Murph pressed. "Don't give me that lie you don't know why your fallback position is an unsecured, unhardened building right near a landing area. What were your *full* orders regarding this building?"

"We were to retreat to this—"

"Yeah, yeah...I got that part. What were you supposed to do if you were about to be overrun or reinforcements wouldn't get here in time?" Murph closed the space between them, standing over the alien in a manner meant to be intimidating, but with aliens all having their unique body language and social cues, who the hell even knew.

"We were to blow the access to the—"

"Silence, you fool!" the other captive hissed. "We forfeit our contract if you—" His sentence was cut short as Crusher kicked him hard enough to send him into the far wall, where he crumpled into a pile and lay still.

"You may continue," Crusher rumbled.

"And be fast about it," Jacob said, looking at the mission clock.

"There is a stairwell under an armored hatch in the secure office back behind us," the alien rushed on. "It's rigged with charges that need to be triggered with a key code, but the only one who knew the code sat in one of the destroyed vehicles."

"That's it?" Murph asked.

"That's it! Just blow the charges and let the whole thing collapse!"

"784, if you would?" Jacob asked.

"Of course," 784 said, walking back into the secure area and scanning for the hatch the alien spoke of. There were the sounds of things being tossed around, and then the tortured shriek of metal being rent as the battlesynth ripped the armored hatch from the floor.

"He appears to be telling the truth," he said. "There is a ladderwell that goes down into what seems to be a panic room."

"Go ahead and check it out," Crusher called. "Be careful. Don't blow your ass up."

There were some more sounds of random destruction, the sounds of weapons fire, a really loud *thump*, and then nothing. Jacob frowned and went back into the room before Crusher could grab him and peered into the hole.

784 had gone into the basement-like area but had then detected a sub-structure beneath and had punched his way in with his plasma cannons. Jacob could just make out the glowing red eyes roaming around the sub-basement.

"You good?" he shouted down.

"Do not come down, this structure is no longer stable," 784 said. "I believe I have found our objective. I will be up in a moment. You will want to stand clear of the hatch opening."

Jacob backed away and, a minute or two later, 784 flew up through the opening, riding on the thrust of his footpad repulsors. He carried two small, flat boxes in his hands.

"That's all that was down there?" Jacob asked.

"There was also a slip-com node of human origin these were connected to," 784 said.

"That's it then," Jacob said. "We got it! Let's get the hell out of here!"

"What about him?" Crusher pointed at the last living member of the security team.

"Let him go," Jacob said. "He's had a bad enough day."

"I certainly have," the alien muttered. "But thank you."

"*Phoenix*, this is Crusher, come get us"

"*Phoenix is inbound*," Jason said. "*We'll drop the transit beam right outside the door for you.*"

"This one should appreciate that," Crusher said, hooking a thumb at Murph. "He almost died during the run across the pad."

Murph opened his mouth to defend his honor, apparently thought better of it, and remained silent.

16

"What are they?"

"They look like old crypto traps," Murph said. "I'm not sure if that's what they're really called. That was the name one of my instructors used."

"So, it's just a secure data core?" Jason asked.

"Much more than that," Murph said. "But that's the essence of it. Someone went through a lot of trouble to hide them down there with their own slip-com node. From what 784 said, they were never meant to come out since there was no access door into that sub-basement."

"When the slip-com node went offline, they were trapped down there," Kage said, looking at the devices. "Talk about a loose end."

"Maybe, maybe not," Jason said. "Even if they contain critical data, nobody would know they were there. That first room they found under the office must have been a red herring, something easily explored even if the charges had gone off. Jacob said there had been a bunch of old servers and terminals lined up along one wall."

The trio was in the *Phoenix*'s portside engineering bay poking around at the recovered devices as the ship flew through the Koliss

System to rendezvous with the *Devil's Fortune*. The locals had indeed been a little pissed about the corvette opening fire on the surface without provocation and ordered the ship out of orbit and out of the area.

The reaction was so tame Jason assumed they were getting ready to coordinate with the ConFed to try and get a warship or two into the system, but since Koliss had no defense fleet of its own, there wasn't much they could do but bluster.

"The initial scans aren't promising," Kage said. "I can see why they call this a trap. If I start pushing too hard trying to get in, it'll probably destroy the data or the core itself. Maybe Cas would have better luck."

"I can take a look if you—"

"Not you, damn it!" Jason said. "The real Cas. You're getting purged from my ship as soon as Twingo gets his hands on you."

"Not a bad idea," the fake Cas said. "The corruption of my matrix is quite irreversible."

"I'd hate to trip a failsafe, but we have nothing else to show for this trip so far," Murph said. "We should probably hand over all of our data so the real Cas will have more to work with. When we cleaned out Elton Hollick's ship, we picked up a lot of data and codes we're missing context for. We lost our tech and our resources at NAVSOC so it's been just sitting."

"Yeah, that reminds me, I need to fly to Terranovus to kill Webb and Welford," Jason said. He tossed it out there as if he were talking about holding a weekend cookout.

"I... Uh, really?" Murph asked.

"I asked them to keep an eye on Jacob." Jason shrugged. "Instead, they tossed him into the Scout Fleet grist mill without sufficient training or backup. It's the least they deserve. Don't worry, they know it's coming."

"I'm not sure that makes me worry less," Murph said.

"Look at the bright side," Kage said, "if it happens soon enough, you can probably avoid that court-martial."

"Go ahead and put these in a protective case," Jason said. "We're only an hour out, so I'm heading back to the bridge before that pilot tries climbing back in my seat again. If we can quickly turn the *Phoenix*, drop these clowns off somewhere safe, and stash the *Devil*, we could be back on-mission in a few days."

"Yeah, the word I'm getting through the Zadra Network isn't good," Kage said, suddenly serious. "There's a lot of chatter about some new hitter who's been killing high-profile targets out in the frontier region. They say nobody even knows what the killer looks like, so it could be Lucky using his holographic abilities."

"We'll talk about that in private," Jason said, shooting a look at Murph. "Let's dock on the *Devil*'s starboard side, and then let Twingo figure out how he wants to shift everything around to get her in the hangar bay."

"I've seen Galvetic toddlers with heavy weaponry do less damage than this!"

Twingo had been in a rage for the better part of two hours. Every new issue he found with *his* ship sent him into a whole new fit. The *Phoenix* had been docked to the *Devil's Fortune* until the SX-5 could be pulled out and anchored to the hard-dock anchor points on the top of the corvette.

The *Phoenix* had then been moved into the hangar bay so the engineer could go through the ship to see what had happened to her in the short time Obsidian had her.

"All we did was fly her!" Sully protested.

"This ship isn't one of your one-size-fits-all combat scows that are just glorified cargo shuttles with armor and guns," Twingo said. "She's unique, *and* she's high-strung. It takes someone with knowledge about her upgrades to constantly keep things adjusted to within nominal."

"Seems tedious," Jacob commented as he walked around the ship. He'd been spending his time down in the hangar mostly to avoid his father, but also because he'd developed a real affection for Twingo in the short time he'd spent with him all those years ago. The engineer was exactly as he remembered, and the familiarity felt...nice.

"Still, it could have been worse," Twingo said. "Back when your father and Crusher took her out for a six-month joyride, it took me almost as long to undo their damage. Not only was he too hard on the engines, but he let her get shot up, and then took her to just any local shop for repairs."

"When was that?" Jacob asked.

"It was... Damn," Twingo said, seeming to realize he'd said too much. "It was after Lucky died. He and Jason lived together on S'Tora, and Lucky had stayed with him during the time Omega Force had broken up, and we'd all gone our separate ways.

"When Lucky sacrificed himself, Jason took it harder than the rest of us. He and Crusher took the *Phoenix* out to the frontier and worked all the settlements as guns for hire, hoping the violence and non-stop work would help them forget."

"Doesn't sound like a great plan," Sully said.

"To put it mildly," Twingo said. "Jason stretches himself too thin trying to protect everybody, so when he fails, it sends him into a tailspin."

"Omega Force broke up?" Jacob asked, frowning.

"Yeah," Twingo said. "Dark times. Dark, dark times. I'll let your father tell you about it since it's his story to tell. By the way, Jacob, I was very sorry to hear about your mother. She and I were friends. We all were her friends. Even Kage."

"Thanks," Jacob said absently. "So, my dad really didn't know she'd died? Before you guys landed in that field when I was there?"

"Not a clue," Twingo said. "Back in those days, there was no way to keep in touch with anybody from Earth. You weren't a spacefaring species, your military was after your father to get their hands on this ship as well as dissect all the non-human crew, and there were too many people finding out about Earth's existence. He didn't even know she was pregnant before he found out she'd died."

Jacob didn't say anything. He just stared at the same spot on the *Phoenix*'s hull as if it had all the answers to his questions. Sully and

Twingo continued without him as he walked to the other end of the hangar to sit on a crate.

His feelings had been thawing towards Jason Burke ever since Captain Webb had punched him in the face, and then explained why he was being a self-absorbed child for harboring such resentments. Now, after talking with Twingo and Crusher, he realized how unfair he had been, but he didn't know what to do about that.

Even if he could just snap his fingers and all the anger and resentment towards Burke evaporated, there still wasn't any sort of relationship to build upon. They were two strangers who met one time when he was a kid. His mom had loved Jason right up to the day she'd died in that car accident, and Jacob had always been bitter by what he saw as her putting her whole life on hold pining away for someone who would never come back.

Taryn Brown had deserved to live a happy, full life. Not living like a recluse in some old cabin while watching the sky every night, hoping to catch a glimpse of that goddamn ship, and then acting embarrassed when Jacob would catch her.

The picture slowly coming into focus was that Jason Burke was a deeply flawed but caring man who tried to do the right thing even when it required great sacrifice. So, what did that say about the son who spit in his face? Not a whole hell of a lot.

Now that Jacob took a rare moment of self-reflection, he had to admit he'd spent far more time whining about his problems than doing anything to fix them, and he'd used his unusual parentage as an excuse and a crutch. Instead of reveling in the gifts of strength, endurance, and durability his father had passed down, he'd bitterly cried it wasn't fair he was different.

"You look like a man who just tasted something he didn't like." Jacob looked up and saw his father leaning against the nose gear of the *Phoenix*.

"Something like that," he said, standing. "What's up?"

"I figure we need to talk to your boss," Jason said. "It might not be a bad idea to do it together...provide a unified front."

"What are we unified about?" Jacob asked, regretting his tone as he did.

"Murph has explained your predicament to me, and I think, regardless of what they're saying now, if you go back to Terranovus with Jansen's head in a pillowcase, you'd have a lot better chance of avoiding the inside of a military prison," Jason said. If he was bothered by Jacob's defensive snappishness, he didn't show it.

"What about Lucky?" Jacob asked. "Sully said you might have a lead on where he's at."

"Lucky is important, but so are you," Jason said after a moment's hesitation. He seemed almost afraid to show any outward affection that might jeopardize the cordial dialogue they'd opened. "If I manage to save Lucky, and there are no guarantees I can bring him back from where he is, and he found out I tossed you to the wolves to do it, he would kick my ass...and that's no small threat in that new body of his."

"New body?" Jacob asked, then shook his head. "You can tell me about it later. Sounds complex."

"Unbelievably so," Jason agreed. "You ready to talk to Webb and lay it out for him?"

"Why not?"

***

Marcus Webb just stared from the screen, his head moving back and forth slightly between the two as the color drained from his face.

"Your audio working, dickhead?" Jason asked.

"I, uh... Yeah," Webb said. "I can hear you. So, it looks like there have been some developments."

"You could say that," Jason said. "We can talk about that more when I come see you in person later. Right now, we need to all get on the same page. As of this moment, Omega Force is helping catch or kill Margaret Jansen. Don't worry, I'm waiving our usual fees."

"I'm still trying to process the idea of dealing with you both at the same time but, fine...let's talk about Jansen," Webb said. "Where are you with that?"

Over the next hour, they briefed the captain on the secret base they'd found on Koliss-2, the person who had contacted them aboard one of the old Columbia-class hulls, and the two crypto traps they'd found in a hidden vault. Webb had a lot of questions about the base and seemed genuinely disturbed One World had managed to put together an operation more ambitious than that of the UEN when it came to force-projection and expansion.

"Have you gotten anything out of the two OSO goons we left you, sir?" Jacob asked.

"One managed to kill himself somehow," Webb said, looking uncomfortable. "The other acts like he's willing to help, but they've not pulled anything useful from him."

"Let me guess, they acted like they were little more than glorified cleanup crews?" Jason asked. "These guys are pros, Marcus. Tell Welford to put the screws to the survivor because he ain't gonna talk just because you asked him nicely. Or don't. Hand him back over to his people and see where that gets you."

"This isn't a frontier mercenary army, Burke," Webb said. "I can't just tell the head of NIS to torture Earth citizens."

Jason just shrugged. "One World has no such hang-ups," he said. "You can play by her rules and play to win, or you can be a gracious loser. You're telling me the UEAS is so different than every other military that's ever existed that you're not going to really lean on this guy? You hopped on a starship to come murder me without knowing why or who I even was back when you were just a SEAL."

"I can't tell Welford how to handle his investigation." Webb put his hands up in surrender. "I'm just saying that, as far as I know, they have nothing useful. What's your next move?"

"As soon as Twingo finishes getting the *Phoenix* back in order and purges that goddamn Cas remnant from the computer, we'll split our teams and try to find this voice that talked to them on that old ship. I have some ideas how we might flush them out since it was obvious they wanted to communicate to Obsidian."

"Whatever you plan to do, you better do it fast. NAVSOC is quickly losing favor with UEAS Central Command, as well as the elected leadership," Webb said. "There have been some media leaks regarding our less successful missions, something I suspect this Office of Special Operations is likely behind. Either way, my connections in the halls of power have been sending me warnings my head is on the chopping block and this command will likely be dissolved. Scout Fleet missions will be handed over to NIS."

"With NAVSOC gone, this OSO outfit will have exclusive access to all clandestine work with the UEAS, which means they'll be the only group with unlimited, unrestricted flight authorization to wherever they want to go," Jacob said. "Not even the trading companies have that sort of free navigation ability. That's a lot of power being usurped by somebody. What about NIS? You think they'll dissolve that as well?"

"It's too visible," Webb said. "They'll just replace all of the top leadership with loyalists, retire Welford in a manner that prevents him from whistleblowing behind their backs, and then they'll control the entire intelligence apparatus."

"Well, now we have the how and why but not where One World fits into all of this," Jacob said. "I think it's obvious they're working together in some way, possibly sympathizers within the OSO, but that doesn't help us find Jansen."

"Or does it?" Jason asked. "Where is OSO headquartered? There's *no* way they're on Earth with the kind of shit they've been pulling lately." Webb furrowed his brow in confusion, and then his eyes widened.

"Oh, no! No way in hell am I giving you that information even if I had it," he said. "They'd put me up against the wall and blow my brains out for letting you of all people know where a top secret governmental agency was headquartered."

"Webb, you're a dead man already," Jason said, his voice quiet. "You know this. If I don't get to you first for the shit you've put my son through when I specifically asked you to watch over him, do you really think these people pulling the strings won't? As soon as they can get you off the radar, they'll pop you just to tie up loose ends."

"Well...this talk has taken a depressing turn." Webb leaned back in his seat. "You're right, of course. I'm dead no matter what I do, so I might as well do the right thing."

"People like you and me don't die of old age, my friend," Jason said.

"I'll see what I can do," Webb said. "Don't start a goddamn war in the meantime. Please."

"Which of us were you talking to?" Jason asked.

"Take your pick," Webb said, stabbing at the terminal to kill the channel.

"I thought that went well," Jason said.

"You asked him to look after me?" Jacob asked.

"Back after I'd met you," Jason said. "He was supposed to keep an eye on you, keep you out of trouble. I suppose I always had fantasies of someday returning to Earth and not being considered public enemy number one but, in the meantime, he was supposed to keep you from making any huge missteps...like joining the Marines and going into a meat grinder like Scout Fleet."

"So, how do you plan to track down the voice?" Jacob asked after an awkward pause.

"I was actually bluffing about that," Jason said with a shrug. "I have no idea. But I've found if you don't concentrate on a problem too hard, the solution just sort of pops up."

"Jesus Christ. How are you still alive?" Jacob muttered as Jason walked out of the com room.

17

"Sit down, Ricardo."

Ricardo Avelar walked the rest of the way into his boss's office and quietly took a seat while she finished typing on her computer. She may or may not have been doing any work. Margaret Jansen was notorious for these little games. Just something to put him in his place and remind him that he's not more important than some random message she was sending out.

Avelar just sat quietly. He didn't shift in his seat or clear his throat, nor did he pull out his com unit and also pretend to be busy. He gave no outward sign she wasted even a second of his day.

"I apologize for that, Ricardo," Jansen finally said. "Coffee?"

"Yes, ma'am," Avelar said. "I'll get it." He stood and went to the sideboard where a small urn-style machine sat with a random collection of old coffee mugs, most of them featuring an orange cat with black stripes. It was easily the only thing in the office that gave any indication Margaret Jansen was actually human.

"Thank you," she said, accepting the mug he'd poured for her.

"My pleasure," Avelar said. "The coffee you have here is amazing. Far and above what we have available down in the bullpen."

"It's called Rocky Mountain Coffee," she said with a smile. "Where do you think it's made?"

"Certainly not the US Rockies," Avelar said. "No way in hell you could grow coffee in that climate."

"It's made on a planet called S'Tora," Jansen said. "What few people know is the proprietor is a man from Earth. He used to live in the Rockies. I like to get it through our suppliers because, when I drink it, I'm reminded of a grave mistake I once made and to never repeat it in the future." Avelar tried to appear interested, but he was simply confused by her seemingly haphazard story.

"I'm afraid you've lost me, ma'am."

"It doesn't matter," she said. "What do you remember of our base on Koliss-2?"

"Mothballed, as far as I know," Avelar said. "If I remember correctly, we still own the property, but we had supply issues, and by the time we were ready to resume production, the Columbia-class ships were horribly obsolete."

"As were the Atlantic-class prototypes never finished," Jansen said. "We've kept the base maintained and farmed security out to one of the local clans. Apparently, the base had visitors. They killed most of our security force but left the base intact."

"The same troublemakers we've been tracking from Captain Webb's command?"

"Good guess, and yes. But not only them." Jansen spun her terminal around, and Avelar saw several images that came from security cameras around the base. One of them was of a ship he recognized as a gunship called the *Phoenix*. The other was of a Galvetic warrior who could only be the one they called Crusher. Rather than answer what he knew, he again feigned ignorance.

"Local raiders? The Galvetic warrior makes that unlikely, but some outcasts hire themselves out as—"

"Did you read the files I asked you to on Jason Burke?" Jansen asked in exasperation.

"I've pulled the files, but I've yet to—"

"You need to read them ASAP and make that your priority," Jansen said. "You also need to read up on the Koliss-2 base because you'll be going out there."

"Ma'am? I'm not field qualified to—"

"Stop. Talking. You're going out there as my representative to meet with the clan and pay off the deaths of their people. Get the local companies working at repairing the damage if there is any to the buildings. There's also something in the operations center you need to verify is destroyed or, if there, retrieve."

"And that is?"

"You'll be briefed on your flight out," Jansen said. "Hodges is waiting for you outside. He'll take you to your ship and introduce you to your tac-team. Welcome to the big leagues, Ricardo. Do this right, and you'll no longer be skulking around offices as an administrative aide."

"Of course, ma'am. I won't fail you."

Jansen just grunted at him as a dismissal, so he gathered his things, downed the rest of the coffee, and hustled out of her office before she could saddle any more of her shit assignments onto him. With Elton Hollick missing, Jansen had been on the search for a new operative she could dispatch in lieu of running field ops herself. Avelar had desperately tried to avoid it, going so far as to carefully playing just incompetent enough to be overlooked, but not so much she'd send him away.

The Omega Force issue was a case in point. He was well aware of who and what they were, had recognized the *Phoenix* and Crusher right away, but by pretending to be so overwhelmed in his job he couldn't be bothered to read a simple dossier, he'd hoped to avoid the type of task he was now assigned.

Flying out to Koliss-2 with that pit bull Hodges dogging his every step and tracking his movements, picking up the damn crypto traps Jansen had left out there she thought nobody knew about, and flying all the way back burned precious time he just didn't have.

"You ready to go?" Hodges asked him as soon as he stepped into the waiting area. The ex-Special Forces operator must have been summoned to come in right after Avelar went into Jansen's office. He felt no shame in admitting the man scared him.

Hodges was strong, experienced in brutality, and all the other clichés you'd expect of someone with his resume. But he was also frighteningly smart. Genius level IQ smart. People underestimated him because of his vocation, folksy dialect, and southern accent, which is exactly what he wanted. Hodges was loyal to Jansen alone, and he was impossible to slip anything by. Whatever Avelar did on this trip, Jansen *would* know about it.

"Ready." He nodded. "I assume my bags have been packed for me?"

"You know the boss lady." Hodges smiled, showing his teeth. "She likes the element of surprise."

"Isn't that something you normally reserve for your enemies?"

"Isn't it?"

"Lead the way, Hodges," Avelar sighed, not in the mood for a verbal sparring match and not wanting to antagonize the man into an actual sparring match. He had the reputation for being physical with the *office dweebs* as he called them, enjoying the fear he generated just by walking by them.

Jansen would have already had clothes and equipment pulled for Avelar and sent up to the ship waiting in orbit. It meant he couldn't retrieve his equipment, talk to anyone on the base or send any messages out, and it kept him off-guard and guessing. These weren't the actions of a good leader, but they were the actions of a political terrorist in exile who had managed to stay one step ahead of her enemies for going on fifteen years.

"I've always liked you, Avelar," Hodges said. "You aren't like the rest of these wilting flowers. This is going to be a fun trip. I can feel it."

"Oh, yes. I'm feeling that, too, Hodges."

"So, you haven't pulled anything out of him? Nothing at all?"

"Sorry, Marcus," Director Welford said. "These guys have some serious training to hold out on interrogations."

"Nobody can hold out forever," Webb scoffed. "What have you been trying on him?"

"The usual methods for a trained operative," Welford said stiffly. "You telling me how to do my job now? You came to me, remember that. It's entirely possible this Easterbrook doesn't actually know anything."

Webb sat back, not used to any sort of emotional display from Welford at all, much less this type of defensive posturing and push-back. This was the second conversation in as many days regarding the captive and Welford hadn't provided him with anything other than some vague excuses about how one had managed to kill himself while in NIS custody.

"We'll table that for the moment, but I don't believe for a second this guy was sent out into the field as part of a sanitation crew to take out a NAVSOC Scout Fleet team, and he doesn't know *anything*," he said. "What have you got for me on this OSO outfit? Do we know who they report to yet? They're obviously not private contractors, so they have to appear on somebody's organizational chart. They're getting money and support from somewhere."

"Nothing my sources have turned up," Welford said. "To be honest, Marcus, we might be missing the forest for the trees when it comes to this OSO thing. For all we know, it's a small group of operators someone has propped up, and they just have an official-sounding name. We've seen that sort of thing before."

"Yeah, the last one was called the Terranovus Colony Project and was headed up by an administrator named Margaret Jansen," Marcus said. "Look how that turned out."

"Apples and oranges, my friend," Welford said. "Have we got a line on Jansen's location yet?"

"Obsidian is still in the game," Marcus said. "I'll know more when they come up for air again and make contact. Right now, they're still operating as if they've been burned."

"They essentially have," Welford said. "You've not gone so far as to disavow them yet, but they're certainly operating outside of their mandate and in opposition to their orders."

"All just legal technicalities. When I met them to take those prisoners off their hands, I signed my career away," Webb said. "So, if I'm understanding you right, out of the single remaining prisoner alive, we have nothing, and we also have no more idea who controls the Office of Special Operations than we did when we first discovered them? This isn't optimal, Michael."

"I'll try some other vectors, but I wouldn't get my hopes up," Welford said. "Whoever this group is, they're damn good at hiding the bodies."

"I'll keep you in the loop on my end," Webb said. "If this is our last ride, let's make it worth it."

"Indeed. Welford out."

Webb frowned as the holograph faded after the hyperlink channel closed. That wasn't the answer he'd wanted from his old friend.

"Thoughts?" he asked aloud.

"He's evading," Ensign Weathers said, walking in from where he'd watched the interaction from the head. He'd had an angle to see Welford's holograph but out of sight from the office's imagers. "His body language and speech patterns were uncharacteristic, and he was definitely lying when he said they'd gotten nothing from Easterbrook."

"No particular insight as to why?" Webb asked.

"No, sir," his aide answered.

Weathers wasn't an injured ex-operator put out to pasture or a trained administrator as most aides in NAVSOC's hierarchy were. Webb had handpicked the man because he had advanced degrees in behavioral psychology and was a savant when it came to reading body language and detecting nuanced cues in people he observed.

He'd come into the Navy after grad school because he wanted to see the galaxy and had gotten on Webb's radar during his first assignment as a screener for Scout Fleet candidates. The captain had immediately seen the advantage of having someone like Weathers around to observe interactions and report back to him.

"His demeanor indicates he doesn't like the fact he's hiding something from you."

"Let's not overreact quite yet," Webb said. "We're navigating some dangerous waters that will likely see me lose my commission. Welford is a career man with his own future to think about, so sharing critical intel with me might be something he's having second thoughts about. I can understand that. When push comes to shove, I trust him to do the right thing."

"Yes, sir," Weathers said neutrally.

Webb stared at him a moment, unsure how to take that. The problem with employing someone who was an expert at reading the meaning in the subtleties of behavior and speech was they were also experts at hiding their own.

"Anyway, I guess we have to start tapping other sources while we still have them," he said. "We have got to find out who the hell owns the OSO. I think we need to head back to Earth."

"Go back to Earth as in physically take the *Kentucky* and go back to the Solar System?" Weathers asked, surprised. "Bold move, sir. But is it the wisest?"

"Face-to-face talks with the people will help speed this along," Webb said. "They won't talk to anyone else, and they sure as hell won't blab covert secrets over a slip-com or hyperlink channel. They're too smart for that. Out of curiosity, what would you have us do?"

"Me, sir? I'm just the psych geek not a tactician. I hardly have the expertise—"

"You're also full of shit. You're too smart not to have some ideas in that big brain of yours. Spill it."

"I'd be flying to Koliss-2. Right now," Weathers said. "One World will have been told the base was attacked. They'll almost certainly send a team to inspect the site themselves. If they cared enough to keep the property and have it guarded, they'll care enough to do a post-battle inspection. Sir."

"Reginald Weathers, you beautiful bastard," Webb said, shaking his head. "I knew you'd come through. You're exactly right. It's an obvious move, but they'd have no choice but to send their own people to look over the damage and to see what Obsidian had been so interested in. But I'm not sure the *Kentucky* is the right ship for that job."

"No?" Weathers asked. "You're going to ask Obsidian to go back?"

"Not just them," Webb said. "Go ahead and take a hike. I need to reach out to someone, and you don't need to know who just yet. Good work, Ensign."

"Thank you, sir."

Once the hatch closed and locked, Webb pulled up a discreet slip-com node and sent a text-only message to an address he had memorized. His aide's idea had been solid. One World might only send some flunkies to scuttle the Columbia hulls and poke around, or they may send a big dog to chastise the security contractors for completely falling on their swords but, either way, it would be a thread that could be tugged and followed.

18

_____

"Yeah, there is _no_ way this is Webb's idea. It's far too elegantly simple and genuinely smart," Jason Burke said as he re-read the message. "I watched his buffoonery when Jansen had him and his team trying to kill me. I doubt flying a desk all these years has made him any better at this sort of thing."

"I feel Jansen might expect us to stake out the base, but they can hardly ignore it. She'll know the failsafes had been tripped in the operations center, and she'll need to verify those crypto traps are secure or destroyed," Murph said, ignoring the stab at his boss.

"From what I've read, Jansen thinks linearly," Jacob added. "It likely won't occur to her that we might double back to intercept her team, but that doesn't mean there aren't more tactically-minded people on her staff who won't."

"This is a low-risk strategy that could yield great rewards," 707 said. "I think it is worth the time."

"Yeah, I think you're right, Lucky," Jason said absently. Someone coughed uncomfortably, and the others looked away. "Sorry. It's easy to slip back into old habits when—"

"There is no need to apologize, Captain Burke," 707 said. "That you miss him that much honors his memory."

"You've no idea how much we all miss him." Jason straightened. "Okay, we have a solid plan of attack here, and we have more personnel than usual to execute it. Cas, is the *Phoenix* ready?"

"Twingo is performing the final calibration sequence now," Cas said, its drone hovering around the perimeter of the group. "The computer core has been purged of my old remnant and a general clean-up was done. She'll be ready soon, but I think it would make sense to reposition the *Devil's Fortune* back in the Koliss System and use her as a base of operations. Then you will be ready for any task-force One World is able to field."

"I'm still weirded out we're taking advice from a floating basket-ball," Murph said, poking at the alabaster orb.

"I am a fully sentient AI borne of a race of hyper-advanced beings whose accomplishments your brain would be quite unable to comprehend. Douche."

"What?!" Murph said. "I don't have to put up with this shit."

"Cas is an irreplaceable member of my crew and brings capabilities to the table that can't be replicated anywhere else in the quadrant," Jason said. "You're just a pain in my ass. So, guess who gets to stay? If you find it's too much to deal with, you can always step outside." Murph just shook his head.

"Touché."

"So, we're all decided then?" Jason asked. "What do you think, Crusher?"

"I don't give a shit." The big warrior lounged in a chair not even looking at the holographic projection the others were working with.

"Useless as always," Jason said. "We'll mark him as a yes. Cas, go tell Doc to change course back to the Koliss System and put us in orbit over the largest moon of the seventh planet."

"Oh, good, I've been demoted to messenger."

"You'll be demoted to the damn recycler if you don't straighten up," Jason said. "Your attitude sucks lately."

"Whatever." Cas bobbed out of the conference room and towards the bridge.

"Thing has a mouth on it for an AI," Murph said. "Although, I admittedly have little experience with them."

"Cas is part of a security system for an ancient super-weapon," Jason said. "It ended up residing in my neural implant for a while, and I thought it was dormant, but it had actually been observing and adapting. A lot of its personality comes from watching interactions among the crew."

"That explains it," Jacob said.

"That concludes the show and tell portion of the evening, kiddies," Jason said. "You've all been given quarters, so feel free to enjoy the ship. Stay out of the cargo bays but, other than that, have at it."

As the others filed out and Jason killed the display, Jacob hung back.

"Hey, you want to grab a drink?"

Jason turned and looked at his son.

"It's still hard for me to get used to you being old enough to drink," he said. "Yeah, there's a lounge on the command deck I keep locked up so Crusher and Kage can't get in there."

"Lead the way," Jacob said. Both men walked out of the conference room stiffly, looking like they were being led to an execution.

The lounge was near the aft end of the command deck, right behind the captain's quarters. It was meant for entertaining VIPs and decked out with all the luxuries one would want when trying to impress.

"Cleaning and Maintenance?" Jacob asked, pointing at a tag near the hatchway.

"Keeps the riffraff out," Jason said. "These animals would get drunk and trash this place just on general principle, and then laugh when I had to give the ship back to Mok."

"Mok?" Jacob asked, startled. "As in—"

"As in Saditava Mok," Jason said, opening the hatch. "The one and only crime lord you stole a cash shipment from. He owns this ship and lent it to us while the *Phoenix* was being repaired. How did you manage to not get killed for that, by the way? Have a seat."

"This," Jacob said, pulling a Blazing Sun marker out of his pocket and sliding it across the table after he collapsed into one of the over-stuffed chairs. Jason picked it up and whistled.

"*I* don't even have one of these, and Mok and I are conspiring to overthrow a government," he said. "It's coded to you?"

"It says I work for the big man himself," Jacob said. "Gives me safe passage and pulls some weight when I need it. Not sure what it'll cost me later."

Jason struggled to contain his emotions. He wanted to rage at his son and tell him how stupid he was for getting involved in these sorts of things, but that would only end the fragile dialogue they'd begun to have. In truth, Jason had to admit he missed the time when helping raise the boy would have even mattered. Jacob was now a man, and he was free to make the same stupid mistakes his father did before him.

"It's hard to say what he'll want," Jason finally said. "As you may have figured out already, Mok isn't your average lord of the criminal underworld. He's ruthless, but I've actually found him to be fair. What's your usual poison?"

"Beer or whiskey," Jacob said. "I try to keep it simple."

"Smart. You can usually find a decent representation of either on most planets you'll visit," Jason said, sliding an unlabeled bottle across the table with a glass. "Give that a try." He waited while his son poured his drink and settled back before getting his own and also sitting at the table.

"I figured it was time we cleared the air," Jacob said after an awkward pause. "Since coming to work for Webb, I've gotten the feeling I wasn't completely fair with my low opinion of you."

"I won't argue a low opinion isn't warranted, you'd hardly be the only one to have that, but I'd be willing to put money on it being somewhat unfair," Jason said. "This have to do with your mom?"

"Mostly," Jacob said. "Or at least I used to think so. I think maybe I resented that she got to have so many memories of you and that was something I could never have. A lot of stuff a dad should be at, and it was always just mom there, until we lost her, too. Grandpa did the best he could, but a seventy-five-year-old trying to keep up with a teenager was hardly fair."

"You guys lived in my old cabin?"

"Yeah. Mom said we should try to keep as low a profile as possible," Jacob said. "There was a time when they used an alias, I guess, because people were hunting them. I was about six or seven when I went back to using Brown."

"I... Look, I had no idea your mom had gotten pregnant," Jason said. "I swear to you, if I had known, I would have come back and figured something out so we could be together."

"She knew that, too," Jacob said, smiling sadly. "She said, if you knew I was there, you'd risk everything to come back home. I think she wanted that more than anything, but during her time with you aboard the *Phoenix*, she realized how important what you were doing was."

"It wasn't that damn important," Jason said, trying to keep his voice neutral. "Certainly not more important than a family I didn't even know I had. Taryn had been aboard during a monumental undertaking. We were fighting against an eco-terrorist death cult that wanted to wipe out entire civilizations, as well as a psychotic synth that had a personal vendetta. I think she thought all Omega missions were like that when, the truth was, most of the time we were just out kicking up trouble along the frontier. All of us, even Twingo, were out here hiding from something. We rarely saw what we did as a higher calling."

"That's not the impression most people have of your crew."

"Don't get me wrong, we try to stay on firm moral ground and help the little guy when we can," Jason said. "Maybe we get more credit than we deserve because we're compared to other merc crews who would torch a school because it's easy money."

"This is damn good," Jacob said, raising his glass. "What is it?"

"Sample batch eleven-B from my crew on S'Tora," Jason said. "They're really zeroing in on what we want using the local grain there."

"You...have a distillery going?"

"A companion company to the coffee business." Jason nodded. "I'm always looking at other revenue streams, and I prefer those to be completely legit. With Earth emerging on the galactic stage, I'll soon be competing with products from my home world, so I've been trying to get the jump on them and have my brands introduced first."

"Coffee company," Jacob said. "You've got to be fucking kidding me. Rocky Mountain Coffee is yours, isn't it?"

"That's the one. Doc was able to quickly get us a variety of Arabica that would grow on the hillsides on S'Tora's northern hemisphere. The volume of processed coffee that's being shipped off-planet to distributors these days is mindboggling. I've done two massive land buys to prop up more capacity, and we're still back-ordered."

"So, you're basically rich off your legitimate businesses alone but still doing this hired gun shit?"

"Not quite," Jason said. "Coffee doesn't grow, process, or ship itself. Right now, everything the company makes I'm pumping right back into it to keep growth sustainable. But yeah, that is eventually my retirement plan. The whiskey isn't quite as labor intensive since we're using an indigenous crop, and we can charge a lot more. All I have to do is not get my head blown off in the meantime, and I should be able to kick my feet up and enjoy myself."

"That sounds decent," Jacob said. "Hopefully, I'll get a chance to visit, assuming I stay out of prison or don't get killed."

"Thanks for the chance to talk," Jason said, sensing the conversation was slowing down. "I won't pretend that this changes anything between us. You have your reasons to be angry, so you'll need to decide what you can come to terms with. For what it's worth, I loved Taryn very much. I loved her so much I realized she would be better off the farther I was away from her. I wish she had met someone and let you live a normal life, but we all have to play the hand we're dealt."

"I guess I can admit things are far more complicated than I

wanted to believe," Jacob said. "When I could blame you for everything bad in my life, and you couldn't defend yourself, it made things simple. Didn't have to make sense, it was just how it was. I honestly can't say where we go from here. Hell, you look like we could have gone to the Academy together, not like someone old enough to be my dad. But I promise to keep an open mind...or at least try to."

"I can live with that," Jason said. "The first thing we need to do before that is to get you out of this mess you've waded into. Helping with Jansen is a no-brainer. I've meant to kill her myself after she sent Webb's team after me, but I've never found the time. The situation with Mok could be a little more complicated. For right now, I'd suggest we keep our relationship a secret from him. He can be... unpredictable. He'd either release you completely or he'd use the fact you carry a marker as leverage against me."

"Between you and I, this has gotten a little out of control," Jacob admitted. "At first, when we killed Hollick and captured the com protocols off him, I really thought we'd just intercept some com traffic to see where she was, then fly out and either capture or kill her. As this has dragged on, I've realized how over my head I am."

"What we need to know is—"

"*Hey...Captain. You there?*" a voice asked over the intercom. "*Where are you, anyway?*"

"What do you want, Kage?"

"*The computer says you're in a maintenance locker. That's weird. What are you doing in there?*"

"What do you want, Kage?" Jason repeated. "I'm busy."

"*Cas and I had a breakthrough with those crypto traps. I think it'll be something you want to see. Twingo wants to keep the* Phoenix *in the hangar bay and is asking permission to rig the SX-5 to the dorsal tie-downs for slip-space flight. Right now, it's just hanging off the docking clamps.*"

"Tell Twingo to stop bothering me with every petty detail. That's what I pay him for. I'll be down to look at what you've got shortly."

"*After you get out of that maintenance locker, huh?*" Kage asked. "*That's...suspicious. I've flown with you for years, and you've never cleaned anything or helped with any maintenance.*"

"Burke, out." Jason killed the intercom channel.

"Is he always like that?" Jacob asked.

"No. Sometimes he's annoying," Jason said.

19

Ricardo Avelar roamed the corridors of the ship, bored and anxious at the same time.

Long spaceflights were not something he particularly liked. To be honest, short ones weren't really his thing, either. He much preferred to have his feet planted firmly on the surface of a planet, but his ambitions meant he had no choice but to endure the personal hell that was a starship. He knew just enough about them to remain completely terrified the entire time the thing was in slip-space and only marginally less so when it dropped back into real-space.

His wanderings brought him to the ship's recreation area, which included a fully-equipped gym. He was unsurprised to find Hodges there. What did surprise him, however, was the man appeared to bench press nearly seven hundred pounds.

Avelar had to look again and counted the number of forty-five-pound plates, and then factoring in the weight of the bar, which was bending under the abuse. The ex-operator was fit and muscular, but there was no way in hell he should be able to lift that sort of weight, much less run through multiple sets of fifteen with it.

Avelar waited until Hodges slammed the bar back into the rack before walking fully into the room. Hodges saw him and nodded.

"What's happening?" he asked.

"Impressive," Avelar said, gesturing to the bar. "You mess with the gravity in here?"

"Why would I waste my time doing that? To impress you? Or the limp-wrists on this ship?"

"You're doing something to lift that much and not even break a sweat," Avelar said. "You've either cheated the deck plating or you— Ah!"

"Ah, what, little man?" Hodges said, walking over to stand in front of him. Avelar recognized the intimidation tactic and stood his ground, looking the man in the eye without blinking. Hodges wouldn't dare touch him unless Jansen told him it was okay.

"I'd heard about the augment program. Didn't know they were into the operational stage yet," Avelar said. Hodges stared at him for a moment with a blank look before he broke into a wide smile.

"I'm the first of the Gen 3s," he said, walking back over to the bench and sitting down. "All the major muscle groups have been supplemented or replaced completely with pseudo-organic muscles. Had all the ligaments, tendons, and some of my bones replaced, too. Fucking hurt like you wouldn't believe, but it was worth it."

The augment program was something Jansen had worked on with partners from Earth. The research was strictly illegal there, but nobody gave a damn what Margaret did to her *volunteers* on any of the half a dozen worlds she kept facilities on.

He'd heard the horror stories about her first rounds of failures until her team perfected the grafting process on humans. The tech was something that wasn't widely available in the quadrant, but it wasn't anything strictly illegal, either. It was prohibited by the Cridal Cooperative and outlawed outright on Earth, hence why Jansen was approached about it. What he didn't understand was why someone Hodges' age would bother going through the invasive, painful procedure.

"Worth it for what? You work in an advisory capacity now. You think Jansen is going to send you back out to the field?" Avelar asked, genuinely curious. Hodges didn't do anything just to do it. The man must have had a good reason to put himself through the augment procedures.

"Top secret," Hodges said. "All I'll say is it was at the boss lady's request."

"Say no more." Avelar held his hands up. "Her ways are mysterious and none of my business."

"She said you were smart enough to know when to keep your mouth shut and not ask too many questions," Hodges said. "The man you'll probably replace wasn't so wise."

"Elton Hollick," Avelar said. "Where do you think he's hiding out?"

"The Reaches," Hodges said without hesitation. "He has contacts there, and it's an area that's almost impossible for us to monitor with any accuracy. He could slip in there and live out a full life without us ever finding him...even if we tried."

"I can't believe Jansen will let a loose end like that just walk, even on principle," Avelar said. He must have caught Hodges in a good mood since the man was never this friendly or willing to talk to anyone who wasn't part of the tactical teams.

"She won't have to." Hodges shrugged. "I've worked with Hollick a few times. The man's ego is immense. He'll come sniffing back around once he thinks he has some sort of advantage to press, either for revenge that the boss lady burned him, or because he thinks he can cut a deal to come back in."

"That does make the most sense." Avelar nodded.

"Hollick is a punk-ass," Hodges said. "Boss lady isn't too worried about him."

"What do you think we'll find at Koliss-2 when we get there?" Avelar asked.

"Jack shit," Hodges said. "The Scout Fleet flunkies will have shot the place all to hell because they have no idea what discreet means. The local contractors will try to cover their asses, so the operations center will probably just be a smoking crater where they blew up the remains to make sure we have nothing left to inspect."

"What do you make of this Omega Force connection?"

"What?" Hodges frowned, his eyes narrowing. "What the hell do those assholes have to do with anything?"

"I was hoping you could tell me," Avelar said, his mind racing. Had Jansen withheld from Hodges the fact the *Phoenix* was on-site and Burke himself was filmed walking through the facility? "Jansen requested I read up on them. I'd never heard of them, and I couldn't figure out why she was so adamant I go through the files."

"She could just be screwing with you." Hodges shrugged. "It's one of her favorite tactics to keep people off-balance. As far as I know, Omega Force hasn't been spotted on this side of the quadrant in over a decade. We caught wind through our intel contacts that one of them was dead, probably Burke himself. Who knows. Maybe she has a new assignment in mind for you once we get back from this sightseeing trip. She knows how much you love long slip-space flights."

Hodges laughed at his own joke, cranked his music back up, and went over to the lat pull-down machine to begin his next series of exercises. Avelar walked out of the gym, wondering why someone Jansen trusted as much as Hodges wouldn't be given all the intel he needed when executing a mission.

What was even the point of holding it back unless Jansen worried Hodges was a blabbermouth, and she didn't want word of Burke's involvement spreading throughout the organization.

Or, she *did* tell Hodges and the man was screwing with him, seeing if he would start spilling sensitive intel so he could report back to Jansen he was an idiot with loose lips. The problem working in an organization with so many evil geniuses on payroll was you couldn't trust anything happening and always had to be a few steps ahead. It was enough to give him a constant headache.

"Ah, sir! I was just looking for you," the ship's XO said as Avelar walked back into the main corridor. "The captain would like you to join him at his table tonight for dinner." Avelar groaned inwardly. One World's *fleet* had steadily been morphing from a ragtag insurrectionist force into an actual military, complete with ambitious officers who would not miss the chance to corner someone they saw as politically connected that could help them later on.

"Tell the captain I would be delighted, of course," he said, smiling.

"Twenty-one hundred hours in the captain's quarters," the XO said, turning to leave.

Avelar idly wondered if the man really had nothing better to do than run messages on a ship that had both an intercom and an internal Nexus all their com units were connected to. Seemed fairly humiliating, actually.

"Thank you, Commander."

"Captain Webb is here to see you, sir."

"Send him in."

Senator, and former Admiral, Josef Schmidt sat behind a cluttered desk and looked disheveled when Webb walked in. Schmidt had briefly been part of the UEN and had been one of the people who had helped draft the UEAS charter the Navy operated under. Once the military was up and running, he retired for a short time before becoming bored and running for public office. He went from the representative of a small district in Florida to a senator within two election cycles.

"Senator, you're looking well," Webb said.

"The hell I do," Schmidt said. "I've been up for two days dealing with the Cridal issue. I assume you're here to beg for your life after losing a Scout Fleet team?"

"Something like that," Webb said. "What's going on with the Cridal?"

"It's nothing," Schmidt said. "Nothing I can discuss with you, anyway. So, what's this about? Your budget so big you just brought a starship across the Orion Arm to visit rather than make a Hyperlink appointment?"

"This office secure?"

"Airtight."

"What is the Office of Special Operations?"

"Jesus, Marcus. You're not even going to ease into it? Where did you even hear that name?" Schmidt asked.

"Some of their people jumped one of my Scout Fleet teams," Webb said. "We captured two, turned them over to NIS, but have so far gotten nowhere with them. Other than the fact they exist, I have no idea who they are or who they report to."

"They attacked your people?" Schmidt asked, frowning. "Did they know they were a Navy unit?"

"This wasn't some accidental skirmish out in the wilds," Webb said. "They were targeting a specific member of one of my teams. A young lieutenant who has managed to be a thorn in the side of One World, breaking up two of their operations."

"And your implication is the Office of Special Operations, assuming it exists, is working with One World, a terrorist faction?" Schmidt asked.

"I'm just giving you what I know," Webb said. "But I think we know each other well enough to just come out and say One World has been having a pretty easy time recruiting sympathizers deep within the military and intelligence community. Who are these assholes, Josef? Come on, give me something."

"All I'd be giving you is a death sentence," Schmidt said. "I'm being completely honest with you when I say I don't know who they ultimately report to, but they just showed up here one day and made their presence felt. People asking who the hell they were got visits from federal agents telling us to keep our mouths shut. The OSO seemed to have dirt on everybody, so people were happy to just keep their heads down as long as their dirty little secrets remained buried."

"I see nothing has changed in this town since the last time I was here," Webb sighed. "Someone props up their private paramilitary unit, has them operating with authority and government funding but, as long as they don't cause trouble, it'll all just be swept under the rug."

"That's a bit harsh but essentially true," Schmidt admitted. "At first, many assumed they were just another black ops unit, maybe an off-shoot of the NIS or even some of your people. Once some of us realized this was something new, they were already burrowed into the power structure here in DC like ticks. If they're coming after your people, you have trouble."

"I need more," Webb said. "These people are operating starships and have access to high-level intelligence. They're not operating in a vacuum or being funded by slush money. They're flying Aracorian hardware, billions of dollars worth of patrol ships, and have them painted up pretending to be with the frontier merc guilds. Someone knows who is directing them, and you probably know who that someone might be."

"I can't help you, Marcus. I hope you can understand the position I'm in."

"And I'd hoped you would understand mine," Webb said, standing up. "They're killing people out there, Senator. Whoever they are, whoever you're protecting, they're targeting and killing human military personnel just doing their jobs. If you can live with that, more power to you because I certainly couldn't."

Senator Schmidt didn't respond as Webb turned and walked out of the office. He hadn't expected the senator to actually give him anything directly, but his evasiveness confirmed not only was the OSO real, but Schmidt likely knew who was involved.

"How did it go, sir?" Weathers asked as he slid into the limo.

"It was a bust," Webb said. "He didn't know anything. I don't know, Weathers. Maybe we're chasing ghosts after all. Anybody could buy ships from the Aracorian yards or through a brokerage for the right price. We catch them, they make up some story about a new shadowy organization, and we're off chasing our tails for months."

"Possibly, sir," Weathers said without expression. The limo they were in had been provided for them when the shuttle touched down from the *Kentucky*. Both officers were well aware it was almost certainly bugged and some three-letter acronym bureau was listening in to every word they spoke. "Where to?"

"Let's head back to the *Kentucky*. If Senator Schmidt didn't know anything, there's nobody else around here who will likely be of much help, either."

As his aide directed the driver to head back to Andrews AFB where their shuttle sat on the transient landing pad, Webb stared out the window as Washington DC rolled by, impatient to be out from under surveillance so he could get back to work.

20

"*Phoenix* is all straightened out," Twingo said, collapsing into one of the bridge seats.

"Don't be so dramatic," Jason said. "You did a double-pass emitter alignment and recalibrated the containment fields. You sit on your blue ass in front of a computer terminal to do that, and the computer does all the actual calculations."

"Can never let me just have a moment, can you?"

"Sorry," Jason said. "Thanks for getting her sorted so quickly."

Twingo, Kage, and Doc just stared at him with their mouths open.

"Did...did you just apologize to someone?" Kage asked.

"How soon until we reach Koliss-2?" Jason asked, ignoring Kage. The *Devil's Fortune* had meshed-in six hours prior, and they were keeping to the established approach lanes and speeds to not stand out in case One World's people were already there.

"Another few hours," Doc said. "You didn't want to mesh-in too close so it's a long flight."

"Okay, Kage, you've been following me around for half a day," Jason said. "What's the news on those crypto traps?"

"Shouldn't we brief everyone all at once?" Kage asked. "I don't want to repeat this all again."

"Cas?" Jason asked. The small white recon drone that housed Cas floated up from where it had been sitting on a chair.

"The reason Scout Team Obsidian couldn't crack into One World's communication networks with the encryption protocols they found in Hollick's personal effects is because they weren't actually com encryption codes, they were passkeys. Some of them were actually to the crypto traps we found in that building," Cas said. "Point of interest, there were many more encryption keys than there were crypto traps, so we must assume Hollick had stolen access to much more than these units."

"That makes much more sense," Jason said. "Com encryptions are regularly rotated and, as soon as Hollick went missing, they'd have purged the access keys and moved to the next one."

"But access to something like these crypto traps or a remote server location wouldn't be so easily changed," Kage said, glaring at Cas. "This would also explain why someone like this Hollick guy would have them stashed away in his dirty laundry on a data card if the story Murph told me is to be believed."

"Skipping ahead to the good part, what was on the crypto traps?" Jason asked.

"The computer is still compiling, but it looks like copies of slip-com messages, some recorded video conversations, and a few that seemed to be secret recordings of people," Kage said. "The interesting part is we have a list of times and locations, and it looks like One World has collected a lot of blackmail material on people on both Earth and Terranovus. There were also some files that mentioned this OSO you were all blabbing about."

"So, One World has infiltrated the OSO," Jason said. "To be expected, I guess."

"No, this looks more inclusive than that," Kage said. "This wasn't just a list of recruited sympathizers or spies. It looks like they have the entire organization mapped out, including equipment lists, budgets, and past mission reports."

"So, Jansen, and we're assuming this is all her data, is getting an unfettered stream of sensitive information from Earth somehow," Jason said. "This isn't completely unexpected but still something to bear in mind. We have to assume she knows more about us than we do about her. Earth's intelligence agencies have kept tabs on us over the years, and they'll certainly have kept reports on all of Scout Fleet's activities. We're not going to be able to surprise her very easily."

"We're two hours from making orbit," Doc said. "Do we have any sort of plan?"

"Since we don't know what these clowns will be flying, or if they're even showing up, we're stuck being a reactionary force," Jason said. "We'll need to monitor the base, and then be ready to move when we see them approach. That could be at any time, but if those crypto traps have current information, I don't think we'll be waiting long. Jansen will need to assess and mitigate the damage ASAP."

"We have both the *Phoenix* and the SX-5 available," Twingo said. "That along with the *Devil* is a lot of firepower depending on what they're bringing to the party."

"Let's get everyone together and hash out a plan," Jason said. "We have the Obsidian crew available, and they appear to have some skills, so let's use them. I also want to keep the *Devil* out of any heavy engagements due to our cargo."

"Ah, yeah," Doc said. "Understood."

Down in one of the cargo bays Jason had instructed his son's people to stay away from, a specialized bank of computers worked non-stop trying to put an ancient AI they called the Archive back together. It was a delicate, arduous task being supervised by Kage and Cas.

When it had been functional, the Archive had easily been the most dangerous thing in the galactic quadrant. Jason had carried the damned thing in his neural implant for years, not understanding its true nature at all until it caused so much degradation to the implant itself it risked injuring him. Until they could either move it to a safe place or figure out what the hell had happened to it on their last mission, Jason didn't want the corvette put at unnecessary risk.

"I'll go round everyone up," Cas said, zipping off the bridge.

"I'll prep the SX-5," Twingo said, getting to his feet with a groan. "The *Phoenix* is ready to go."

"Let's get this over so we can get back on task," Jason said. "We've burned up too much time here already."

———

"Not a bad-looking joint," Hodges commented, surveilling Koliss-2 from the bridge windows of the Aracorian cruiser they flew. "I can see why the boss lady likes it so much here."

The ship had a fully human crew, no Ull anywhere aboard, which was becoming more common these days. The ship was a basic class built by the shipyards that orbited over the planet Aracoria, but she'd been fitted to human specifications. There had been six cruisers purchased in the order, three of them still sitting without crews as One World rushed to fill postings.

This ship, the *Thomas Truxton*, had the most flight time and the most experienced crew. It made Avelar somewhat nervous Jansen sent her best ship on what she swore was just a simple retrieval and inspection operation.

"When will we be over the base?" he asked.

"We'll make our first daylight pass over Koliss Base in forty-six minutes, sir," the captain said. "It's early morning there, and we're adjusting our orbit to put the sensors in optimal range. CIC will pipe the images up here as soon as we get them."

The view out the forward windows made Avelar a little queasy. He'd made no secret of his distaste for space travel and looking out over the planet as the *Truxton* flew around it just made him feel like he was constantly falling despite the artificial gravity. The thought he would soon be climbing aboard one of the cruiser's cramped utility shuttles didn't do much to settle his stomach.

"Here we are now," the captain said. "Long-range optics have eyes on target."

"Damage looks minimal from this angle," Hodges said as the

enlarged images came up from the analysts belowdeck, complete with callouts and arrows pointing to changes from the last time a One World ship had visited the base. "Operations Center is partially caved in, Assembly Building Four has some evidence of fighting around it, but nothing was leveled or blown up completely. Webb's loser squad must have been here for a specific target and got it, or they were just bumbling around and ran when the shooting started."

"The fact the Ops Center looks imploded from these images says it's probably the first thing." Avelar moved up and pointed to the area north of the building. "Looks like someone was engaged on this hillside, too."

"That's the direction the security contractors would have come from if they'd just been camped out in their HQ and not patrolling the grounds regularly like they're paid to," Hodges said. "We'll be sure to bring that up to them."

"The shuttle and your escort are prepped and ready, sir," the captain said. "We can launch at your discretion."

"One more full pass, and then we'll head down," Hodges said. "Send the fighters to secure the landing area, and then we'll bring the shuttle in. How many troopers are we taking?"

"Twenty-five."

"That should be sufficient," Hodges said before turning to Avelar. "You have your tac-gear fitted and ready?"

"I do." Avelar nodded, ignoring the condescending tone.

"Go get kitted up, and I'll meet you in the launch bay," Hodges said.

Avelar walked off the bridge, tempted to remind Hodges he was in charge of the mission but, ultimately, deciding it wasn't a fight worth engaging in. So far, Hodges had not only been unusually cordial to him, he'd opened up a bit and offered some valuable insight.

Normally, the man ranged from indifferent to openly hostile when it came to the administrative staff that Margaret Jansen employed. Avelar had heard some hushed stories about how Elton Hollick and Hodges had gotten into multiple physical altercations within the office space, damaging equipment and the building.

"You okay?"

"I'll be fine," Avelar grunted.

"You want to be boss lady's right-hand man, you'd better get over your spaceflight queasiness," Hodges said. "You're embarrassing yourself in front of the cannon fodder." Avelar looked back into the shuttle bay and, sure enough, the security troopers laughed and elbowed each other as he gritted his teeth and sweated through the bumpy atmospheric entry.

"I thought *you* were her right-hand man," he said.

"Nah." Hodges grinned. "I'm just her trained attack dog."

"I didn't expect you to be so self-aware," Avelar said. "No offense."

"I know what I am." Hodges shrugged as much as he could in the seat harness. "She didn't recruit me to run spreadsheets."

The ride smoothed out as the shuttle passed into the lower atmosphere and the airfoils bit into the air. They had a short flight within Koliss-2's normal air traffic patterns before descending and veering north to the base. The fighters escorting them zipped away, diving to overfly the base and clear the area as the shuttle descended and flared to land on the VIP pad near the ruined operations center.

"Fighter escort has called an all-clear," the shuttle pilot said over their headsets. "Standby for touchdown."

"After we're out, take off again and find someplace south of here to loiter," Hodges said. "The fighters should stay in the area. If we have any trouble from the local contractors, I don't want our ride back to the boat sitting as an easy target."

"No argument here," the shuttle pilot said.

"You expecting the contractors to act up?" Avelar asked.

"Wouldn't surprise me. We're about to climb into their collective asses with both feet for the failures here. They could take that personally."

The shuttle cycled its landing gear and touched down with a firm bump onto the tarmac to announce their landing. The light ring outlining the main entry hatch went from a dim red to a bright green to indicate they were clear to disembark.

"Get up, get out!" Hodges barked at his troopers. "Secure the landing pad until the bird leaves, then clear the ops center. Be careful of any structural hazards."

The troopers popped off their harnesses and charged off the shuttle, setting up a secure perimeter around the craft with their weapons pointed outward. Hodges and Avelar walked off a moment later. As soon as the hatch closed again, the peculiar whine of the Aracorian atmospheric engines spooled up, and the shuttle lifted smoothly from the pad, turning south, and accelerating away.

"Com check," Hodges said into his headset. One by one, their twenty-five troopers, the two fighters, the shuttle pilot, Avelar, and the *Truxton*'s ground support technician all checked in. "Let's go."

The troopers broke their defensive ring and jogged the hundred meters or so to the operations center. From the ground, the two-story concrete building looked in decent shape. There were some windows blown out here and there, presumably from the pressure of the blast when the locals triggered the failsafe charges in the sub-basement.

As they'd practiced on the *Truxton* during the flight out, the troopers quickly breached the main entrance and leapfrogged through the building, setting up a picket as they pushed through the inactive security checkpoints to the heart of the building. It didn't take long before they came to a cave-in that would allow them to go no further.

"Tough building," Hodges grunted. "This is as far as we go. Turn the spiders loose."

"Copy that," one of the troopers said, kneeling and opening a small black case. Twenty tiny, six-legged drones scrambled out and, as they'd been pre-programmed to do on the *Truxton*, clambered onto the rubble and found their way down into the secret chamber under the building.

"This could take a while," Hodges said. "You want to go out and meet with the head of the clan that shit the bed on our security? He should be here in a few."

"Let's," Avelar said, appreciating Hodges was at least pretending he was in charge. "Redeploy the team as you see fit."

"Will do," Hodges said. "Everyone from the main security portcullis back, head out, and wait by the entrance. The rest of you maintain security here and wait for the data from the drones. Our main mission is to figure out if we still need to fly in heavy equipment from the ship and excavate under the building."

"*Three ground vehicles approaching your position,*" Fighter One called in. "*Non-armored, minimal weaponry, three occupants each. No sign of heavy weaponry or odd behavior.*"

"Go ahead and buzz them," Hodges said. "We're on the way out."

"Right on time," Avelar said.

"I've dealt with these dipshits before," Hodges said. "They'll probably beg and grovel to keep the contract and, in the end, they'll require us to sign a statement saying the security shortfalls on the base were our fault."

"Huh?"

"They know we'll just hire one of the other clans, but they won't want word getting out it was because they fucked up so badly."

"Sounds very...corporate." Avelar could only shake his head. The more he interacted with alien species, the less and less *alien* they seemed.

21

"Fighters are still in the area, the shuttle has moved three hundred klicks south and is flying a lazy-eight over somebody's farm."

"And the cruiser they came in on?" Murph asked.

"Moved back up into a standard holding orbit," Doc said, highlighting the Aracorian ship they'd observed moving into the area. "They're keeping a low-profile so they're not bothering to station keep over the base."

"Pointless," Jason said. "These Tier Three planets never give a shit what you're doing as long as you're not creating any debris fields by opening fire on each other above their planet. This one is even laxer since they don't have any defenses of their own to speak of. Pretty planet, though."

"It smells nice, too," MG said.

"That's always a plus," Crusher said. "What about those fighters?"

"Running two randomized, overlapping patterns above the base," Doc said.

"What do you think?" Jacob asked his father. Jason rubbed his chin, looking at the holographic representation of the base in the *Devil*'s main conference room.

"Taking both ships is overkill and actually limits what we can do down on the ground," he said. "I hate to say this, but I think we should leave the *Phoenix* here and pile everyone into the SX-5. Can you handle that ship in air-to-air combat?"

"No problem," Sully said. "It's a standard Eshquarian helm and fire control. That ship should have no trouble against two fighters. What about that shuttle?"

"We'll splash it with the *Devil*'s guns while their cruiser is on the other side of the planet, then Doc will leave orbit and take her towards the larger moon," Jason said. "The cruiser will investigate a crash, but they probably won't suspect anything at first since the shuttle pilot will never see the shot coming. They'll just disappear off the net."

"That traps the ground team on the base, at least for a little while," Murph said. "Smart. Then Sully can take the fighters."

"It'll be better to hit the exposed ground forces first," Crusher said. "The fighters won't react in time to stop him, but it'll cut the number of troops we'll have to face once we bail out. Who is going on this joyride?"

"From Omega Force, it will be me and you," Jason said. "Jacob can pick his team, and I assume the battlesynths are coming along."

"Of course," 707 said.

"I'll need a copilot," Sully said. "Preferably one with experience in that ship."

"That'll be me," Kage said.

"We'll take my entire team," Jacob said. "None of us will be any use here aboard this ship."

"Once we're on the ground, we'll want to take the operations center back," Jason said. "I'll lead that charge with Crusher and 707. Obsidian and 784 will engage the troops we see moving away from the building. Try to pick out someone who might be in charge. The point of this op isn't to kill everyone. At least, not right away."

"That's it?" Murph asked. "We're not going to plan the details any
further than that?"

"We find that usually just screws us up," Crusher said.

"They're as bad as us," MG said.

"They're as bad as us *since Brown took command*," Murph corrected.
"I'm beginning to see the common denominator now."

"Everybody is a fucking comedian," Jason growled. "Get your shit
and get up to the dorsal docking hatch. Ten minutes."

As they filed out of the conference room, Jason's emotions were a
mix of pre-combat jitters and debilitating fear as he realized his only
son was accompanying him into what would almost certainly be a
fight. It didn't matter that Jacob had been running his team on his
own for over a year now. Logic meant nothing to his gut.

He also felt a keen sense of guilt for secretly being glad Jacob
would likely be arrested and imprisoned for his rogue actions against
One World. If Jason could keep him alive through this mission, he'd
be out of the game completely. Maybe he'd wait a few months, and
then mount a rescue mission to spring him out. Webb and Welford
owed him that much.

The composite team quickly geared up and mustered near the
ladder that would let them through the dorsal hatch and into the SX-
5. Sully was already in the small strike craft doing his pre-flight with
Kage by the time Jason pulled himself up and tossed his gear in the
corner. He hadn't even bothered to put on his body armor yet.

"We're about ready, Captain," Kage said when he turned and saw
who had come aboard. "Doc has given us a downlink so we'll be able
to track targets with the *Devil*'s sensors until he and Twingo break
orbit."

"Sounds good," Jason said, sinking into one of the seats lining the
starboard side of the open bay and closing his eyes, mentally
preparing for what he was about to do. Or, at least, he tried to do that.

"Why the hell are we even taking you losers? Haven't you fucked
this mission up enough already?" Crusher's obnoxiously loud voice
floated through the open hatch.

"*We* fucked it up? We were on-mission before you jumped

through a ceiling and attacked us unprovoked!" Jason recognized the voice of MG, Obsidian's weaponeer and resident hard-case. He and Crusher had been sniping at each other the entire flight, and it was as annoying now as it had been for the first fifteen hours.

"You have one of those, too?" Sully called over his shoulder.

"One of what?" Jason asked.

"A huge pain in the ass like MG. Someone who serves no purpose when there's no shooting other than to complain, eat, and smell up the ship."

"We actually have two," Jason said. "You're sitting next to the other one."

"We leaving yet?" Crusher demanded, his head poking through the floor hatch.

"Yes, dipshit," Jason said. "We're about to thrust off with your fucking head sticking through the open hatchway and the rest of the team stuck below staring at your ass."

"Whoa! Where the hell is this coming from?" Crusher asked. "I was just asking a question!"

"I hate this goddamn job," Sully mumbled from the pilot seat while the others scrambled up into the SX-5 and Jason was finally able to close the hatch.

"Tell Doc he's clear to close up the dorsal hatch," he said. "We can leave at your discretion."

The team quickly found their seats and strapped in as the ship pushed gently away from the *Devil's Fortune* and accelerated towards the planet and their entry vector. Jason stood in the middle of the deck and strapped on all his gear, checking his weapons.

When he looked up, he saw Jacob staring at him with an unreadable expression, but not a hostile one. He took that as progress and strapped into the station just behind the flight crew for the ride down.

Jason always found it an odd feeling to sit in a ship he wasn't piloting. His skills at the controls were a great point of pride for him and had taken him years to hone and perfect. When he'd first come to space, he barely understood how to fly an airplane on Earth, much

less an interstellar combat ship. After a few moments of observing
Sully, he concluded the guy had a natural instinct for flying. He'd
never been in a Jepsen SX-5, but he was already smooth and confident in his inputs.

"Ten minutes, and we'll hit the ground," Kage said. "We're setting
up for a single strafing run before dumping you idiots out the back,
and then we'll take out the fighters. Doc is about to— Ah, there he
goes. Their shuttle was just blown out of the sky. The *Devil* is turning
out of orbit and moving away at full power."

"Ten minutes!" Jason called over the team channel. He got a few
thumbs up and one middle finger that had a sharp claw on it.

The SX-5 swooped down from the upper atmosphere and into the
established traffic patterns. They'd reach their departure point in a
few minutes, and then Sully would drop them to the deck and try to
come in between the two patrolling fighters without being seen.

The contingency plan if they were spotted was to take down the
fighters first, but that was risky with all of them still in the ship. If it
was shot down after they were out, it was only two people lost. If they
took a hit before, they could lose the whole damn team.

"Here we go," Sully said, pushing the nose over and bringing the
power smoothly up. The SX-5 rocketed towards the ground and
angled north. The area they overflew was mostly farmland or unde-
veloped wilderness, so he didn't worry about the sonic boom as they
pushed up over Mach 2 and leveled off at around seventy-five meters.

"We're good to go," Kage said. "Both fighters are moving apart and
leaving the middle open for us. Sending the targeting package to
you."

"I got it," Sully said. "Fish in a fuckin' barrel."

The troopers heard the ship coming at them a split second after it
was too late to do anything about it. Sully lined up main guns and
opened fire, walking the plasma shots through the bunched-up One
World troopers and into the three open-air ground vehicles that
looked like some of the locals. The vehicles, and their occupants,
exploded spectacularly, indicating there was more on them than just
fuel.

"Most of the human troops are down. Few squirming around, but you're clear," Kage said. "Expect more from that building judging from the thermals."

"Understood," Jason said. "Put us on the ground."

"What the hell was that?!"

"Get up!" Hodges yelled, dragging Avelar to his feet. "They're coming back around!"

But they weren't. The sleek ship of a type Hodges had never seen before flew off after that first, devastating pass. It pulled into a tight, spiraling descent and came to a hover near the far side of the operations center. He couldn't see what was happening, but he assumed it was dropping off ground forces. The ship had been too big to be a fighter but was far more capable than any combat shuttle he'd ever seen.

While the toady Jansen had told him to keep an eye on still struggled to get to his feet, the engines of the strange ship spooled up, and it shot away to the east, not the direction it had come from.

"Fighters, you have incoming! We were just attacked by an unknown ship. It's just flown off towards the east!"

"*Copy Ground Lead,*" one of their escort pilots said. "*We've lost contact with Shuttle One...assume it's been lost. Moving to intercept now.*"

"Shit!" Hodges yelled. A few others shook their heads and stood, looking disoriented.

"What?" Avelar asked, now looking steadier on his feet.

"They took out our shuttle, too. The *Truxton* won't be back around for another ninety minutes, so we need to hold out for that long. They're moving to the ops center, so we need to get the hell out of here," Hodges said, pointing towards a squat, concrete structure about sixty meters to the north of Assembly Building Two.

"The drones—"

"Will be pointless if we're all killed," Hodges said. "We need to take cover and wait for support and dust-off from the *Truxton*. Now, *MOVE!"*

As Avelar and the five uninjured troopers stumbled and began running for the bunker-like structure Hodges knew would be open, the wily old operator checked on the others strewn about the still-smoking ground. He and Avelar had been damn lucky.

They had been a bit behind the main group he'd sent ahead to secure the local contractors before meeting with them just in case they tried something stupid. The blast had tossed them and a few others into a shallow depression in the hillside that had shielded Hodges and the others from the worst of it.

More of his people might have survived the initial strafing if whatever the local assholes had been carrying hadn't exploded. When their trucks lit off, it wiped out all his troopers in the immediate vicinity. He found three were alive, but they weren't anything close to combat capable.

He shot the first two he saw as a mercy killing, but the third looked to be in good shape save for the missing foot. The kid was tough and had already activated his uniform's tourniquet and sat up, checking his weapon.

"You still with me, trooper?"

"Yes, sir. Not mobile, but I can still shoot."

"Good. These clowns will probably come from the operations center and move this way once they find out their target wasn't in there," Hodges said. "Can I count on you?"

"I'll make them sorry they came this way, sir, don't worry. Get the VIP clear, and I'll hold them up."

"Good man," Hodges smacked the top of his helmet and ran off towards the building he'd sent Avelar to.

He knew it was eventually going to be an auxiliary power station to support the shipyard operations, with a fusion powerplant buried deep within the reinforced concrete structure. He also knew it hadn't been finished when he read through his brief for this mission. He didn't like trapping himself inside a building, but at least that one would have a chance of holding up if that gunboat came back around.

As if it had read his thoughts, there was a sharp explosion from the east, and Hodges knew he'd likely just lost one of his escort fighters. He took one last look behind him and saw that the trooper he left behind moved into position to engage anyone coming from the ops center, knowing he would be killed immediately by the return fire. It was one nice thing about One World recruiting zealots: it was easy to convince them to throw their lives away when you needed them to.

Hodges leaned into it and poured on the speed, his cybernetics whining as he accelerated to over thirty kilometers per hour. Maybe he and Avelar would be able to hide out until Webb's team—and he had no doubt that's who this was—searched the area, and then left empty-handed.

22

"Splash one!"

"Good shot," Kage said. "We've got another fighter trying to come around the edge. He's using the southern ravine for cover."

"Let's keep this away from the base," Sully said.

He yanked the SX-5 into a sharp climb, pouring on the power as the sleek ship roared up and away from the compound. This small vessel was quickly winning him over with its combination of power, maneuverability, and weaponry. It was so nimble and responsive within the atmosphere he almost forgot he was flying a ship as big as a wide-body passenger jet from back home.

At five-thousand meters of altitude, he chopped the power and kicked the Jepsen into a lazy hammerhead turn, bringing the nose back around and re-acquiring the target. The fighter, still committed to its run up the ravine to try and attack from the east, didn't react to Sully's maneuver. Either it was running passive sensors to try and stay hidden, or the pilot was an idiot.

"Looks like we're being ignored," Kage said. "Strange."

"Shit!" Sully said, slamming the drive to full power. "He's going for that building. He'll try to destroy it with our team inside."

"But their people are inside, too," Kage said, gripping his console as the SX-5 shook under the stress of the powered dive.

"They're cultists...they don't care," Sully said, angling his nose over a bit and opening fire into the path of the fighter. The plasma shots slammed into the ground well ahead of it, but it made the pilot veer off hard into a climbing turn to avoid it. It also took them offline to hit the building and returned the speed and position advantage to Sully. The fighter now tried to climb away while the more powerful Jepsen dove into it. The display lit up with detection warnings as the pilot, knowing he'd been spotted, brought up his active sensors and tried to target the SX-5.

"We're being hit with a targeting scan," Kage said. "Bringing the shields up. They'll take a good amount of punishment, but try not to fly right into any missiles."

"Noted," Sully grunted, concentrating on the fighter as it tried to get back into the ravine and use the topology to its advantage.

"*Kage, those fighters have called out to the cruiser,*" Doc's voice broke in on the com. "*They're accelerating along their orbit and will be over your position within the next fifteen minutes.*"

"Got it," Kage said. "You get that, Captain?"

"*I heard,*" Jason said. "*Take that fighter out, and then get clear.*"

"I've got him," Sully said.

He pulled out of his dive, leveling their flight, and moving along the ground to get above the ravine the fighter tried to dive into. He chopped the power and deployed the speed brakes, rolling left and letting the ship slide around, kicking the nose over and slowing enough so the racing fighter shot underneath them, realizing its mistake too late.

There seemed to be a moment of indecision when the pilot didn't know whether to slow to match Sully's maneuver, or kick it in the ass and run for it. That proved to be a fatal mistake. The SX-5 now skimmed along the top of the ravine, directly behind the fighter as the pilot's maneuvers became more desperate and erratic.

Sully fired the main guns again, sending plasma shots streaking into the ravine. Multiple shots peppered the right airfoil and engine nozzle, causing the fighter to yaw violently to starboard before the pilot could correct it. They returned fire with the articulated turret on the tail, but the underpowered guns splashed harmlessly against the SX-5's shields.

His mouth a grim line, Sully went to work walking shot after shot into the fighter until, finally, it rolled over and fell into the ravine, exploding into a fireball upon impact.

"Good fight, buddy," he said, throwing a salute. "Ground team, the last fighter is down. We're bugging out to the north."

"*Copy that, Sully,*" Jason said. "*Good work.*"

"Give me another grenade!"

"Goddamn it, Crusher! Stop playing around and clear that portico!" Jason shouted.

MG had been standing closest to the big warrior and handed him a grenade from his harness. It had a red stripe on the bottom marking it as an incendiary. Crusher smiled at the stocky weaponeer, pulled the safety, and double-clicked the trigger before tossing it around the corner. He and MG stood there giggling when it went off, and the two troopers trying to hold the security checkpoint were flash-fried.

"Aw, Christ! That smell!" Murph said.

"Clear!" Crusher called out.

"Stupid son of a bitch," Jason ground out as he stalked forward.

As with most plans, theirs had completely blown up before they even hit the ground. Once Sully mowed down pretty much everybody out in the open, Jason had decided not to split his force up and get them under cover before that cruiser could come back around and call out their positions to the fighters. The issue now was that Crusher and MG seemed to be having a competition to see who could kill in the most creative way possible.

They'd pushed in and quickly took out the first six. Crusher had just barbecued another two, which meant there were maybe three more holed up near the debris of the cave-in. So far, they'd been lucky, and the only injury had come from a ricochet that had clipped Mettler, leaving a nasty gouge in his left arm.

Jason knew that if he let those two morons keep playing with explosives, however, there was a decent chance the already compromised structure would collapse on them.

"No more fucking grenades!" he yelled. "We're near a cave-in, and I don't want everyone killed when you bring the roof down."

"707 and I would probably be fine," 784 said.

"Don't start with me," Jason warned as he walked up. "Listen up in there! All your friends are dead, but we'd don't want to kill anyone else unless we have to. Toss your weapons out and surrender, and you'll walk away from—"

A burst of automatic weapon fire through the opening cut him off. They were using old-school firearms, and the smell of honest to God gunpowder made Jason more than a little nostalgic. It also told him they didn't have much that would stop what he had in mind next.

"You want us, come get us Navy scumbag!" someone shouted in English from within.

"Damn. Inter-service rivalries have gotten a lot more heated since I was in," Jason remarked, stepping away from the opening. "707? You feel like helping out a bit?"

"Would you prefer them alive?" 707 asked, sounding bored.

"Either or," Jason said. "We're not taking prisoners with us, so don't do them any special favors."

"Very well," 707 said. Both battlesynths switched over to combat mode, their eyes blazing red and weapons deploying.

"You dumbasses had your chance!" Crusher laughed.

707 and 784 walked through the security archway and immediately took fire. The bullets from the conventional firearms pinged harmlessly off their armor, and both battlesynths ignored it. About the time Jason would have expected 707 to take control of the situation, all hell broke loose.

A powerful plasma blast from a battlesynth arm cannon came out of the security portico and blasted the armored front entrance of the building. Six more shots fired in rapid succession blew out the entire front wall while sporadic small arms fire continued unabated.

"What the—"

"Evacuate! They have rigged explosives!" 707's voice rang in their headsets. Jason immediately knew what that meant.

"Through the hole! Everybody! Now! *Move, move, move!*"

The composite team was made up of skilled operators who didn't waste so much as a millisecond of confusion or questioning. At his order, everyone broke for the hole the battlesynths had punched through the wall. Jason reached it first, turned, grabbed Jacob, and threw him through the opening. When he turned back to usher the others through, Crusher grabbed him in much the same way and tossed him out of the opening.

Father and son sprinted towards a low wall running the perimeter of the concrete area in front of the building. Jason watched as the others all came through, with MG and Crusher as the last. 784 appeared in the opening when there was a bright flash, and a pressure wave knocked Jason off his feet. Later, he would say he couldn't remember if he'd actually heard the explosion or not.

784 was flung through the air by the force of the explosion, firing his repulsors to help direct his ballistic flight away from the biotics tossed across the grass. He came down on his feet with a *thud*, spinning towards the building just as it completely collapsed in on itself.

Two stories of concrete and steel caved in with still no sign 707 had made it to the doorway. Jason struggled to his feet as his nanobots deployed to fix his inner ear. By the time his balance came back, Crusher was already standing, as was Jacob. The rest lay on the ground, dazed but alive.

"Well...shit," Crusher said.

"Did 707 make it out?"

"No," 784 said. "He was at the epicenter, trying to disarm the device."

"He was right *next* to it?" Jason asked. "That's...not good. That was a powerful blast. Could he have survived it?"

"Possible, but the odds are not in his favor," 784 said. "He is also not showing up on the net, but that could be from interference or his systems knocked offline. Do not give up hope, Captain...we are a tough species."

"*Did everyone make it out of that?!*" Kage's voice came over the com.

"We're short one battlesynth, but we're not ready to call it just yet," Jason said. "Where are you?"

"*Fifteen klicks east, seven thousand meters up,*" Kage said. "*Our optics picked up the explosion.*"

"Is that cruiser doing anything?"

"*No,*" Doc said. "*We have it on sensors, and it's moved into a geostationary orbit right over your position.*"

"That's too high up to try and hit us with its weapons," Jason said. "What's it up to? They know we took out all of their people."

"Did we?" 784 asked. "We are assuming everyone on the hillside is dead, and the entirety of their remaining force was in that building."

"Sully, overfly our position and get us a full-spectrum sweep of the immediate area," Jason said. "Let's see if there are any stragglers."

"*Copy. On our way,*" Sully said.

A moment later, the SX-5 flew gracefully overhead at only a couple thousand meters, slow enough for Kage to get a good read on the area with the ship's sensor suite. Jason held his breath, half-expecting someone to take a shot at the ship as it flew by so exposed.

"*You've got one alive in that field,*" Kage said. "*He looks injured, but thermals show he's still very much breathing. There's also some disrupted grass going straight towards that structure just north of the large building in front of you. It looks like maybe some people went that way, can't tell you when or how many. The building itself is too solid to scan through.*"

"You get anything on 707 when you overflew the rubble here?" Jason asked.

"*Nothing definitive, sorry. There were a few active power signatures the computer couldn't identify.*"

"Copy that. Doc, tell Twingo to start coming up with a plan to excavate that mess with what we have on hand," Jason said. "We're not leaving if there's a chance he's alive. I'll handle our lone survivor out there, and then we'll check out that building."

"I'm coming, too," Jacob said. "But I want the rest of my team pulled out in case that cruiser moves down and decides to sanitize the base from orbit." Jason stared at his son, about to tell him to piss up a rope and that he'd be withdrawing with his team, but that wouldn't be right. This was his mission, and he wasn't a little boy Jason could order around.

"You copy that, Sully?"

"*On my way for pickup*," Sully said.

"Would there be any point in arguing this command decision?" Mettler asked. "Why are you benching us, LT?"

"In case they've got another building rigged to collapse on us and there aren't any battlesynths to blow a hole in the wall to escape through," Jacob said. "We're still on-mission, and if I get the entire team wiped out, then all we've been through and all we've done will be for nothing. Taylor's death will be for nothing. If I don't make it out, Murph takes command and executes the mission as he sees best."

"Understood," Murph said, cutting off MG.

"What?!" MG asked.

"Mission first," Murph said. "If we still have a chance to get Jansen, all of this won't have been for nothing."

When the SX-5 settled on the tarmac and dropped the ramp, a dejected-looking Obsidian crew climbed aboard, leaving their lieutenant in the care of Omega Force's heavy hitters and the remaining battlesynth. Murph looked back as he walked up the ramp and tossed Jacob a salute before Sully closed the ship and moved away.

"Let's go wrap this up," Jason said. "That cruiser isn't just going to sit up there forever."

"I will take point," 784 said, switching back to combat mode and moving off across the grassy area towards the squat, bunker-like building they suspected the survivors fled to.

Jason dialed up more magnification on his optics and flicked the velocity mode on his weapon to low. The survivor on the hillside wasn't moving, but he put two rounds in him for good measure, feeling a pang of guilt as he did. The guy was just someone doing a job, not involved in the bullshit politics of the people ordering him around.

As they approached, Jason still couldn't figure out what the building was supposed to be. It looked unfinished, but it was clear from the way it was overbuilt and oddly proportioned it was meant to fill a specialized function and wasn't just some random utility building. There were two entrances, one of them a large access opening that had an alloy door already in place and locked, and a person-sized door at ground level that was wide open.

"Probably not a great idea to just walk through the open door," Crusher said, pointing to the footprints in the loose dirt on the concrete that showed a handful of people had gone directly into the opening.

"Let's go around the side and see if there are any other openings," Jacob said, pointing to their left. Jason was just glad to get out of the open where anybody from within the building could have taken a shot at them if they'd had a weapon with some range.

Once they made it around, they found what they were looking for. It was a louvered vent almost a meter and a half across, but it was also over ten meters up the smooth concrete wall. Without waiting for a prompt, 784 fired his footpad repulsors and floated up the vent, quickly cutting away the mounting flanges with one of his lasers and pulling the vent and fan assembly out of the wall.

He descended slowly and gently put the five hundred pounds of machinery on the ground, barely making any noise. Jason made a gesture for him to proceed, and the battlesynth took off again, this time disappearing into the opening.

"All clear," he said over the com after a minute. "You will find yourself in a large air duct I have cut through. I am standing on a catwalk high above an open bay."

"On our way," Jason said. "Good thing we didn't bring any of the normies." He crouched and launched himself up, easily grabbing the edge of the hole and pulling himself up and through. Jacob followed after him and, by the time he dropped through the opening to stand next to 784, Crusher had come through the hole.

He looked over the edge into the darkness below before switching his ocular implants to mid-wave infrared. His neural implant also provided a false-color overlay so he could perceive depth a little easier while seeing in that part of the spectrum.

"I can hear someone talking," Jacob said quietly. "Sounds like they're pretty far down there, though."

"Confirmed," 784 said. "There is a network of ladders and stairs across this bay that will allow us to access the lower levels."

"Then let's get at it," Jason said.

23

"Where the hell did they go?" Avelar asked.

"Quiet!" Hodges hissed.

The pair of them hid in a recessed alcove on the main floor while the troopers they'd brought with them explored the lower levels, possibly for an access tunnel that led either to the construction cradles or the assembly buildings. Hodges had wanted to cover the entrance himself, and Avelar decided to stay with him.

They observed members of the Scout Fleet team, led by one of those damned battlesynths, following the path they'd cut through the tall grass. Implausibly, it also looked like they'd had a Galvetic warrior along with them. Maybe Marcus Webb had a little more juice than he'd been led to believe if he was recruiting some of the galaxy's most notorious badasses into his little club.

Hodges watched them approach, kicking himself for not taking a weapon that had any sort of range to it. The plasma carbine he carried had an effective kill range of maybe fifty meters, more than enough for close-quarters combat, but anything beyond that and the plasma charge diffused, and it would do little more than announce his presence. So, instead, he'd stayed pressed against the walls and waited with his weapon trained on the doorway, ready to light them up the instant they came through.

But they never did.

The small group had walked over near the sealed access doors to the left, and then walked away from the doorway to the point he could no longer hear them. If they had any sort of competency and, so far, they'd shown they did, they would circle the building looking for another ingress, of which there was none. Eventually, they would have to either come in through the doorway he covered or leave and blast the building from orbit.

A metal-on-metal clattering well above him caught his attention. It wasn't much. It might have just been something in the building shifting or the normal creaks as it expanded in the midday heat. Or had they found another way into the building? Hodges had looked it over when they arrived, always intending to use it as a bugout shelter, and hadn't seen anything. Could the battlesynth have just cut through the walls without him or Avelar hearing? Unlikely.

The voices of the troopers he'd brought with him wafted up from the ramp that led below into the guts of the building where the powerplant would have lived. Their lack of discipline after having most of their team wiped out was exactly why he called them cannon fodder right to their faces. They were marginally better trained than your average infantryman, but a far cry from Special Forces.

Unfortunately, their incessant chatter made it impossible to listen to what might be happening above them. He could break com silence and tell them all to shut the hell up, but they were just using basic RF-type radios, and the signal could probably be tracked by the battlesynth. There was so much mythology around the species he had no idea what was true and what wasn't, so he decided to err on the side of caution.

"—turns the lights on, I think. Tired of walking around in the dark."

The voice came clear as day from near the ramp as the troopers made their way back up after scouting for an escape tunnel. A second later, bright floodlights flickered to life inside the cavernous bay, bathing the entire area in white light. Hodges and Avelar were still partially hidden in shadows, but with the lights up, he was able to see a grinning Galvetic warrior negligently lob a grenade down the ramp with an underhand toss.

There were some confused shouts below from their troops, and then a sharp explosion. The big warrior tossed his head back and laughed uproariously as he and the battlesynth stomped down the ramp to finish off any survivors.

"What the hell part of *'we need survivors to question'* did he not understand?" a voice said from somewhere Hodges couldn't see.

"There might be some down there," another said, this one easily recognizable. It was Lieutenant Brown, the one Jansen had warned them about.

"So, you two dipshits going to keep hiding in that corner, or are you going to toss your weapons out and make this easy?" the other voice asked. Hodges just let out a sigh. He felt embarrassed he actually thought he had enough cover in the alcove.

"How long did you know we were there?"

"Since we came in through the vent up there," Jason said, tapping near his eye. "Thermal vision. Spotted you right away."

Jacob watched as the man tossed a few weapons aside, raising his hands. The other guy just looked like some bureaucratic weasel and hadn't even been armed, but the other one looked like he could handle himself. There were also some odd mannerisms in the way he moved that set alarm bells off in Jacob's head.

It was the same telltale hitches he'd spent years learning to suppress. This man had been modified in some way and was still trying to get used to appearing normal. He looked over to see if his father had noticed, but Jason Burke still wore that same, smirking, bored expression that seemed to be semi-permanent on the man.

"I know who Lieutenant Brown is," the man said, nodding to Jacob, "but I've never seen you before, and it seems like I should have. You two actually look a little similar. Brothers? Cousins?"

"If you think I don't see that holdout pistol you're inching that hand towards, you're sadly mistaken," Jason said. "If you don't play nice, I'll chop those arms off. Seems like whoever paid for all of that cybernetic gear you're sporting wouldn't love that."

"How—" the man began.

"It's easy to spot if you know what to look for," Jason said. "You can tell you only recently had it done. If you survive this, you need to work on making your movements appear more natural."

"Thanks. I'll do that. My name is—"

"Not yet," Jason said. "We'll get to all that once Crusher finishes off your people below."

"*Captain, you have incoming!*" Doc's voice broke in on the team channel. "*Two shuttles coming down from the cruiser. Sully is moving to intercept, but he's out of position.*"

Jacob watched the man with the cybernetics and saw his jaw tighten slightly, and a half-smile tugged the corners of his mouth. He'd just been alerted by his people the cavalry was on the way.

"You think they'll get here in time?" Jason asked.

"What?" the man said, feigning confusion.

"The shuttles full of reinforcements you were just told about," Jason said, stifling a yawn. "You think they'll get here before we have time to ice you, and then get picked up?"

"I guess we'll see," the man said.

"I'll go grab that other pistol," Jacob said. He put his carbine on the ground near Jason and walked over to where the captives stood. This guy looked dangerous, and he would need both hands to put on the restraints. He didn't want to give the guy a chance to kill him with his own weapon.

He was halfway to them when the floor bucked, and a tremendous explosion shook the building. Jacob and the two captives were tossed off their feet. Jason managed to remain upright. Half of the lights went out as Crusher and 784 came running back up the ramp.

"What the hell was that?" Crusher demanded.

"Ground team, you have locals coming down the hillside in technicals," Sully said. *"The building you're in was just hit with rocket fire."*

"Why the hell are the locals shooting at us?" Jason asked.

"You killed their advance team," their captive said. "They take that sort of thing personally."

"I hate sore losers," Jason muttered. "Sully, stay clear of the area until we get this sorted. Go ahead and let the shuttles land. Let them deal with each other."

"Smart move," the captive said. The other one still hadn't said a word.

"Shut up," Jason said, bracing as another round of explosions shook the building. "One more word, and I'll shoot you. 784, we need eyes out there, but I don't want you risking a direct hit from a rocket."

"I will go back up into the vent shaft," 784 said. "The opening is relatively small, and I can move out of the way of any lucky shots."

"Where do you want me?" Crusher asked, watching as Jacob pulled the rest of the weapons off their captives. The one who looked like a bureaucrat had, oddly enough, a beautiful Czech-made pistol that wasn't something an armory would just have lying around for him to use.

Jacob looked him up and down again, trying to see if he'd missed something in his first dismissal of the man. The other one, not surprisingly, had blades, sidearms, and even a telescopic baton hidden on him.

"You and I will cover the doorway," Jason said. "I don't think we'll have much to do until these two forces are done fighting each other or they join together and come after us. Sully, if the second thing happens, it'll be up to you to save the day."

"Understood," Sully said.

"So, who are you, tough guy?" Jacob asked as he tightened down the standard wrist restraints he carried. Those weren't normally something he had on him, but the mission had been to try and snag one of these guys alive to question.

"I'm nobody," the man answered. "Just some flunky they send out to run errands."

"That just happens to have extensive cybernetic upgrades? Sure," Jacob said. "You were ready to be all chatty a minute ago. What changed?"

"Maybe I don't like your face. Who's the merc you're running with? He looks a bit like you except he's definitely a killer. You're not. Webb hiring out the tough jobs now?"

"You got a name to go with that mouth?" Jacob asked again.

"His name is Hodges," the other man spoke up for the first time. "He's Margaret Jansen's fixer. Be very careful with him. He's a genius and a sociopath in addition to his cybernetic enhancements. He will kill you without remorse, just because he can."

Hodges's eyes bulged from his head as he stared at his companion as if he couldn't believe what he heard.

"Have you lost your fucking mind?" he spat.

"And you are?" Jacob asked, stealing a glance to where his father and Crusher watched the doorway.

"My name is Ricardo Avelar. I'm the replacement for Elton Hollick, the man you had the misfortune of crossing paths with on occasion," Avelar said. "Now that we can't find Mr. Hollick, I handle certain tasks within One World's administration."

"Hollick is dead," Jacob said, looking at Hodges. "I killed him. Left his corpse in a filthy alley on some shithole planet." That wasn't technically true. Jacob had killed Hollick, but they'd taken the body with them and disposed of it so as not to leave evidence.

"Ah," Avelar said, nodding knowingly.

"You're dead, Avelar," Hodges said. "You just committed suicide."

"For someone with a hundred and sixty IQ, you're surprisingly dense sometimes," Avelar said. "The game has changed, Hodges. You're no longer the scariest thing in the room."

The sounds of real fighting outside drowned out any reply Hodges might have made.

"*Both shuttles have unloaded their troops,*" 784 reported. "*A small envoy moved out to talk to the locals, the locals killed them immediately. Now, they're all in a close-quarters gunfight, and the One World troops have no cover to get behind.*"

"This is going to be fast and nasty," Crusher shouted.

"Ah, shit...here they come," Jason said, raising his own weapon and opening fire. "Jacob! They're going to try to take cover in here, I think we can hold them off and bottle up this doorway."

Jacob stood there, feeling useless but knowing somebody had to watch the prisoners. The one named Avelar just stood there calmly, his hands bound behind him. Hodges, however, seemed to be a coiled spring, vibrating with energy. The sounds of an especially intense spat of fighting drew his attention towards the doorway where Jason and Crusher had moved to block the One World troops.

An odd snapping sound caused him to jerk his head back just in time to see Hodges had broken his restraints and ducked his head just enough to not catch the incoming blow to the face.

Hodges's off-target hit still carried enough force to send Jacob flying. He hit the ground with a clatter, his weapon skidding across the floor as he fought off vertigo. There was no time to try and draw his sidearm as Hodges didn't bother going for a weapon, just dove onto Jacob to try and finish the fight quickly. Hodges went for his throat as Jacob was able to get a knee up and keep him from gaining complete control of him on the ground.

In a panic, Jacob shot his left arm across his body, and then swept down to clear Hodges's hands from his throat. This pitched him forward where Jacob could land a solid palm-strike that went a little higher than he aimed and hit Hodges between the eyes.

Jacob used the distraction to shove with his pinned leg, sliding Hodges off before rearing back with both feet and kicking him full force, the blow connecting solidly and sending his opponent flying backwards. Jacob rolled to his feet, still a bit dazed from that first hammer blow, and went for his sidearm. Hodges was already there, moving much faster than he would have believed possible.

"Oh, no," Hodges said, slapping the pistol from his hand. "We're keeping this— Ugh!"

Jacob took advantage of the man wasting the time to taunt him to catch him in the throat with a left-handed jab. As Hodges took a step back, Jacob launched off his back foot and drove his right fist in with all his strength. He was used to the people he'd fought before having no ability to block, or even survive, a hit delivered with all the power available in his enhanced muscles.

But Hodges was far from normal.

The punch slammed into Hodges' sternum but, instead of the expected bone-cracking and blood flying, Jacob felt three of his fingers break and all his target did was grunt. Son of a bitch had a reinforced skeleton. Pulling his ruined hand back in close, he knew he was in trouble. Hodges smiled and moved towards Jacob as the Marine backed away.

"You should have shot me when you had the chance," he said, lunging.

Hodges was actually quite disappointed with Lieutenant Brown. He'd expected a much better fight than what he was getting. The problem was obvious to him after the first exchange. Jacob Brown was faster and stronger than almost any other human, but he was inexperienced and not particularly skilled as a fighter. He relied on his power to overwhelm his opponents and, when he met someone his equal, he didn't know what to do.

The punch that shattered his hand against the alloy plate in Hodges' chest had been a perfect example. It was a reckless, stupid move that might work in the movies but would get you killed in real life.

"This will be a hard final lesson for you, boy," he said, moving in as the Marine cradled his hand against his side. Hodges slipped to his right, moving away from the injured hand because he wanted to force Brown to use his weaker left hand to defend. He didn't bother with trying to take him down, just came in close and delivered five light-ning-fast hits to the body before skipping back out as Brown threw a wild left-hander that missed by inches.

Changing tactics, Hodges shifted quickly to the other side, now going after the injured arm with the same rapid combination he'd used before but, this time, Brown was ready. The kid stepped away just enough so Hodges missed, and then came in hard, turning to his left and hitting him in the temple with an elbow that rang his bell. He stumbled away a couple of steps and shook his head, pissed at himself for letting the little bastard get a free shot like that.

"Point to you, kid," he said. He moved in again, still intent on keeping this a standup fight where he could use his superior arm strength to just pummel the little bastard to death. But, credit where credit was due, Brown wasn't going to just stand there and be a target.

He'd figured out Hodges's strategy quickly and still had a lot of fight left in him. When the older man went for a feint, followed by a knockout swing aimed at the head, Brown ducked under it and, ignoring the broken hand, hit him in the gut with a right-hand punch that felt like it tore something loose inside him. The Marine pressed his advantage and followed with a left up under the chin, snapping Hodges' head back.

Brown separated and turned, looking for a weapon. Hodges, now fearing for the first time the kid might get lucky after that gut check, rushed and tackled him, driving him into the concrete.

"I can't believe your punk-ass actually killed a Ull one-on-one," he said. "You can't even stay on your damn feet."

Brown's head hit the concrete despite his best efforts to keep his chin tucked, and he was obviously dazed. Hodges looked over at Avelar and saw the weasel just standing there, still in his restraints. The dumb bastard hadn't even tried to pick his gun back up. In fact, the idiot smiled at him.

Hodges turned back to his work and, after securing Brown's unin-jured hand, pulled back to end it. The young Marine was strong and fast, but still just as fragile as any other man. A couple hits, and that would be all she wrote.

Just as he was about to strike, a savage roar filled the room. Hodges, fully expecting to see that goddamn Galvetic warrior, looked up and saw the human merc, his face contorted with rage and hate. For the first time in a long time, Hodges felt a thin tendril of fear wrap around his heart.

"Hodges, meet Jason Burke. You've already met his son, Jacob Brown," Avelar said, still smiling.

24

Jason's mind was blank. In place of reason was a burning, white-hot rage.

He'd walked back in now that the One World troops had stopped trying to get into the building to check on the prisoners and saw the big one had slipped his restraints. The fucker was straddling Jacob, who looked half-concussed, and was about to finish him off.

All the fear and anger he'd been carrying since learning Jacob was out in space fueled his turbocharged adrenal response. He launched himself across the room, dropping his weapon, and diving for the piece of shit trying to kill his son. The guy was still sitting there with the same stupid, surprised look on his face when Jason hit him like a freight train, sending them both flying across the concrete.

Jason rolled over backwards and was on his feet just as his target did.

"You're Burke, huh? I thought you'd be bigger."

"And you're a dead man. You just don't know it yet."

"Then come on! I'm not afraid of you!"

"You will be."

Hodges was in trouble.

Burke had slammed into him with enough force that there were warnings scrolling through his field of vision as his systems tried to mitigate the damage. He'd moved so fast across the floor Hodges could scarcely believe it.

What the hell did this guy have done to himself? How could he even control that sort of speed? Even more unbelievably, an impact that had managed to damage his cybernetics appeared to not even have fazed Burke. He was just standing there, hands open and loose at his sides, breathing slowly but still looking enraged. This was a real fighter.

Ignoring the warnings from the computers that managed his cybernetics, Hodges came in again, this time more cautiously. He tried to keep just out of reach to see if Burke would give him an opening but, instead, the merc just came at him like a wild badger. Not uncontrolled, but fast and vicious.

Hodges brought his arms up into a guard as Burke hammered him with blows. Unlike his son, Burke didn't seem to be affected at all when he smashed his fist into one of Hodges's alloy subdermal plates. If anything, the hits just got harder and harder until the flashing warnings started again, saying he was taking too much abuse, so he had no choice but to separate.

He'd barely managed to get four or five solid blows and each time Burke just shrugged them off as inconsequential even though Hodges had his actuator gain maxed out. Theoretically, that should have smashed through human bone like balsa wood, but all Burke had were a few pressure cuts.

Hodges, on the other hand, started to feel the effects of overloading his cybernetics as the heat built. He'd run too high of a power setting for too long, and the warnings being fed to him from the processors were coming fast and furious.

Burke let him separate, still keeping his hands up in a loose guard and smirking. The lack of respect enraged Hodges, but he hesitated. It turned out Burke had been right. He *was* afraid.

"You okay?"

"Yeah...just...stay back," Jacob said, climbing to his feet. He had significant injuries. He looked over at Ricardo Avelar and saw he was still in his restraints and keeping his distance before Jacob looked back at where his father now appeared to be toying with Hodges.

"Don't be too hard on yourself," Avelar said. "Hodges is a killer with decades of experience. His cybernetics make him overconfident, however. Your father is about to teach him a lesson in humility. Right before he kills him, that is."

Jacob watched as Hodges tried yet again to get Jason in close where he could use what he thought was his superior strength. Again, Jason would let him burn energy before answering with hits of his own. So far, the fight had been a standup affair, looking more like a hybrid boxing match than a street fight.

"Ugh!" Hodges grunted, falling to his knees after Jason slipped through his guard and landed a rib shot that deflated him. Jacob frowned as his father again backed off and let Hodges collect himself.

"He's not doing it out of any misplaced sense of nobility," Avelar said, seeming to read his mind. "He's prolonging Hodges's suffering."

Jacob said nothing to the prisoner. He wasn't sure what he was watching. It was sort of like when you watched the heavyweight bouts, and they seemed to be moving slower and more carefully than the middleweight fighters, but the blows they landed hit with much more force. Both fighters were incredibly strong and fast but seemed to be hesitant to get in too close where they could be grabbed by the other.

"You're looking a little red there, bud," Jason said, moving in like a cobra and snapping Hodges head back with a nasty left uppercut. Hodges countered with a wild swing of his own, but Jason had already danced out of the way. "Slow, too."

"Damn you!" Hodges grunted through gritted teeth.

"Feeling the temperature going up?" Jason asked, feigning another left before ducking under the block and throwing a basic sidekick into Hodges's hip, knocking the man down again. "It's the problem with primitive cybernetics like yours. You're running your systems too hard, and they can't get rid of the heat. You're literally cooking yourself. That's what you smell. You turned the safeties off, didn't you?"

Hodges didn't answer. His breath steamed in the air despite the room being a moderate temperature, and Jacob could swear he smelled what might have been pork and electrical wiring burning. He was also starting to look like a boiled lobster and sweated profusely.

Jason, a cruel smile on his face, came in and hammered Hodges in the side of the head with a haymaker. Hodges went flying, not even trying to defend himself at this point, and landed in a heap.

"And now, we're at the end," Avelar said, sounding indifferent.

———

It had been one of the stranger fights Jason had ever been in.

There hadn't been a lot of blows exchanged by either fighter, and it hadn't been the most skillful or technical display he'd ever put on, but it got the job done. Once his ocular implants showed him the dumbass's cybernetic gear was cranked to maximum and heating up quickly, it was simply a matter of forcing him to expend energy and help the process along. By the time Hodges realized he was cooking from the inside out, it was too late.

Now, he sprawled on the ground, eyes wide and unable to move his limbs except in an uncontrolled, spastic way. His eyes were completely red where they'd begun to bleed, and his mouth was open in a scream of agony that wouldn't come out. Jason would have felt some pang of sympathy for the man had he not walked in and seen he was about to crush his son's skull. After that, he'd tried to prolong the man's agony as long as he could. He knew it was sadistic, but he didn't care.

"You might have just been doing your job, but that's my kid you were about to kill," Jason said to the man. "Just can't allow that." He reached down and picked up the beautiful CZ pistol with the anodized orange grips, racked the slide, and put a round in each of the man's eyes. The 9mm slugs bounced around inside the alloy-reinforced cranial shell doing irreparable, total damage to the brain.

"This is a damn nice pistol," Jason said to the man standing by Jacob. He popped the magazine out and cleared the chamber before setting it gently on the ground. No point tossing around something that nice on a concrete floor.

"Thanks for being careful with it. I'm sort of partial to it."

"You okay?" Jason asked Jacob, walking up and looking him over.

"I will be," Jacob said. "Got in a bit over my head there...thanks." The last word sounded like it was a real struggle to get out.

"We're just lucky he had crap hardware installed," Jason said. "I've fought the Viper one-on-one, and even at half that guy's size, she was a handful.

"You've *actually* fought Carolyn Whitney? Is there any footage of that?" Avelar asked, perking up.

"Okay, so who are you really, Avelar?" Jacob asked. "I've seen One World types commit suicide before betraying Jansen. You with NIS?" Avelar laughed at that as if it was the funniest thing he'd ever heard.

"No, I'm not NIS, but you're right, I'm not exactly your typical One World recruit, either," he said. "My name really *is* Ricardo Avelar. We've also already talked once before."

"The voice on the ship," Jacob said. "You were the one with the warning."

"We don't have time for this," Jason said. "Bring him with us. Don't forget that nice pistol he carried."

"Thank you," Avelar said.

"784, report." Jason was already walking off.

"*The One World forces have retreated to the far side of the operations center away from this building. The local forces have followed them and have taken out approximately seventy-six percent of their total numbers while losing only five percent of their own*," the battlesynth said. "*It looks to be coming to a quick close, Captain.*"

"Sully, do you see any place for a dust-off within a klick or two?" Jason asked.

"*There are two large buildings directly south of you. I can drop in behind the last one*," Sully said.

"Moving now. 784, get your metal ass down here! Jacob, police the body of your buddy over there. Go ahead and give the corpse a couple of good whacks if it'll make you feel better. Ricardo Avelar, you're walking with me."

Jacob gave his father a flat, unfriendly look before going and rooting through the pockets of Hodges. The stink of burning electronics and cooking flesh made him gag as he pulled a couple of data cards and a standard Fleet crypto key out. He took a long look at the face, now stuck in a rictus of pain and horror.

Jacob had been cocky after besting that Ull. He assumed he was the top of the heap when it came to human fighters. That hubris had almost cost him his life. Had he fought with more skill and care, could he have beaten Hodges?

The lesson to learn was there was always a bigger, badder dog than you. He was lucky there was an even *badder* dog on his side who stepped in to save his dumb ass. Watching his father come raging in and kill Hodges for the threat of killing him broke something loose inside Jacob.

No matter how shitty he'd been towards the man, Jason was still willing to go to war and put it all on the line to protect him, risking his own life without hesitation. You didn't do that for someone you just sort of cared about or felt obligated to. That had to come from the heart. The entire Omega Force crew cared about him, too. In the heat of the moment, he felt like he needed to take a hard look at the grudges he held.

"Hey, dipshit! You coming, or are you losing another fight to that guy?" Crusher shouted through the doorway, killing the introspective moment.

"Or maybe they're actually the assholes everyone says they are," Jacob sighed, turning and collecting his gear before shuffling out the door, holding his injured side.

"Okay, Avelar...talk."

The flight up to the *Devil's Fortune* had been uneventful but long. Sully and Kage decided not to tempt fate and had flown far south through the normal air traffic before requesting an orbital ascent. That kept them well out of range and off the sensors of that Aracorian cruiser still sitting there, watching its people get chewed up by the locals.

The fact Hodges and Avelar weren't coming back would put the captain in a bit of a bind. Would he stay and try to recover his principles or abandon Koliss-2 and face Jansen's wrath? If they stayed, it would give them a little bit more time to plan their next moves.

They pulled Avelar into the plush conference room after they'd searched him and scanned for trackers. He was released out of his restraints, given a decent meal, and allowed to collect his thoughts while 784 stood watch. After an hour, everyone filed in to see what useful intel he might have or if he could be used as a bargaining chip with the cruiser's captain.

"It's actually Special Agent Avelar, of the United States Secret

JOSHUA DALZELLE

Service. I can't tell you what a pleasure it is to finally meet you, Captain Burke."

"Okay...I didn't expect that," Jason admitted. "What the hell is a Secret Service agent doing out here? Looking for counterfeit dollars?"

"That is one of our functions on the investigative side, yes," Avelar said. "But my job was primarily counterterrorism...at first. I have been on a deep-cover assignment for the last four and a half years, reporting directly to the president and his cabinet."

"Undercover within One World?" Jacob asked.

"No. But we'll get to that, I promise," Avelar said. "Some things are about to come to light that will...disturb some of you."

"I'm disturbed by how boring this already is," Crusher mumbled.

"It will get better soon, I promise, Guardian Archon." Crusher just glowered at the use of his formal title.

"Showing off your security clearance won't impress too many here. Lots of people know who Crusher really is," Jason said. "Come on, let's get to it."

"Sorry, Captain," Avelar said. "I was placed undercover within the NIS because it was suspected the service was a hotbed of One World sympathizers. No offense, Agent Murphy."

"It's not exactly a secret." Murph shrugged. "From what I gathered, there was some effort to recruit young agents by appealing to their egos. Everyone secretly wants to believe they're James Bond, and a secret organization working behind the scenes plays into the fantasy. By the time they realize what they've done, they're in too deep."

"Before this goes any further, you have any way to support your claims?" Jacob asked. "I assume you're not still carrying your service badge."

"Of course not. I can give you a slip-com address that will put you in touch with my handler. From there, we will be routed until we get to someone you're sure to recognize who can vouch for me," Avelar said.

"Kage can help set that up," Jason said. "But why are you being so overly helpful? Jacob tells me you contacted them when they were on this base before, so you obviously want something from this Scout

Fleet team in exchange for whatever information you have. What is it?"

"Fair enough. I think Lieutenant Brown and his team have a chance to put an end to my assignment. Margaret Jansen is exposed and vulnerable right now, but she would need to be taken out properly. An internal assassination from within the organization—even by someone later found out to be an undercover operative, namely me—wouldn't chop the head off the snake. They would retool, and they have contingencies in place to replace Jansen if the worse were to happen.

"But if one of Marcus Webb's teams was to take her captive or kill her in a surgical strike, that would be something else entirely. The reason is that Jansen isn't really in charge of One World. In fact, One World is little more than a marketing tool right now to keep the recruits within other organizations coming into the fold. They don't really exist other than as a name whispered in dark corridors. The real power of this organization is the Office of Special Operations."

Everyone at the table sat in stunned silence for a moment. Finding out One World was just some clever branding and there was an altogether different and unknown shadowy organization pulling the strings was disquieting. That Avelar seemed to be intimating they had a much larger reach than what the assumptive power of One World had was also a concern.

"Com node is set up down here," Kage said. "Just punch in the address at your station." Avelar leaned forward and entered the slip-com node address from memory before grabbing his coffee mug and leaning back again.

"This really is excellent," he said, raising the mug to Jason. "You'll be able to leave the exciting but growth-limited mercenary business soon and retire a very wealthy man. Assuming you want to, of course."

"Seems your intel on our little operation is thorough," Jason said sourly.

"I've been trusted with a high level of access," Avelar said. "The things I know aren't commonly passed around among the various agencies."

"Thank you for contacting Turner Merchant Marine Logistics and Outfitting. How may I route your inquiry, sir?" a young human woman on the main wall display asked. She wore a blue Polo shirt, headset, and looked like she sat in a cubicle.

"Hello, miss," Avelar said. "My name is Cyril Christos. I believe I had an appointment?"

"Just let me look here," the woman made some pretense of clicking around on her computer for a few seconds. "Ah! Mr. Christos. I will route you directly. Have a nice day."

The process was repeated a mind-numbing seven more times, each person Avelar connecting to asking a series of specific questions designed to determine if he was under duress or being coerced. By the time the screen flickered and the scene shifted again, most of the people in the room were half-asleep. When the face of a middle-aged man appeared, looking like he'd been woken up, all of the Scout Fleet personnel snapped upright in their seats.

"Good evening, Mr. President," Avelar said. "I apologize—"

"It's night here, actually," the president said. "I see you've made some friends, Agent Avelar. Is this a— Holy shit! Is that actually Jason Burke I'm looking at?"

"Yes, sir," Jason said. "I'm afraid you have me at a loss. The last US president I knew of was Hightower."

"She's the one who briefed me on your involvement in bringing the Cridal to our rescue that day. My name is Weinhaus, and you have a supporter in me, son. If you'd like, we can see about getting things smoothed over so you can come back to Earth again."

"Very generous of you, Mr. President," Jason said. "But, for right now, we were just trying to verify the identity of your wayward agent here."

A message popped up on the glass table surface in front of Jason. It was from Kage.

Voice pattern and facial recognition a match to Earth media. Computer detects no manipulation. I'm confident this is who he says he is.

Jason nodded his thanks to his code slicer as Avelar took back control of the conference.

"This has to do with the One World issue, sir," he said. "We just had a gunfight with One World units at a base on Koliss-2."

"Who the hell is *we?*" Weinhaus demanded. "Aren't you supposed to be with One World right now?"

"The situation is fluid, sir," Avelar said smoothly. "I was sent by Jansen to recover a set of crypto traps she left secured on their unused base. By the time I got here aboard one of their cruisers, a Scout Fleet team had already been here and got a hold of the units. In the resulting firefight, I was able to escape with the Scout Fleet team in a way that will lead Jansen to assume I'm probably dead."

"And we want this?"

"Yes, sir. It gives me back the freedom of movement I need and, if the crypto traps hold what I think they do, the tools we'll need to start pulling apart the entire operation for good."

"Who is in charge of the Scout Fleet team?" Weinhaus asked.

"I am, sir," Jacob answered. "Lieutenant Jacob Brown, Scout Team Obsidian, sir."

"You're executing this operation on Captain Webb's orders?"

"Not exactly, sir," Jacob said, swallowing. "We're...sort of a rogue element right now. We captured information from a One World traitor we thought we could exploit to get to Jansen, but we didn't trust that our chain of command wasn't compromised already. Webb hasn't officially disavowed us yet, but I expect that will happen soon."

"Oh, dear Christ," Weinhaus said, rubbing his eyes. "Avelar, you've teamed up with a burned spec ops unit to take on Jansen?"

"And a notorious mercenary unit led by one of Earth's most wanted men who also has Galvetic royalty in it, sir," Avelar said unhelpfully. "So, there could be some additional political fallout."

"I... Whatever," Weinhaus said. "I don't want to know. What's the timeframe we're looking at, Agent Avelar? Things are happening legislatively here, and there are global political ramifications to the decisions being made. The sooner we can expose this triad, the better."

"It'll be soon or not at all, Mr. President," Avelar promised.

The channel closed without prompting, causing Jason to look at Kage.

"Wasn't our end. It was manually killed on the other side."

"You get used to that," Avelar said. "The president or his cabinet members who are read-in on this operation try to keep it short. Less chance of being overheard."

"Okay...so you're you," Jason said. "Now, give us the rundown."

"Margaret Jansen is currently on the planet Plaki Prime," Avelar said. "She has a small hold-out base there from which she runs the One World side of an operation we call the Triad. One of the second components is the OSO, and we've yet to discover who the third party is, but we're guessing it's someone major.

"Jansen has a small defense force on Plaki while the bulk of her military power is spread out throughout the Orion Arm. She's paranoid and as afraid of her own people as she is of the Earth governments hunting her. Hodges, the man Captain Burke beat to death—"

"I actually shot him in both eyes. It was pretty cool."

"—was a large part of her personal security. His cybernetic enhancements were done illegally on some planet where she had connections that could perform the procedure. She relied on him completely, so when she sent him to babysit me, it meant either she was on to me and was going to have me killed, or the crypto traps you found were of critical value to her. Since Hodges never made a move to kill me even when we were being overrun, I can only assume it was the latter."

"So, there's a lot of information you're still missing as well," Jacob said.

"Of course," Avelar admitted. "If I had this all buttoned up, I'd have called in the cavalry months ago and gone home already. But I think we're very close. Those crypto traps are the last key."

"What do you think is on them?" Murph asked. "What would she want to hide in a secret subbasement vault on a planet erased from Fleet navigation charts?"

"My best guess? Her blackmail material on all the power players,"

Avelar said. "She's managed to stay in power long after her usefulness had run out. Earth didn't put much effort into tracking her down after her failed military coup with the Terranovus fleet, either. This indicates she has serious dirt on the people who would have the political juice to protect her."

"What about her Ull contingent?" Jason asked. "Last time I tangled with her, we had to deal with those bastards, too."

"All but gone," Avelar said. "There is a small group of non-combatant Ull still on Plaki Prime. They still want that jump drive technology, but they're beginning to see Jansen isn't going to give it to them. There are maybe six or seven of them there, none of them soldiers or even particularly brave. If the shooting starts, they'll run."

"How *lightly defended* are we talking here?" Jason asked.

"Some automated gun emplacements I know how to deactivate, and less than two dozen security troopers." Avelar shrugged. "Like I said, she's hiding and relied on Hodges to keep her safe. Now, there is one issue with her preparations we will need to deal with. The woman has escape vectors built in *everywhere*. I'm talking tunnels, slip-space capable ships in hidden hangars, safe houses all over the damn planet. If we can't take her by surprise, and she gets any sort of warning, she'll be in the wind. I have no idea about the details for most of it, so don't bother asking."

"So, maybe the answer isn't brute force," Jacob said. "Your cover isn't blown yet, is it?"

"I already don't like where this is going," Jason said.

"Think about it. OSO goons already tried to grab me once," Jacob said. "Avelar comes back with me in restraints, says he found me unconscious next to a dead Hodges, and then we can get close without her rabbiting."

"Your plan relies on the assumption Margaret Jansen is a moron. I assure you, she is not," Avelar said. "If I came back with you in restraints and Hodges missing, and her cruiser captain reporting I never came back, she wouldn't let us get within a hundred meters of her. We'd be separated and imprisoned while her people extracted the truth from us. You would never see her face-to-face."

"I hate giving up on a perfectly good plan just because it won't work," Jacob sighed, wincing.

When they'd come aboard the *Devil's Fortune*, he'd been taken straight to the infirmary where Mettler and Doc had worked on his injuries from the fight with Hodges. Doc had used the advanced equipment aboard to set and bond the broken bones, and then gave him a booster of nanobots instructed to go to work on any soft tissue damage. Within an hour, Jacob had gone from being in agony to just being merely uncomfortable.

"We're on the clock here, so we need to figure this out fast," Jason said. "Once that cruiser leaves, we'll have a harder time getting close to her. It's already reported back it's lost people, but once they leave, we'll know they gave up and likely found Hodges but not Avelar. Jansen will be on high alert after that."

"They'll stick around for a few more days and sift through the rubble," Avelar said. "Assuming they can get the locals under control. The captain won't want to face Jansen with a big pile of unknowns like that. He'll be thorough, and he has the manpower to search the construction area of the base where the fighting was."

"Let's take a pause here, get some rest, and then decide within the next twelve hours what we're going to do," Jason said before turning to Jacob. "If that's okay with your team?"

"Not a bad idea to stand down for a hot minute and make a plan when we're calm and rested," Jacob said. "We also should probably let Captain Webb know what's been happening here."

"I'll take care of that," Doc said. "The last I heard, he was taking his ship to Earth, so he'll probably either still be there or on the way back to Terranovus or Olympus."

"Meet back here in ten hours then," Jason said. "Avelar, we'll get you some proper guest quarters since I think you've passed the trust test. The brig in this ship isn't very comfortable, even as far as brigs go."

"Much appreciated, Captain Burke," Avelar said.

Everybody trudged out of the conference room, exhausted. It had been a long ground op, and even the people who stayed aboard the ship felt the strain.

Jacob went straight back to his quarters and gingerly stretched out on the rack, not even bothering to take his boots off. Thanks in part to the narcotics Doc had given him, he was sound asleep by the time the lights automatically dimmed from his lack of movement.

✦

25

"A secret base on a hidden planet. Incredible."

Webb stood on the bridge of the UES *Kentucky*, already in the Koliss System by the time the *Devil's Fortune* had messaged him with an updated brief. After his meeting on Earth, and the dead-end he ran into there, he'd set course directly for Koliss-2 to see firsthand what One World had been up to out there.

"The fact this system was erased from our charts and replaced with a no-go hazard zone is...troubling," Captain Duncan said.

The ship's CO had been promoted from Commander last year and had been asked to stay on with the NAVSOC command and control ship even though his rank would have entitled him to a more prestigious command within the regular fleet. He'd been a solid officer and a trustworthy confidant for Webb, so he would cynically hold onto him for as long as he could.

"It suggests this conspiracy runs a little deeper than just recruiting radicals in the training centers," Webb agreed. "Navigational charts starships rely on are sacred documents only a few people have the power to change at will. Once this gets out, captains will no longer be able to trust the data they're getting from Fleet Ops. They won't be willing to put their crew or ship in danger. Bad, bad precedent to set."

The *Kentucky* was a highly specialized ship made to look like a bulk freighter of indeterminate origin but, in reality, she was one of the most advanced warships in the Navy. Her primary mission was a command and control platform that allowed Webb to run the entirety of NAVSOC operations from a mobile platform, but she was also armed and armored to a degree that made her more than a match for most ships up to a destroyer class.

Right now, Webb had Captain Duncan moving the ship into position within the holding orbits over Koliss-2 so they had a down-firing solution on the One World cruiser. The ship had been flying shuttles to and from the surface base, and the *Kentucky*'s optics showed they were on the ground looking for something. Or someone. They'd been lining bodies up in one of the open grassy areas and dividing them up by species.

"The ship we've identified as the *Devil's Fortune* is sitting in orbit over the third moon, sir," a lieutenant called from a sensor station. "She has what looks like a small strike craft anchored to her dorsal hull."

"Which means the *Phoenix* is either in the hangar or flying around here someplace," Webb said. "God only knows what those lunatics are up to."

"Speak of the devil," Duncan said, accepting a tablet from an ensign. "Literally. The *Devil's Fortune* has just sent a slip-com channel request. It's priority tagged as normal traffic."

"I'll take it in my office," Webb said, walking towards the back of the bridge where there was an open hatchway into a small office he used while aboard.

"Sir," Jacob Brown said as the image resolved. "I'm here with Jason Burke and Alonso Murphy as well."

"Relax, Lieutenant, this isn't being recorded," Webb said. "What's going on?"

"We've pulled out a deep-cover operative working within the One World power structure. He's been filling in the blanks for us and helping us get a plan of attack together to hit Jansen. We even now know where she is," Jacob said.

"Deep cover from whom? NIS?" Webb asked.

"The US Secret Service, under the direction of the president personally, if you can believe that," Jacob said. "We've already cleared him. Woke the president up, and he vouched for him."

"You woke the fucking president of the United States up to vouch for an operative?" Webb asked, his eyes bulging.

"Not our idea, sir. Anyway, it's all good. We found out she's keeping a low profile and is under-protected right now. We're hashing out the details now, but the agent thinks we can take Jansen and expose the people behind the OSO and One World at the same time."

"You working with an operative under presidential orders almost puts you back on the legal side of things, Brown...but don't think you're off the hook with me," Webb said.

"Nor are *you* off the hook with *me*," Jason Burke's voice said from somewhere in the room. Webb suppressed a shudder at that and pressed on.

"What about this cruiser we're shadowing?"

"What?" Jacob asked. "You're here? In this system?"

"That's right." Webb smiled. "The *Kentucky* is in a high orbit, looking downhill at the Aracorian cruiser you told us belonged to One World. They're moving a lot of people down and back from that base."

"Looking for the operative, no doubt," Jacob said. "He took Elton Hollick's place in Jansen's organization. They'll need to at least recover his body before going back to her."

"How pissy will the locals get if we shoot it down?" Webb asked.

"I wouldn't do that," Jason said. "You could disable it if you think you can hit it clean and get away. If you tumble it out of orbit, as low as it is, you're risking a lot of civilian lives below. Morality aside, the ConFed *will* show up for something like that."

"I'll see what I can do," Webb said. "We have enough Marines onboard right now we could try a boarding action. Maybe."

"If you even just keep them tied up here so they can't get back, that would help," Jason said. "From what this Secret Service guy is saying, the One World fleet is spread around the area. This one was the only ship Jansen had except for her private frigate."

"Why is that?"

"Paranoid," Jacob answered. "She's as afraid of her own people taking a shot at her as she is of you or the NIS finding her."

"She's not wrong," Webb said. "I only worked for her for three months, and I thought about shooting her at least four different times. We'll try and keep the cruiser pinned down here. Go do what you have to do, Lieutenant."

"Aye-aye, sir."

"Murph, I'm about to tell you to do something you're not going to like," Jacob said once the channel to the *Kentucky* closed.

"I haven't liked anything you've ordered me to do since I've met you, so this shouldn't be a stretch," Murph said.

"You're not coming with me."

"What the fuck are you talking about?" Murph asked

"I talked it over with Avelar last night, and then with my father before you walked in," Jacob said, turning to Jason. "Maybe you can explain it better."

"I can't risk taking the *Devil* into an unknown situation like Jansen's stronghold no matter how lax Avelar says the security is," Jason said. "I'm ordering my crew to take her back to S'Tora to keep the cargo she's carrying safe and let Kage and Cas continue their work on it. I'm taking the *Phoenix* and loading up Crusher, Jacob, and 784 to go get Jansen."

"Any reason why we're being left behind so you can run wild with these mercs?" Murph asked stiffly.

"Because, win or lose, I'm either dead or in prison. I'll be turning myself in after this operation regardless whether Jansen slips away or not," Jacob said. "Omega Force has promised to give you shelter, and you have access to Obsidian's funds. I want you to fix the ship up, or buy a new one, and figure out a new life that doesn't include sitting in Red Cliff."

"We all made this choice, Lieutenant," Murph said. "It's not right, what you're doing."

"Probably not," Jacob said, "but I'll end my stint as team leader as I started it, with no fucking clue what I'm doing. Avelar thinks a smaller unit will have an easier time getting in, so you would likely be asked to stay on the ship, anyway. This just makes more sense. I don't want you guys killed or rotting in a military prison because I made a grave miscalculation after we got Hollick. Hell, you may still be able to go back to the NIS once this has calmed down."

"We could find a use for MG and Mettler," Jason said. "They wouldn't just be sitting around doing nothing."

"Not my ship, so I can't force myself aboard," Murph said finally, still looking stiff and angry. "Might I make a suggestion before we part ways?"

"Of course."

"Leave now. Before the others wake up. Mettler might be a professional about this, but MG is going to lose his shit."

"That was the plan," Jacob said, looking away. "Avelar and Crusher are already prepping for departure."

"Well then," Murph said, standing and knocking his chair over. "Good luck."

He stormed out of the com room without looking back. Jacob blew out a long breath through pressed lips, feeling like an absolute shitbag officer.

"You're doing the right thing," Jason said. "Even if it doesn't feel like it. We're going to be hitting this place hard and fast. We need Avelar to get in but, after that, your normal human crew will be a liability. Even as good as you are, you'll be hard-pressed to keep up once Crusher, me, and 784 are in action."

"You ever have to make choices like this when you were in?" Jacob asked.

"I was never an officer," Jason said. "I was only a staff sergeant when I got out, so my decisions didn't have quite the reach yours will.

You're also being a stand-up man by admitting you were wrong and trying to protect your men from that mistake.

"I wasn't kidding when I said what this ship is carrying is the most precious and dangerous thing in the known galaxy. I can't, and won't, put it at unnecessary risk, and that includes the risk of it falling into enemy hands. It's why I needed the *Phoenix* back. I can't take this ship out to the borderlands to try and hunt down Lucky. It sticks out like a sore thumb in a place like that, and we'd be fighting off every pirate from here to the Avarian Empire. We have a good plan. It's worth the hurt feelings to execute it and save your team...and mine."

"I appreciate you doing this," Jacob said. Gratitude was a new emotion when attached to his father, so he rolled it around in his head for a moment, seeing how it felt. "If I had known Lucky was in trouble, I'd have never taken the *Phoenix*. I think, at first, I looked at it almost like a funny prank when Cas let me aboard."

"You're a lot more advanced than I was," Jason said. "When I was younger, I only stole a neighbor's dirt bike not an unlicensed interstellar warship."

"We'd better bounce before the other two wake up. I don't need another scene like the one with Murph, and I really don't want to have to fight MG in your hangar bay."

"Let's roll," Jason said, smiling.

"What're you so excited about?" Jacob asked as they stepped out into the corridor.

"You're not?" Jason asked. "This is always the best part, right when a mission kicks off. It's the excitement that's kept us in the game all these years."

"Yeah. That and the fact you look like you're only a year or two older than me," Jacob griped. "Another mission like this one and, pretty soon, people will think I'm *your* father."

"You need to get yourself a brilliant outlaw geneticist on your crew so he can tinker with your aging process like I did," Jason said. "It's just too bad he hasn't found a way to make Crusher any smarter."

26
────────

"We still don't know the extent of the damage. The *Truxton* is still trying to account for all the bodies. Goddamn local clans opened fire on our people as soon as they landed."

Margaret Jansen paced her office, talking to someone over a slip-com node. Annoyingly, the man still insisted on disguising his voice. As if she didn't already know who he was.

"And the crypto traps?" the voice asked.

"Buried beneath the rubble of the ops center in a hidden vault," she said. "There's no reason to believe they were compromised."

"That was a foolish, dangerous risk you took storing them there. What the hell were you thinking?"

"I was thinking it would be smart to have copies of the only thing keeping you from coming at me full force in a place you didn't know about," Jansen said. "Don't pretend you haven't thought about pruning the tree a bit now that the OSO is up and running."

"That's ridiculous talk, Margaret, and beneath you. There will always be a place for you here. Now that we're leaving Terranovus, it won't be long before it will be safe to bring you back in. How are the Ull doing?"

"They're impatient and increasingly angry we haven't handed over the jump drive," she said. "Honestly, just give them the damn thing. We don't need it anymore, and they haven't a snowball's chance in hell of being able to reverse engineer that heap of trash."

"Not my choice to make. I actually don't know where the *Traveler* wreckage is currently. It was moved since the last time I was on Earth. It might have been taken out to the Ceres Vault. Who the hell knows at this point? Just keep pushing the Ull back until we can finally get rid of them."

"I won't miss them," Jansen said. "Disgusting, arrogant creatures."

"It's almost over, Margaret. Once the last dominos fall on Earth, we'll be able to fulfill our obligation to—" the audio cut off with a hiss of static.

"You there?" she asked. "Computer, check connections. Computer? What the hell?"

She stormed out of her office, intent on ripping a new ass into her tech supervisor, but the bullpen was empty. An eerie silence hung over the room as not even the machines made their normal hisses and beeps.

"What the hell?" she said again, now hesitant. Was this some sort of prank?

She walked out into the office area, and that's when she saw the blood. Lots of it. The carpets were soaked, and she could see it was on the walls and even the ceiling the farther out of her office she walked. She reached into her suit jacket and pulled out a small pistol, the weight of the puny weapon offering her no comfort. She desperately wanted Hodges to be there with her. This was his area of expertise. Direct action was not something she was comfortable with.

After trying multiple com stations in the office, she realized the entire network was down, so there would be no calling outside for help. There was also only one set of doors leading out of the bullpen, so if she wanted to make it outside to escape, she would need to go through them. She almost wished there were the sounds of a struggle or screaming so she could figure out which places to avoid.

"The tunnel!" she exclaimed, feeling foolish for not thinking of her emergency escape route first.

She ran into her office, closing and locking the door behind her. She went to the middle of the office and pulled up the corner area rug, exposing a recessed handle and keypad. Under the rug, and attached to it, was a steel hatch. After she went through and closed it, the rug would fall back into place and buy her a few more minutes depending on how good the team was that came after her.

She punched the code in, saw the green light flash, but there was no comforting *thunk* of the bolts retracting. Margaret yanked on the handle, but the hatch wouldn't budge. She tried the code twice more, each time the green light flashing to indicate the code had been accepted, but the actuators for the locks never engaged so she could open the damn thing. How could someone have come inside and sabotaged it without her knowing?

"Guess it's the front door," she whispered, now feeling a level of fear she hadn't experienced in many years. With shaking hands, she opened the safe behind her desk and pulled out a plasma carbine, a weapon she had a passing familiarity with. Steeling herself, she went back out into the bullpen and through the double doors on the other side.

If the blood in the office area had been disturbing, then the sight that met her when she walked out into the common area just beyond was nothing short of horrific. The bodies of not only her office staff but everyone who would have been in the admin building were piled up in a bloody heap right in the middle.

The dozen or so corpses all had their throats cut, and a grotesque slick spread in all directions. The smell was overpowering, and her mind absently noted there was also the body of an Ull in the pile. It looked like the attaché that was always hanging around the building.

"Hello, Margaret," a familiar voice said. Her head whipped around, and Hodges stood there, unarmed and his hands at his side.

Her mind raced, and she started to bring her weapon up. Had

Hodges killed all these people? Why? Why wasn't there any blood on him? How did he do it without her hearing?

"How are you here?" she asked. When he walked a step towards her, she yanked her weapon up. "Stay back!"

"Margaret, you're stressed. You need to put the weapon down," Hodges said. His voice sounded...off. No, that wasn't right. His voice was fine, but his tone and language were all wrong. Hodges didn't speak like a host on public radio.

"I said to *stay back!*" she shouted at not-Hodges. "What are you? Some sort of shape-shifting alien?"

"That's just silly, Margaret," not-Hodges said. "There's no such thing as shapeshifters, and you know it. You're just having a panic reaction to seeing your colleagues like this. It's understandable. Put the weapon down, and I'll explain it all to you."

"Why did you do this?" she asked, lowering her weapon. It wasn't that she particularly cared about the lives of her people other than the massive inconvenience it caused. What it did was tell her that not-Hodges would spill blood—a *lot* of blood—for no other reason than convenience.

"I didn't do this." Not-Hodges gestured to the pile. "You did, Margaret. Your actions have brought me here."

"You're going to kill me?"

"Of course. But first, you need to see something."

Margaret tried to raise the gun to fire, but *something* seemed to shoot out of not-Hodges, and there was a searing pain in her right hand. She dropped the weapon and looked down, seeing her right hand was a raw mess of exposed muscle and bone, all but one finger missing.

When she looked up, not-Hodges was mere inches away. She'd not even heard him move. Up close, her panicked, hyperactive brain took in some subtle details. There were some missing scars, and the proportions were slightly off.

This Hodges was from some years ago. A new pain in her right arm snapped her back into the moment, and she looked down, seeing that not-Hodges had applied a makeshift tourniquet with what looked like electrical wiring.

"I can't have you bleeding out just yet, Margaret," not-Hodges said softly. "I have to show you something. Come along."

He led her back into the office area and sat her in a seat facing the large wall monitor she used for staff meetings. She didn't resist. Whatever this thing was, she knew there was no way to escape. The part of her brain that refused to give up clung to the hope the crew of her personal ship would notice the drop in communications and send a rapid response team to investigate.

"That's good," not-Hodges said. "Just watch this, and then it will be over." A video began playing on the monitor, and a familiar face filled the screen. This time, there was no voice modulation, unlike when she'd spoken to the man not ten minutes ago.

"Hello, Margaret," he said sadly. "I'm sorry it's come to this, I really am. I just want you to know it's not personal. We had our differences in the beginning, but I came to respect your tenacity and grit.

"The problem is that, now, you're a liability to the group. One World has served its purpose, now it's time for it to move aside. We've had discussions, and we've agreed you won't see reason and take a lesser role in the organization, and there's too great a risk of you pulling a power play later on. Just realize even this is a compliment to your effectiveness."

The video winked out and, still, no cavalry had come charging to the rescue. A strange calm came over her as she realized what was coming was inevitable.

"The contract states I am to make it painless if you so desire," her captor said. "If you would feel better putting up a fight, you may, but it will only prolong your suffering."

"What are you? Show me that much before...it...happens," she said.

Not-Hodges shimmered and winked out of existence, replaced by a sleek, black...*something* underneath. It must have been some sort of kill-bot with holographic generators that let it mimic a person. The illusions weren't perfect, but they were enough to throw her off and let it get close.

"You're sentient?" she asked. "Some sort of new synth, maybe?"

"Some sort," it agreed, walking forward. Without warning or preamble, it deployed a spike from its forearm and shoved it into her head. There was a bright flash, and the last thought that Margaret Jansen had was of her home in Georgia.

"I'm not seeing Jansen's frigate on sensors," Avelar said.

"Does she ever deploy it without her being aboard?" Jacob asked.

"I've never seen it happen," Avelar said. "Doesn't mean she hasn't, though. On the surface, there's not a lot I'm privy to she doesn't explicitly tell me."

Jason frowned but kept the *Phoenix*'s weapon systems armed and ready. They'd meshed-in close to Plaki Prime, ready to engage Jansen's ship in a surprise attack. When they'd arrived, however, the ship was nowhere to be found. A deep scan with the active sensors accounted for all the traffic in the system, with no sign of a frigate-class vessel.

"Let's push ahead with the plan," he said. "We're already here and if she's on the planet with her ship missing, all the better."

He put the *Phoenix* into a standard orbital approach and requested a landing clearance that would let him put down in the open area Avelar had indicated on a map of the continent. It was a remote, wilderness area the agent swore would give them a backdoor into Jansen's compound. He was confident 784 would be able to overcome any security provisions they ran into that he wasn't aware of.

"This is strange. All coms seem to be down at the base," Avelar said. "I'm not even getting the nav beacon for shuttle landings."

"That should be broadcasting constantly if it's an approved airfield," Jason said. "Crusher, what do the sensors say?"

"Buildings all look like they have power," Crusher said from the sensor station. "Nothing moving around on the ground the optics can see. Doesn't look suspicious, just not busy."

"There's not a lot of people at this compound," Avelar said. "Most are at the main base farther south, but there should still be people and vehicles moving about."

With a growing sense of unease, Jason circled and descended, keeping just out of the line of sight of the compound. Jansen knew what his ship looked like so he didn't need to advertise they were coming before they even walked off the ramp.

The plan was simple, yet elegant. Avelar wanted to take advantage of Jansen's low-profile, hiding-in-plain-sight approach to security at the smaller compound along with one of her many escape plans to sneak up on her within her inner sanctum, bypassing security completely. Once they landed, and Jason secured the ship, the four biotics geared up while 784 went outside and looked around.

"Seems all clear," he said as the others joined him on the ground. "According to Agent Avelar's directions, we are approximately six kilometers from the tunnel entrance."

"Let's get to it," Jason said, taking off at a steady, ground-eating run the others could easily keep up with.

He looked back to make sure Jacob was with him, and then pressed on. His son was still nursing several serious injuries from his fight with Hodges, and Avelar was just a normal human, so he kept having to rein himself in and keep his impatience in check.

Thanks to the brutal terrain and their inability to take a direct route, it was nearly two hours later when they reached an overgrown, unassuming concrete structure with a steel security door that looked like it could have belonged to a public utility company. Avelar nodded, and 784 walked up, taking multiple readings of the door, and scanning it in every wavelength available to him.

Satisfied there were only the mechanical locks to contend with, he reared back and kicked the door. He overestimated the strength needed, however, so instead of breaking down the door, he'd actually just kicked a hole through the steel plating.

"Damn," Jacob said, looking through the hole. "That's half-inch plate you just booted through."

"I will try again," 784 said, getting ready to kick it again.

"Easy there, Baby Huey," Jason said, stepping in the way. "Let's try a little finesse here."

"This coming from you?" Crusher snorted.

Jason ignored him and reached through the battlesynth foot-sized hole and felt around for the lock release. It was a large, mechanical quarter-turn lever that would pull all the locking bolts in simultaneously. When he pulled the lever, it moved smoothly and silently. Apparently, Jansen kept up with the maintenance of her escape plans.

"Clever," Jacob said. "Can only be opened from the inside, unassuming, and works even if they kill all the power or use a tight-beam EMP."

"It also doesn't draw attention like a biometric reader or keypad would," Avelar said.

"No cameras?" Jason asked.

"Not tied into the compound system," Avelar said. "There's a closed-loop circuit with the monitor right inside the door here."

"What's this?" Crusher asked, pointing to a hole that had been neatly punched through the concrete near the locking mechanism. It looked recent and couldn't be seen from the outside because of the overgrowth.

"Vent hole?" Jason asked. "Maybe to make sure it doesn't get stuck because of a vacuum?"

"That looks like it was just done within the last few days," Avelar said. "So, I wouldn't have been around to see what was going on."

The team moved into the tunnel and found it actually wasn't dark, just very dimly-lit.

"What was the rest of this plan?" Jason asked. "She comes out here and goes for a hike in the woods?"

"This plan required a pickup from her ship," Avelar said. "There's a clearing up on a hilltop to the northeast. I'd have directed you there, but the *Phoenix* would have been too exposed and too close to the base."

The tunnel ran a full half a kilometer before terminating in a stairwell that went up to another door, this one laying horizontal and presumably set into a floor. Avelar climbed the steps first and inspected the door. There were a few stifled curses, and then the light of his flashlight bouncing around as he took a closer look.

"Problem," he whispered. "This door has been tampered with. From this side."

"How so?" Jason asked, keeping his voice down in case Jansen sat right above them.

"This side has a shielded, hardened electrical lock system with a keypad recessed into the floor. The wires going to all the solenoids that would pull the bolts back have been cut, disabling the door."

"Someone wanting to make sure she couldn't leave through here," Jason said, looking back down the tunnel and thinking of the perfectly bored hole near the handle of the other door. "Can you force it open?"

"Each bolt will need to be pulled back manually," Avelar said. "There are twelve."

"Will they remain open once pulled?" 784 asked.

"They should. They're not spring-loaded. Power would need to be applied to lock them back in place."

"Please, step aside," the battlesynth said. "And, everyone, ready yourselves."

784 climbed the stairs and, moving so fast his hands were a blur, pulled all the locking bolts and shoved the door up and out of the way. He switched to combat mode and fired his repulsors, flying into the room above while the others sprinted up the stairs.

"Clear," 784 said. "My sensors aren't picking up anybody in the vicinity."

"Abandoned?" Jacob asked, sounding defeated.

"Not quite," Crusher said. "Take a deep whiff."

"Dead bodies," Jason said, sniffing. "Come on."

They moved cautiously out into the area outside the lavishly appointed office. Once they came around the cubicle walls and the front desk, Jacob just let his weapon drop and let out a huge sigh.

"Fuck," he said, pointing at a very dead Margaret Jansen sitting in a chair, her open eyes staring at the wall monitor ahead of her.

"All this blood isn't from her," Jason said. "784, check out there."

"Someone blew her hand off." Avelar sounded clinically detached as he inspected the corpse. "Then it was wrapped with wire to stop the bleeding. The death blow was something piercing the skull here. No other injuries."

"Huge pile of human bodies in there," Crusher said, pointing a thumb behind him as he and 784 walked back in. "All throats cut and one Ull decapitated."

"What in the fuck happened here?" Jacob asked, awestruck. "There's no real sign of a battle or any marks from weapons fire. How did a team come in here and kill everyone like this?"

"Either way, it's over," Jason said.

"Not quite yet, Captain," Avelar said. "We still need to recover the physical encryption keys to fully unlock those crypto traps, and I'd like to take a look at who our mysterious assassin is."

"There are cameras in this place?" Crusher asked.

"Oh, yes," Avelar said. "Jansen was nothing if not completely paranoid. Rightfully so, it would seem."

27

"Here's the vault," Jacob said. "You think you can get it open without ruining the contents?"

"Easily," 784 said, stepping up to go to work.

Jacob and his father had ripped the office apart, operating under the assumption Jansen would have her most important stuff closer to her so she could grab and dash if the compound was compromised. They'd found it behind a false panel in one of the bookshelves. None of her hiding spots for her safe or bugout tunnel were particularly clever, but they were quick to get to.

Avelar sat at Jansen's desk, working at her terminal to access the secret surveillance system she'd had installed along with the primary system everyone could see. Jacob had noticed the agent logged right in, apparently having compromised Jansen's first layer security credentials some time ago.

"I can access a lot of stuff from here, but any deeper, and I'll need her biometrics. She's been sitting at room temperature too long for a retinal scan to be valid. Her eyes looked a little milky," Avelar said. "But I can definitely get to her camera system. She had this installed more to keep an eye on her people and make sure they were actually working than as a serious security measure. Here we go— What the hell?"

"What?" Jacob asked, walking over. "Is that Hodges?"

"Yeah...three days after he was killed on Koliss-2." Avelar frowned. "And, apparently, he grew his hair back out to a style he wore two years ago in the time it took him to resurrect himself and fly here."

Everyone except 784 huddled around the terminal to watch as *Hodges* walked into the compound unchallenged by the gate guards, whom he killed first. A blade seemed to deploy out of his arm and damn near decapitated the guard.

"Oh, no," Jason whispered. "Oh, fuck."

"What?" Avelar turned.

"Shh!" Jacob hissed, pointing to the screen.

The computer automatically tracked through the different feeds to follow Hodges after Avelar framed him on the screen. He went and killed everyone in the common area, dispatching four before anybody had even caught on to what the hell was going on. Once they started to panic and scatter, Hodges moved so fast the image flickered as the camera's refresh rate was too slow to track all the movements.

Once everyone in the common area was dead, Hodges's form shimmered and, suddenly, he was Margaret Jansen. *She* walked into the bullpen and quietly ordered everyone to stand up and file out into the common area, which they hurried to do without complaint.

Once out in the other room, Jansen morphed back to Hodges for some reason, and then got to work killing the rest of them, efficiently slicing their throats with that wicked blade that came from his forearm.

Hodges then piled all the bodies up in the middle of the room, another inexplicable action. He was almost done when an Ull came into the room, taking in the scene with an unreadable expression.

"Hodges! What have you done!" it asked. "Jansen will—" it was cut off as Hodges crossed the distance in the blink of an eye and lopped its head from its body.

"This is...intense," Crusher rumbled.

784 walked over just as Jansen walked out of her office and encountered the thing that killed all her people. The interaction chilled Jacob to the core. He knew what was coming, but he couldn't look away. The calm, detached mannerisms and the way it led her to be slaughtered were more frightening than if a team of Korkarans had come in and ravaged the place like wild animals.

"Here we go," Avelar said, turning the audio up as Jansen was led to a chair.

"Just watch this, and then it will be over."

When the video started on the wall monitor, nobody could believe who was on the screen. As soon as a clear image of the person's face came up, Avelar paused the video and leaned back, exhaling loudly.

"Holy fucking shit," Jacob hissed. *"Director Welford?!"*

Many, many things fell into place for Jacob with this revelation. He knew Welford was a confidant of Captain Webb, which would explain why One World was always one step ahead of Scout Fleet.

"Wait," Crusher said. "Isn't that the asshole who posed as a lieutenant *way* back years ago on Earth when we killed Deetz?"

"That's him," Jason said quietly. "He was CIA back then. Later, he was assigned to Terranovus and helped us defeat Jansen there. He apparently flipped once he was given the directorship of the NIS...or he's been playing us the whole time, and he was never our ally."

"Captain Webb is going to shit a brick over this," Jacob said.

Avelar resumed the video, and they listened as Welford implicated himself in a massive conspiracy involving both the OSO and One World. Then, before Jansen was killed, the thing mimicking Hodges dropped the disguise. Crusher and Jason both groaned, the other two humans just looked confused. 784 didn't react at all.

"Friend of yours?" Jacob asked.

"Sort of," Jason said, glancing at Avelar. "He's an assassin. New player in the game."

"I'm going to go check to see if that video is still on the unit out there," Avelar said, appearing to not care or not notice Jason's discomfort. Once he left, Jacob turned on them.

"So...who is he?"

"He goes by the name Seven," Jason said. "He's who we're going to be hunting soon."

"Yeah, I can't wait for that," Crusher grumbled.

"Wait...you mean—"

"Seven used to be Lucky," Jason sighed. "We think Lucky is still in there...somewhere. For right now, though, he's become something dangerous, and it's our fault for meddling in things we didn't understand."

"We will assist you, Captain Burke," 784 said. "777 is one of us. He is our responsibility as well."

"We'll need the help," Jason said. "Thanks."

"Unit was wiped clean," Avelar shouted from the outer office. "The only copy of that video is on the surveillance footage."

"You better call in Webb," Jason said. "This site will need to be sanitized, and he has some serious decisions to make."

"I'll do it from the *Phoenix*," Jacob said.

"I'll go with you. We can just fly her back here and put down. No point walking miles through the woods over and over."

As he walked with his father through the tunnel, and then the forest to get to the *Phoenix*, Jacob's mind was in freefall. People had died, friends of his, and it turned out the real enemy wasn't some splinter faction. That was a front for a group within the government pulling the strings and using the One World boogieman as a cover for their activities. Commander Mosler and Sergeant Taylor were both dead because of Michael Welford's betrayal.

He now understood what Avelar had meant when the agent had told him he was tilting at windmills. One World never really even existed. He'd been chasing a ghost the whole time, trying to grab onto smoke and choke the life out of it because he was too naïve to look at the problem from all angles.

His faith in their institutions was likely irrevocably destroyed, he was facing a long prison term while the people involved in One

World would likely not, and now he wondered what the hell the point had been all along. He used to see himself as a patriot and a guardian of humanity. Now, when he looked, all he saw was a useful idiot.

Captain Webb sat in his office, staring off into space.

He'd just been briefed by Jason Burke and Lieutenant Brown about the fate of Margaret Jansen and what they'd learned about One World. Knowing Welford had been involved the whole time was a hot knife twisting in his gut. He'd known Welford since the old Terra-novus days and thought they were fighting on the same side.

Finding out the man was actually the enemy he'd been chasing this whole time was tough to handle. The video footage of the assassin Welford had hired to send after Jansen was also terrifying. Webb had little doubt it would be sent after him soon. The director was tying up loose ends now.

"*Sir!*" Ensign Weathers broke in over the open com channel. "*They found a survivor in the rubble. It's 707! He was just sitting in the subbase-ment waiting for someone to clear the building off him.*"

"That's good news, Reggie," Webb said. "Keep me in the loop but start bringing the crews back. We'll be departing the system soon. Tell the local clan leader I'll be down to finalize our agreement in an hour or so."

"*Aye, sir. Weathers out.*"

"Some good news, at least," Webb said to the ceiling.

Once Omega Force had left the area, the One World cruiser recalled its shuttles and left shortly after. Webb had debated following and engaging but, in the end, let them go. He didn't want to risk the *Kentucky* for such a minimal mission gain. Instead, he sent people down to the base to survey the damage and comb the area, seeing if anything was left behind the One World people missed.

When the locals had shown back up, Webb thought they were in for another fight but, instead, the clan leader had come and offered his apologies and assistance. Webb came down on a shuttle to talk to them and cemented a new agreement for them to watch over the base on behalf of him personally—paid for out of NAVSOC's slush budget —and asked them to move in equipment to begin clearing the collapsed building.

While they were doing that, his people brought up the body of the man named Hodges to begin investigating where his cybernetics had come from. They were quite a bit more primitive than what someone like Carolyn Whitney sported. Hodges had still been a tough nut to crack.

He'd beat down Jacob like it was nothing, so they needed to make sure this secret cabal wasn't getting ready to unleash a whole damn army of modified soldiers on them.

"Captain Duncan," Webb said into the intercom. "Prepare the *Kentucky* for departure. We'll be heading to the Plaki System as fast as she'll fly. I have to go down to the surface for a bit, so don't leave without me."

"Of course not, sir. She'll be ready to go by the time you get back."

Webb tossed back the rest of the drink he'd poured himself after Brown's news and reached for his service coat. There were a great many unpleasant tasks ahead of him in the coming days, and those were just the ones he knew about. God only knew what was coming at him that he didn't.

28

Michael Welford was running short on patience. There were so many things happening all at once and, out of the blue, Marcus Webb said he was on his way to Olympus and wanted a face-to-face meeting. He claimed the information he had was too sensitive to trust over Hyperlink.

Webb wore himself down, buzzing around like a little bee thinking he was still integral to the game. Little did he know the legislation to dismantle NAVSOC was already working its way through the system, and he would likely be arrested once the oversight learned about all of Scout Fleet's less-than-legal actions. Welford would do his best to make sure Webb didn't spend any time in Red Cliff. He owed the man at least that much.

The meeting room was in the operations center of NAVSOC's new base. The building was beautiful, and everything smelled new. Welford had a pang of regret knowing this would all be either repurposed or torn down completely as the military moved to Olympus.

When he walked into the room, the lights were dim, and several monitors on the wall glowed with the 3rd Scout Corps emblem. Strangely enough, one of them had the wings and skull crest of Omega Force.

"What the hell? Webb? Where are you? I don't have time for this silly shit."

The door slammed shut behind him, and the screens all came to life. At first, he was annoyed, then concerned when he saw what was on them. One was the video he'd recorded for Margaret Jansen the assassin was supposed to play for her. Had she survived? He'd received proof of death from Jorg.

The other monitors showed things even Welford didn't know about but involved him. He quickly realized this must be from Jansen's cache off her crypto traps. The woman had been secretly recording everything, positioning herself to take out anybody at any time with information they didn't even know she had.

"Do we have your attention?"

Welford spun at the voice as the lights came up, and he stared at Jason Burke. Crusher sat in a chair in the corner, and two battlesynths were along the wall.

"Where's Webb?"

"You don't get to make demands here, Michael," Jason said. "But because I'm a nice guy, I'll tell you. Webb isn't here for plausible deni-ability. The *Kentucky* isn't even in this star system. She left with Webb aboard three days ago."

"Listen, you—" Welford didn't get to finish his sentence since he was flying across the room from a savage snap kick Burke sent his way. He hit the far wall and collapsed, wheezing and trying to get his body to at least start breathing again.

"That assassin you used to kill Jansen, how did you find him?"

"What?" Welford asked, completely confused. "The assassin? That's what you want?"

"If I have to ask twice, I'm going to shatter both your kneecaps," Jason said.

"I contract these things out, Burke. He came highly recommended from my broker within the Raplix Guild, someone named Jorg," Welford said. He climbed shakily to his feet and walked over to the conference table, slumping into a seat. "Is that all?"

"All I care about." Jason shrugged. "But, as you can see, Webb has your balls in a vice. He may use this all as leverage on you, or he may hang you out to dry. No idea. As it turns out, old friends seem to change over time."

"Oh, grow up," Welford snapped. Now that he was confident this was just a shakedown, his confidence returned. "You know the stakes we play for. I've been deep into the game since I stood in a freezing cornfield trying to talk you out of a gunship that could have changed the balance of power on Earth overnight."

"So, this is all about power?" Jason asked. "Seems...thin."

"I'm doing this because, if I don't, someone else will. Whether we like it or not, Earth is forever changed by our association with alien powers. If we keep wasting time and energy arguing with each other, we can't focus on the real threats out *there*," Welford said. "Soon, the power that controls the UEAS will change, and whoever controls the Navy and the ability to move about in space controls everything. All the old borders will fall, order will be imposed, and we'll finally begin working as a singular species towards like-minded goals."

"Whatever." Jason waved him off. "I don't believe any of that horse-shit any more than you do. You sound like a politician, but you're no different than any other power-hungry sociopath I've ever met. You and Crisstof Dalton would have been close friends."

"Is that all then? You're just looking for a new contractor for wet work?"

"Pretty much," Jason said, turning to leave. "Oh! I almost forgot. There is one more thing. Do you remember what I asked of you before I left Earth after the Cridal came?"

"You said a lot of things. What specifically am I supposed to remember?" Welford leaned over the table, holding his midsection where he'd been kicked.

"I said to look after my son and keep him safe. Remember?" As he'd been talking, Jason had approached the table across from Welford. He looked it over and saw it was a nice, heavy, solid wood piece. Perfect.

"And I did! He's been given opportunities to—"

"He's been used as cannon fodder and has had the dogs put on him, dogs you hold the leashes to," Jason said, leaning into the table. "Do you remember what I said I'd do to you if I found out you endangered him?"

"You're not going to kill me in the middle of a Navy base, Burke," Welford scoffed.

Jason just smiled at him and, fast as a rattlesnake, grabbed the back of his head and slammed his face into the surface of the table. Teeth and blood went everywhere as Jason pulled Welford's head back and slammed it a second, harder time. This time, the skull fractured, and the orbital bones collapsed.

The third hit finished the former director of the Naval Intelligence Section off completely. Welford's legs thrashed and kicked under the table for a moment before he went still and slid out of the chair onto the floor.

"Fucking gross," Crusher complained. "Why can't you just shoot people like a civilized person?"

"You guys can clean this up?" Jason asked the battlesynths.

"Of course," 707 said. "We will deliver him to his co-conspirators, and then I will join you on S'Tora. 784 will remain here with the rest of Lot 700 until we decide where we will ultimately end up."

"Sounds good," Jason said. "If you can't make the drop without being identified, just toss his ass out the airlock."

"We will handle it," 707 said, looking at the mess that used to be Michael Welford. "I am sorry, Captain Burke. We have failed you miserably in keeping your son safe."

"That's not true, and you know it," Jason said. "He's a man and has the right to make his own decisions. You backed him up along the way and guided him and, for that, I'm eternally grateful to you. I'm also grateful you'll be coming with us to go get Lucky. He's going to be a handful."

He stuck his hand out, and 707 reached over to shake it. The battlesynths had observed this ritual among humans and placed great significance in it. Any human who would shake hands with a battlesynth was telling them they trusted them completely. Most

species went out of their way to avoid battlesynths, much less willingly let one grab them.

"Let's go. I'm hungry," Crusher said, stretching.

Jason took one last look at Welford as 784 shut down the displays.
It felt less like justice and more of a promise kept. Either way, he'd
sleep like a baby tonight.

"President Weinhaus, it's an honor to meet you, sir."

"Sit down, Captain," Harold Weinhaus motioned Webb into a
chair. They weren't in the Oval Office, which had disappointed Webb
a bit, but in a secure SCIF underneath the White House. His liaison
had explained the Oval Office was for press appearances and was
monitored continuously. The real work was done below.

"My analysts have been going over the trove of intel you pulled
from Jansen's spider hole," Weinhaus said. "She was a thorough
recordkeeper. The briefings have been...hair raising. I know you're
aware of some of it, but once those crypto traps were fully unlocked,
there were things in there that would melt your brain. We're lucky
those idiots didn't drag us into a war with the stunts they were pulling
on other people's planets."

"They were an ambitious lot, sir," Webb said.

"We've been busy making arrests. Carefully and quietly, given
how connected some of these people are. We've shut down the Office
of Special Operations, and NIS is being stood down pending an
investigation. Director Welford is in the wind. We know he traveled to
Olympus, but then there's no sign of where he went from there. He
never returned to his ship, and we don't think he's still on the planet."

"He's slippery despite that fussy, bureaucratic persona," Webb
said, keeping a straight face.

He knew for a fact the corporeal remains of Michael Welford had
been propped up in an easy chair in the DC townhouse of a prom-
inent US Senator who had been one of the main power backers of
the group running One World. The warning had apparently been

received since the news announced last week that, to everyone's shock, he wouldn't be seeking re-election.

"Yes," Weinhaus said slowly, his eyes never leaving Webb's. "Very slippery."

"Is that why I'm here, sir? You'd like me to find Welford?"

"We have people for that," Weinhaus said. "I'm here to tell you NAVSOC will also be stood down during the coming investigations and you'll be removed from command regardless of what happens afterwards."

"I...understand, sir," Webb said, his mouth flooding with a hot, bitter taste. It wasn't like this was unexpected, but it was strange to have the big man himself telling you that you were going to be fired.

"I don't think you do," Weinhaus said. "You're being removed at my request. Within the coming weeks, as we dig the traitors out of the ranks, we'll be propping up a whole new clandestine service. Something that reports directly to this office and not to the regular UEN chain of command. I want you to be the man who heads that up for me."

"Me? Sir...that's well above my—"

"False modesty is not a virtue, Captain," Weinhaus said. "I can already see in your eyes what your answer will be. My idea is to move Scout Fleet out from under the UEN and let it stand as its own entity. NAVSOC will be retooled as something else more in line with the original forward observer mission and given back to the fleet."

"It's an intriguing offer, sir," Webb said. "I guess I have no choice but to accept."

"The details will be forthcoming. Consider yourself working for me now, Captain, and the official paperwork will catch up. We'll be pulling personnel out of the UEAS and assigning them on orders to your command, so it's going to get really muddy, really fast. The details will be handled by Fleet Ops, but I wanted you to hear it from me personally and to say thank you. It took a brass pair to send a scout team out like that to ferret out Jansen."

Webb squirmed at this. The president knew damn good and well Jacob had gone rogue and Webb was on the verge of disavowing the team but, now, he made it clear he was giving him the credit (or the blame) for the entire thing.

"Just doing my duty, sir," he said with a wan smile.

"Well, I need you to keep doing it," Weinhaus said. "We're on the precipice right now. Humanity is marching inexorably towards a unified planet and a single form of representative government, but we're just not there yet. For now, it keeps the peace to allow people the chance to acclimate to this wide galaxy we've been thrust into while retaining the comforting familiarity of their own little corner of the planet. We'll get there, but when we do, it won't be because a group of power-mad lunatics forced us into it."

"Well said, sir," Webb said.

The rest of his time was spent doing the usual White House routine. He was taken up to the Oval Office for a photo-op with Weinhaus, introduced to the staff, and then sent on his way in the back of a limo. Once he was off the grounds, he breathed a huge sigh of relief. They'd actually pulled it off. Mostly.

The group behind One World wasn't fully dead and buried, but they were scattered and frightened right now and, for the time being, that was just as good. He pulled his com unit and checked for messages before opening a channel to his ship.

"Sir?" Ensign Weathers answered.

"Tell Captain Duncan we'll be leaving as soon as I'm aboard."

"Destination, sir?"

"The planet S'Tora."

29

"It's seven serving six, you filthy cheaters!"

"It's six-six, Crusher," Twingo said.

"Whose side are you on, you little bastard?" Crusher snarled, turning on his friend.

Both Obsidian and Omega Force had found their way back to S'Tora and had spent time relaxing on the beaches and in the small town Jason called home. Captain Webb was on his way down, having just made orbit, so they were all gathered at the hangar for one last barbecue and beer bash.

Someone had set up a volleyball net in the sandy strip of beach on the road leading up to the hangar, and the two teams were now locked into a tied battle for bragging rights.

707 had made it a week earlier and was still trying to acclimate himself to being around so many emotional, unpredictable biotics in such a close setting. He and Jason had worked out a plan of attack to track down Lucky as the Obsidian crew spent a tense month waiting to find out if they'd be heading to prison or not. The fact Webb was coming out personally didn't bode well.

"Incoming!" one of the locals Jason had invited shouted, pointing to the sky.

Jacob looked up and saw the outline of a Sherpa-class Navy shuttle coming in on final approach. They all cleared off the small beach before the repulsors gave them a sandblasting and walked back up the road towards where MG and his father had the classic Camaro pulled out in the sun, animatedly talking about cars. MG was originally from the Los Angeles area and was a complete car nut, a hobby Jacob had little interest in as someone who'd never actually owned a car.

The shuttle flared and landed softly near the far edge of the landing pad. From what Jacob understood, his father had built this base by hewing the hangar right into the mountainside so it was hidden from view to ships in orbit. The pad was also irregularly shaped so computers wouldn't as easily identify it as a landing pad like they would a round or octagonal shape.

He trudged up the hill towards the shuttle, breathing in the fresh sea air and lamenting an otherwise very pleasant day was probably about to end with some very bad news.

"Lieutenant." Webb nodded as he, his aide, the captain of the *Kentucky*, and Agent Avelar filed out of the shuttle.

"Hey!" Jason yelled, waving as he walked over. "Everything go okay?"

"Agent, I'll let you brief them," Webb said. "And by brief, I mean be short. I'm smelling the grill and seeing Crusher swilling a beer, and I'm not about to stand around here talking shop."

Jacob cocked his head at Webb's exuberant tone. It'd be really fucked up if he was here to party, and then put him in cuffs afterwards.

"One World is done," Avelar said. "The director of the NIS was implicated officially but has gone missing. Shame about that, really. The data we've pulled from both Jansen's devices and Welford's hidden servers has allowed us to begin pursuing the other players in this organization. Just so you know, and this is *not* to go beyond this meeting, we believe that the Cridal Cooperative may have been behind this the entire time. We can't prove it, but it seems Seeladas Dalton was interested in installing a puppet government so she could get her hands on Earth's rapid technological expansion."

"Like father like daughter." Jason shook his head.

"Indeed," Avelar said. "We'll be playing that one very carefully, but we're confident now the ringleaders are being collected, she'll pull her tentacles back. For now."

"What about us, sir?" Jacob blurted, unable to handle it anymore.

"3rd Scout Corps, including Scout Team Obsidian, is being reassigned to the new Scout Fleet Command," Webb said. "We will be an off-book, clandestine service that answers directly to the president and the Joint Chiefs, used at their discretion. NAVSOC is being shut down for now, pending a restructuring as a more traditional force.

"Sadly, this means our new shiny base on Olympus won't be our new home. The president has asked me to find suitable accommodations for our new force."

"Always more room on this planet," Jason said. "Not near me, of course."

"Tempting, but this place is too far away," Webb said. "Thankfully, I just found out a fully established base that already exists on Koliss-2 just became available. Just need to clear out the old tenant's junk first. Scout Team Obsidian, commanded by team leader Lieutenant Jacob Brown, is hereby ordered to report to Koliss Base no later than sixty days from this date. Congratulations, you avoided Red Cliff."

"Yes, sir," Jacob said, breathing a sigh of relief.

"Just remember you're still in the military," Webb said. "If you want to play space cowboy again, resign your commission and come out here with your father."

"What about me?" Murph asked.

"Special Agent Alonso Murphy will be remaining in Scout Fleet as a liaison, serving in Obsidian," Ensign Weathers said.

"This will be an official posting, so you no longer have to pretend to be a Marine sergeant," Webb said. "Now, if you want to read a book, use words over three syllables, or eat something other than crayons, it won't blow your cover."

"Losing my staff sergeant pay I guess," Murph sighed. "It was good while it lasted."

"Don't pretend I don't know about the secret slush fund you guys have going," Webb said, waving a finger at all of the Obsidian members. "You clowns are richer than half the mainline families in America, so spare me your tears about no longer double-dipping. As long as it doesn't compromise your ability to perform your mission, I'll keep looking the other way."

"Okay, enough of this bullshit," Jason said. "You guys staying for the party?"

"You actually have to ask?" Webb asked.

"Tell your shuttle crew to get their asses out here and grab a beer," Jason said. "Twingo should have the grill fired up by now."

During the evening, Jacob felt the tension he'd been carrying since Commander Mosler had been murdered ebb away. The food was amazing, local fare brought by his father's business partners at both the coffee plantation and the distillery. They all ate and drank too much, watching the surf while sitting under the tail of the *Phoenix* inside the hangar.

As the sun settled behind the horizon, the party showed no signs of slowing. The locals, a more conservative group, had left early. It was strange watching them interact with Jason like he was a legitimate businessman and a pillar of their little community.

By the end of the night, the members of Obsidian found themselves outside at a table, separated from the others, and sharing a bottle of the whiskey Jason made on the planet. The sense of accomplishment and relief at avoiding prison had settled over them and, for once, even MG had nothing to complain about. Jacob poured one more round and passed the glasses out, raising his own.

"To fallen friends," he said. "To Commander Ezra Mosler and Corporal Taylor Levin...rest easy, boys."

"Cheers!" the others said, raising their glasses and downing the whiskey.

The rest of the night got a little hazy after that, but it was the best damn time Jacob couldn't remember having.

30

It was almost three weeks later before Obsidian was finally ready to leave S'Tora.

When Captain Webb said they had sixty days to report, what he hadn't mentioned was he had no intention of taking the team with him on the *Kentucky*. When they'd all finally regained consciousness the next day, the shuttle was long gone, and the ship had already left orbit.

So, with few other options, they relocated to the starport they'd first landed at before stealing the *Phoenix* and got to work on the *Boneshaker*. The ship was still a heap of garbage, but the local crews on S'Tora were highly-skilled, enthusiastic, and surprisingly afford- able. The level of work they did was amazing considering it cost half as much as they'd paid on Pinnacle Station just to get the piece of shit to the bare minimum of space worthiness.

Once the crews were done and paid, the *Boneshaker* went through two days of rigorous testing by Sully and Mettler. Jacob had been worried his pilot was going to leave Scout Fleet and go back to the regular Navy after he caught wind of the restructuring.

When asked, Sully had laughed and said he wasn't going anywhere. Despite being injured seriously a couple of times, after being in Scout Fleet, he couldn't imagine going back to the Fleet and being a shuttle pilot on some cruiser, picking up dinner for VIPs.

"She's fueled and ready," Sully said. "We can leave anytime."

"Go ahead and finish prepping her," Jacob said. "I'll just be a minute."

The Omega Force crew came up from their base to see them off. Jacob walked over to where his father stood apart from the others, an unreadable expression on his face.

"You have everything you need?" Jason asked.

"We do," Jacob said. "Thanks for everything...I mean that. I don't know where we stand right now, but I know it's not where we were. I'd like it if we could maybe talk once in a while."

"I'd like that, too," Jason said, sticking out his hand. Jacob took it and shook it with a firm grasp. "I'm proud of you. It's not the life I would have wanted for you, but you took on something big and you saw it through while standing by your friends. If you ever need my help, don't be afraid to ask."

"I won't," Jacob said, releasing his father's hand. "I-I'm not sure how to—"

"I know," Jason said. "I'm not sure, either." Jacob smiled and clapped his father on the shoulder.

"See you around, old man."

"Stay out of trouble, kid."

Jacob walked away and saw Crusher gave MG some sort of nasty-looking curved blade and hugged him. Jacob just shook his head and walked past. As he stepped up the ramp, he heard Murph and 707 talking.

"So, you're going to be rolling with Omega Force for a while?" Murph asked. "Not going to lie, I was hoping you'd stick with us. You're a fun guy for being so serious all the time."

"I will help Captain Burke hunt down and handle the situation with Lucky," 707 said. "It is my duty to help one of my comrades, just the same as you would. When that is over, however it ends, I may return to see how you are faring without me. Poorly, I would imagine."

"Oh! Another joke?!" Murph laughed. "See? We're rubbing off on you already."

"So it would seem," 707 said. "Take care of yourself, Agent Murphy."

"You, too, Combat Unit 707."

"You may call me Tin Man," 707 said, turning and walking away from a slack-jawed Murph without looking back.

"Was he joking?" Murph asked Jacob.

"I don't think so," Jacob said. "I think he was letting you know you've earned his respect and friendship."

Once they were all in and settled, Sully wasted no time firing up the engines and getting them off the ground. The longer they stayed, the harder it would be to make themselves leave. It spoke to that very human need to have a home, any home, and the longing to be there.

As the *Boneshaker* ripped into orbit and turned onto a new course for their mesh-out point, Jacob tuned out the jabbering of his team and thought back to the time spent with his father. Having that deep resentment of Jason Burke burned away had left him with a little bit of an identity crisis.

He had to admit, after spending time with his dad, he understood why so many people admired and respected him. Jacob was also coming to terms with the fact, unfair as it was, Jason not being around while he grew up had been what was best for everybody, and that it hurt Jason just as much as it hurt him.

The fact he loved Jacob enough to risk his life over and over to help, never questioning him, made him realize that, just because his family wasn't typical, didn't mean it wasn't a family.

"Next stop, Koliss-2 and our new home," Sully announced. "Now, get the hell off my flightdeck."

EPILOGUE

"You dragged her all the way back here from Olympus?"

"The engineering crews finished the refit," Webb said. "She actually flew here under her own power."

Jacob and the rest of Scout Team Obsidian stood on the tarmac of the newly named Mosler Station on Koliss-2, the new home of Scout Fleet. In the hangar was a welcome and familiar sight: the *Corsair*. The custom, human-built ship was sleek and menacing even sitting in the hangar.

"Thank God," Sully whispered.

"The *Boneshaker* will be kept here for mission use," Webb said. "It's ideal for getting into rougher places without anybody taking a second glance. For what you'll be tasked with in the future, however, you'll need to have a more capable ship, so I'm handing her back over to you. Try not to leave it sitting on a gangster-controlled planet this time."

"No promises, sir," Jacob said.

"Anyway, take a few weeks to get re-acclimated to the ship and move all your crap in," Webb said. "Don't expect any mission taskings for a couple of months, at least. We're still getting this base propped up, and the political fallout from the information you pulled from Jansen's files is still settling back on Earth. Lots of sudden retirements from politicians hoping to avoid prison."

"What about the Cridal Cooperative?" Murph asked. "It's pretty clear they were pulling the strings from the top this whole time."

"Above my pay grade, but I do expect some sort of response," Webb said. "The Cridal have their own problems right now. The Saabror Protectorate is making aggressive moves towards them, and the ConFed fleet has harassed some of their worlds after Admiral Colleran took her taskforce into an open rebellion. For now, I think Earth wants to keep their head down and see how that all shakes out before confronting the Daltons. Expect to be at the forefront of what-ever we do."

"Count us in, sir," Jacob said.

"You say that as if I was asking you, *Lieutenant*." Webb patted his pockets. "Which reminds me...these are for you." He tossed him a small box. When Jacob opened it up, silver captain's bars gleamed in the midday sun.

"I...didn't expect this," Jacob said. "I was honestly just happy to avoid the court-martial."

"We're still going to have some long talks about your disregard for orders and how you don't know as much as you think you do, but President Weinhaus requested promotions for the Scout Team that took down Jansen and Welford," Webb said.

"So, that means we're all bumping up a pay grade, sir?" Sully asked.

"It does, Lieutenant Commander Sullivan," Webb said. "Even Murph is now Senior Special Agent Murphy. There's a party for you tonight at the club. Attendance is mandatory, dress uniforms are required. See you then."

"Shit," MG muttered. "I have no idea where my uniforms are."

"Everybody hit supply and make sure you have the proper uniforms with the correct ranks," Jacob said. "Do it now, and then take the rest of the day off. See you all tonight."

Jacob left his team standing there and walked up the ramp into his ship. He'd only flown on the Corsair one time when he first joined Scout Fleet, but there was still a sense of homecoming as he walked down the ship's main corridor. She was a military ship and not nearly as well-appointed as the *Devil's Fortune*, but she was a damn sight better than that flying deathtrap they'd stolen from Mok.

He walked into the cabin that used to be Commander Mosler's and now belonged to him. As he sat at the small desk, there was a sense of closure, having come full circle after a One World traitor had murdered Mosler to leading Obsidian when Jansen's organization was brought down.

Even though One World was just a smokescreen for a much broader threat, they'd still managed to get the job done and even came out of it with promotions for his team. He could tell Captain Webb wasn't thrilled about Jacob being rewarded for insubordination but, for now, he'd decided it wasn't a smart battle to pick in the current political climate. Politicians didn't like seeing people they'd propped up as heroes later prosecuted for those actions.

Jacob felt...different. The mission that forced him to put aside his feelings and work with his father had opened his eyes to the way things really were, not the way he tried to make them. Jason Burke wasn't the self-centered, ego-driven thrill junkie who walked out on Taryn Brown as Jacob tried to paint him. Getting the chance to let go of the insecurities and the blind hate for him had taken a load off his soul he hadn't even known was there.

That's not to say he and Burke would now just magically have a close bond or traditional father and son relationship. Part of the problem was, thanks to Doc's genetic tinkering, Jason barely looked a year older than Jacob, so it was hard to think of him as *Dad*. The other part was that Jason was still more or less a stranger to Jacob, but he was beginning to realize that was okay.

Learning to separate the legend of the man from the person he'd just run an operation with was part of taking these first steps. He had no idea what the future held for him and his father, but what they had today was a hell of a lot more than they did yesterday, and he couldn't help but think his mother would be happy about that.

"I told you Jansen was a loose end that needed to be tied off years ago. Now, we'll all be lucky if we're not executed."

"Don't be so dramatic," the man in the dark suit said, rolling his eyes. "This is a significant setback, certainly, but not insurmountable."

"We've lost the NIS, OSO, and One World in one fell swoop," the mousy man behind the desk insisted. His name was Elliot Pembroke, and he was director of a little-known governmental agency called the Office of Global Resource Management. An innocuous, boring name for an office that controlled the flow of money and material to and from the planet. "Welford's mangled remains were dumped in the fucking easy chair of Senator Braxton's home!"

"That was a nice touch," the man conceded. "Braxton should take that as a sign to get better security. Don't worry. We cleaned the place and disposed of the body. As far as anybody is concerned, Michael Welford just up and disappeared."

"Do we know who killed him?" Pembroke asked.

"The ME who looked the body over said his face was slammed into a hard, smooth surface. Three hits that did so much damage it killed him and left him an unrecognizable lump of meat. Whoever did it was either sending a message or was highly pissed off."

"Or both. An Ull maybe? They're strong enough to do something like that."

"No Ull could make it on and off Olympus without being detected. This was an insider job, and the signs all point to Marcus Webb as the facilitator. That means it could have been one of his battlesynths, which is unlikely given the savage, personal nature of the attack, or it could have been his enhanced Scout Team leader. Either way, Welford is dead, and we need to adjust our plans accordingly. Seeledas Dalton was not pleased all her help has been wasted and we are starting over."

"I'll begin drawing up a new roadmap of how we can achieve our goals," Pembroke promised. "I'll start immediately."

"That would be wise," the man said, standing and straightening his suit. Nobody knew his name, and he'd made it clear he had no intention of telling them. He was a ghost that came and went, herding members of the secret group around where they needed to be or eliminating those who outlived their usefulness. He wasn't someone you ever wanted to see standing at your door. "I'll be in touch."

After the man left, Pembroke poured himself a tall drink and sat back down to try and calm his frayed nerves. He'd agreed to help this group and use his office's not-inconsiderable power and influence because he agreed with their goals but, now, bodies were being dropped in people's living rooms, and a covert military operation had just wiped out fully half of their resources.

He had no way of knowing if that would be the end of it or if Marcus Webb was just getting warmed up. He'd just approved massive requisitions for material and personnel to Webb as he was setting up a secret base on some alien planet, putting him further out of their reach.

Things were getting dangerous, and Pembroke wasn't a man who had a high tolerance for risk. He needed out, but he needed to find a way to do it that kept the man in the suit away from his door. He closed his computer terminal and grabbed his jacket. There were a few people in DC who might be able to help him set up an arrangement that kept him out of prison, or worse. He pulled out his com unit and hit the icon for his virtual assistant.

"Please, contact the office of Senator Josef Schmidt and tell him Elliot Pembroke needs to see him," he said. "Tell him I need to get in contact with Captain Marcus Webb, and that it's urgent."

ALSO BY JOSHUA DALZELLE

Thank you for reading *Vapor Trails*.

If you enjoyed the story, Lieutenant Brown and the guys will be back in:

Heavy Metal

Terran Scout Fleet, Book Four

Subscribe to my newsletter for the latest updates on new releases, exclusive content, and special offers:

Connect with me on Facebook and Twitter:

www.facebook.com/Joshua.Dalzelle

@JoshuaDalzelle

Check out my Amazon page to see my other works including the #1 bestselling military science fiction series: *The Black Fleet Saga* along with the international bestselling *Omega Force* series.

www.amazon.com/author/joshuadalzelle

AFTERWORD

This was the mashup between two series that the readers of both Omega Force and Terran Scout Fleet have been expecting since we learned that Jacob Brown was actually the son of Jason Burke. I hope it wasn't too jarring for the Scout Fleet readers who don't follow the other series or that you got lost in the back and forth.

Moving forward the two series will diverge again onto their own respective, parallel timelines within this shared universe. To maintain the individuality and integrity of each, there won't be any of these crossover stories again, or at least there are none planned in how they're both mapped out. I want Scout Fleet to remain a more military sci-fi story while Omega Force will return to its usual genre-straddling adventurism following a band of outlaws.

When I wrote the ending to have Lucky be the one who actually killed Margaret Jansen I realized there were probably going to be a lot of readers confused as to why I didn't have Jacob, Murph, or even Jason do it. The reason I made Jansen's death somewhat anticlimactic was to reinforce the theme (and title) of the book: One World was now only smoke and mirrors, a distraction to keep your attention while the real power worked behind the scenes. I also wanted to keep Jacob from killing a defensless person in cold blood. When he killed Hollick, it was in a stand-up fight against a skilled opponent. I'd prefer to keep Jacob's conscience more clear than his father's.

Thank you to those that helped prop up this side-project by going all-in when "Marine" was released. That book was a Dragon Award finalist and its audiobook version hit #1 on all of Audible. That's huge. This series won't be an open-ended project like its Omega Force cousin, but I will try to maintain it for as long as there is a demand from readers and I feel like there's a story there worth telling.

Cheers!

Josh

Made in United States
Orlando, FL
08 May 2022

17674319R00161